THE DEATHS AT MANSFIELD GRAMMAR

NATASHA JARDIM

THE Q QUARTER

About the Author

Natasha Jardim is from Victoria, Australia and holds an M.A. of Cultural Heritage and an M.A. of Secondary Teaching, which she puts to full use while writing. Her murder mysteries are intended to be entertaining and thought provoking, sometimes emotional. Her characters are human, gifted and flawed all at once. Some are unhinged and others are loveable – that's the fun in chasing a killer. When she is not writing or teaching others how to do so, you can be guaranteed she is cooking, travelling or reading crime thrillers with her husband.

Note from the author

I would like to say thank you in advance for your generous readership. If you have a moment, I welcome all reviews across platforms. They truly make a difference! Thank you dear reader, and I look forward to entertaining you with future novels!

To keep in touch, you can find her on the following platform:
Instagram: n_jardim_writer

For my love, Christopher

Prologue

D EATH WAS A RITE of passage, like any other.

Stephen Graham climbed the tree with ease, convinced of the truth in the idea. His long fingers carefully fastened the rope to the strongest branch, after which he sat back to catch his breath, and surveyed the view. The vision of Mansfield Grammar was breathtaking. The drums of salute thundered around him, building steadily as the ghosts of the manor woke in the white light of the moon to bid him welcome. He had spent many a creative evening in this tree, conjuring the history of the building, igniting the lost stories so as to fuel support for his writing career.

He had been destined to be a writer. A poet. A wordsmith. A storyteller. A conjurer of worlds. A teller of tales. A failure. He had failed, ultimately. He cried, watching the school, watching *that* window. There was no tale that could speak of his wretchedness. There was no sonnet to tell of his longing. Nobody understood. How could they? They had not loved as he had loved. They had not been betrayed as he had, no. Keates and Poe would have to weave words inspired by other worldly powers to sufficiently tell of the grief and mocking that had shredded and shackled him to a prison where time was the warden. Time was endless.

Stephen placed the noose around his neck as though it were a necklace. This was his place, his seat. They were here; the imprints of the manor, guiding him to join them in the stone halls. The beat of the final tune rang strong. *Peace*, he thought and slipped from the branch.

He was free.

Chapter 1
The Faculty

"**I**'M TURNING IN NOW."

Minnie double checked the arrow on her GPS before turning as instructed. The stone majesty of Mansfield Grammar was a short drive from the high wrought-iron entrance gate. An ominous cloud threatened to crawl across the sunny sky, signalling the fading of the summer and the rise of autumn. Mansfield Grammar was a wide, grand building; a postmark for the wealth of the former colony of Victoria. Built in 1865, the school had welcomed and taught the wealthiest and most powerful people in Australia's history. To its credit, and for its exclusive education, even the English nobility had sought to send their children for a term of 'fresh, Australian air' since before Federation. Minnie, having only taught in two schools previously, neither as private nor grand as Mansfield Grammar, felt the creeping intimidation the stature of the building was intended to evoke.

"God, that was a drive."

"I'll say," said Minnie, watching an arborist and gardener amongst the wide, intimidating high border trees as they cut and organised the slain branches. The arborist, hanging high in neon safety gear, was fervently gesticulating to the gardener on the ground.

"Did Rob say he'd be out the front?"

"Yes, but I don't expect him to be there."

"He better be."

"He's seventeen, Charlie. He has better things to do than meet me."

"Actually, speaking of..." said Charlie, her voice flowing with remarkable clarity through the Bluetooth speaker considering the mountainous region of Mansfield. "Did they say anything else once you put your forms in? Did they mention Rob?"

"Yes, the Principal rang," said Minnie, distracted by the row of teenagers riding past her on horseback. Many of the students rode horses, it was part of the curriculum, only it was one thing to read about such extracurricular activities in education and another to witness it. "She didn't seem to mind once I explained that we were friends and Rob just so happened to be a student here."

"Easy then." A great clang erupted from the speaker. "Shit. Absolute shit..."

"What happened?" Minnie demanded, slowing down as she turned into the staff carpark. The school loomed over her car like a gothic shadow. A group of students were walking around the side of the school. One of the students, a sandy-haired boy who seemed to have mistaken the brisk autumn day for high summer, had thrown his school jumper over his shoulder and was breathing deeply from a small contraption in his hand. He paused, let out a great gust of smoke, and quickly stashed the device in his trouser pocket before following his friends to the front of the school.

"Fucking pan fell on my foot."

"You need to stop cooking," said Minnie, putting the car into park. "You're a disaster."

"Well, until my blessed husband gets back, I'm stuck with it," she said distractedly.

"I'm here. This school is enormous. I can tell you exactly where your fifty-five thousand a year is going."

"Take a deep breath."

Minnie looked at the speaker and laughed. "You know me too well."

"Yes. And my fifty-five thousand a year is going down the drain if Rob doesn't work harder. Make sure he does his homework, will you?"

"I'll do my best," said Minnie, collecting an empty coffee cup, chocolate wrappers and a water bottle; the debris of her four-hour long drive. "Ok, I'm going to go. I'll call you tonight."

"I'll message, Rob."

"No, leave him. He's fine."

"Sure?"

"Sure. Thanks for keeping me company on the drive."

"Minnie..."

"Mm?"

"You're going to be fine."

Minnie nodded. A swell of sadness swept over her. "Yep."

"Absolutely fine."

"I'm going now."

When the phone hung up, Minnie sat in her car for a few short moments. She was an ugly crier and did not want to be introduced to her new colleagues with the patchy redness that seemed to stain her skin for hours afterward. The steady crunch of the rocky ground sounded only a moment before there was a sharp knock on the passenger window of her car. A thin man with a priest's collar in square glasses and perfectly square teeth gave a cheery wave. Minnie recognised him,

Father Baldwin. She hastily stepped out of the car as he walked around to meet her.

"Welcome!" he said cheerily, extending a long-fingered hand.

Minnie shook it with enthusiasm, feeling mildly less anxious. Being welcomed by a familiar was considerably more comfortable than walking into the school alone and with no idea where to go. Father Baldwin had been part of the panel that interviewed her for the position of Senior School English and Literature Teacher. She knew she was not the first choice, especially of the Head of the Senior English faculty. The world of Grammar education was small, and rumours swirled that Mrs Edna Richardson, the Head of Senior English, was in talks with Rupert Devi from Edenfield Grammar. Whether the remuneration was a dispute or a change of heart, no one had a concrete answer for why Mr Devi remained at Edenfield and Minnie, a public-school teacher, was offered the role.

"How was the drive?" asked Father Baldwin.

"Good. Long though. It's good to finally be here," she said.

"Let me help with your bags."

"Thank you."

"Well," he said, when she opened the boot of the car and revealed two full-sized luggage and a few overnight bags. "You packed lightly."

"I thought I overpacked."

"Miss Vincini came with a packed car and a courier van," said Father Baldwin, extracting the luggage with ease. "You'll be sharing your apartment accommodations with her."

"What does she teach?" asked Minnie, loading an overnight bag on top of each luggage to roll up to the school. She dreaded the strain but was determined, just like in her travels through Europe, to breathe through the pain and pull the load as quickly as possible. *Cardio*, she thought. *It's just cardio.*

"Mathematics," said Father Baldwin, straining under two overnight bags.

The books, thought Minnie, watching as he worked out which carrying method would offer less strain.

It was then that a lanky boy of sixteen turned the corner with an air of both begrudging compliance and bashfulness. "Hey," he said, approaching with the gait of a boy not quite used to his height.

"Wagner?" asked Father Baldwin.

"I'm here to help, Minnie," said the boy. "*Miss Fox*," he added purposefully, looking at Minnie with an expression that told her his mother, Charlie, had just been on the phone.

"How are you, Rob?" asked Minnie.

"Fine. Tired." He took hold of a luggage and two overnight bags with ease.

"I'll get the rest in due time," said Minnie, locking the car after pulling out another bag. "No point breaking our backs."

Not far from the staff car park, they turned to the main grounds where the front of the school, signalled by the wide stone steps, played host to dozens of secondary school students from junior to senior school, engaging in various states of rest or entertainment. Two teachers on yard duty milled between two groups of boys lying in the perfectly manicured, lush grass, deep in conversation while hugging mugs of coffee. One of them seemed to spot Millie and Father Baldwin and waved.

"Ah, Miss Lo and Miss Greenwood," said Father Baldwin. "Science and Humanities. You'll meet them soon," he added, leading the way up the stone steps.

Rob was already through the grand doors and waiting in the foyer. The entrance of the building was of magnificent stone and mahogany, reminiscent of the detail afforded to grand houses in Europe. Minnie eyed the brilliant lionhead door knocker as she entered. The dwindling smell of paint tickled her nose; a warning sign indicating as much stood a few feet from the door. *Warning: wet paint. Kindly do not lean on the walls.* The entrance hall was rather more modern than Minnie expected. It was evident this area of the school had undergone major refurbishment and while the essence of the mid-Victorian entrance remained, the refurbishment bluntly juxtaposed the Victorian Tudor-Gothic architecture. The familiar scent of old wood and polish tickled Minnie's nose. An immaculately dressed older woman with a blunt haircut and thick-rimmed green glasses sat behind a corner desk.

"Our newest arrival!"

"Mrs Jeong," said Father Baldwin. "Miss Fox has arrived."

Mrs Jeong smiled and reached for an A4 sized box. "I'm Olivia. Only Father Baldwin insists on titles. Was it a long drive from Melbourne, Miss Fox?"

"Four hours," said Minnie, noticing her name marked on the box in thick permanent marker. Olivia Jeong looked an efficient woman; her desk was immaculate, down to her organised post-it notes, and three coloured gel pens lying side by side as though spaced by a ruler.

"We have to do some boring paperwork," said Olivia. "It won't take long. What's Wagner waiting for?" She peered at him over her glasses and pointed to him with a wonderfully long acrylic nail.

"Bags," said Rob shortly.

"You can leave them here, Wagner. You know the rules. No students near teachers' apartments." Olivia's tone suggested a futility in any attempts to justify the need for assistance. She continued to peer sternly at him over her glasses.

"Sure," he mumbled. "Tell mum I helped, ok," he muttered to Minnie before leaving.

"Good boy, but rules are firm," said Olivia as he disappeared outside.

"Of course," said Minnie. She had no intention of getting on the bad side of the woman who, as was the case in most schools, ran the day-to-day administration and knew both the secrets and rumours. The school administrator, as indicated by Olivia's badge, was one of the most important and underestimated people. In Minnie's experience, the school administrator, or the 'S/A' as they were known more colloquially, could make a teachers' life easier or harder depending on how they felt.

They have the ability to start and end a rumour, her mentor had told her. *They're useful but never tell them anything you don't want repeated within a minute.*

After half an hour of administration, including being photographed, finger-printed, and signing various documents pertaining to her lodgings, Olivia handed her the box and welcomed her to Mansfield Grammar.

"I'll help you get these to your apartment but then I must go," said Father Baldwin, leading her through the security doors. He tapped his pass key on the scanner to the left. "I have to prepare for chapel. Do you attend?"

Minnie withheld the urge to reply honestly. "When time allows it," she responded, stumbling with the weight of the bags. They left half behind due to the loss of Rob's assistance. The familiar smell of old, polished wood and carpet accompanied a sweetness in the air that she could never quite place when in old buildings. The space was magnificent. The refurbishment must have included halving the original open foyer, allowing access only to the front desk, behind which, through a set of hardened glass security doors, was the staircase, elevator, and apartment foyer. Minnie attempted to take in as much detail as possible. From the grand chandelier in the carved ceiling to the portraits that stared down at them; Minnie was in awe.

Who were these people?

The carpets bore the look of honourable wear and tear and the staircase was so intricate it bordered on garish. Minnie followed Father Baldwin into the elevator, an ugly imposition in such a building, where he pressed '2'.

How did they get approval to impose these modern updates? Surely this is Heritage Listed.

On the second level, a short journey down a wood-floored hall led them to Apartment 3. "Home sweet home," he said, motioning for her to use the new security pass that hung from her lanyard. "I'll get the rest of your bags."

Aware that she was sharing with Miss Vincini, she knocked before entering. The space was lovely. Large windows to her left allowed for light to flow into the small lounge. Dozens of candles in various states of existence; new, mushrooming, tunnelled, and flattened, littered the room, from shelves to the floor. Files, textbooks, and stacks of paper littered the coffee table; Minnie had crafted the scene many times before in her own home. She put her bags to the corner and walked the area, taking in the hints of original décor and admiring the remarkable, sleek updates. She would not have minded if the rooms were in their original state. The history of the building was part of its charm. She was grateful to see a split cooling and heating system. At least there was little chance of suffering the extreme weather that Mansfield was known to afford; stifling summer and unrelenting winter. A pair of running shoes outside of the first bedroom door indicated the room was taken. Minnie knocked then carefully opened the second door. She had chosen correctly. A good-sized bedroom was complete with Scandi-style furniture, including a chest of drawers, a plush armchair and bed glowed in afternoon light that streamed in through a long, six-paned window. Minnie made to open it but found it stuck and unrelenting. Panting, she spotted a lock on the top and pulled the security bolt. With another strong effort, she pried the window open and sat on the bed as reward for her work.

"Oh good, you managed it."

A woman stood in the doorway, sweaty and flushed. She had black curly hair, twisted into a messy bun, and an athletic figure that made Minnie immediately suck in her stomach and mentally promise never to eat another bag of fun-size chocolates again.

"Kate," she said, extending her hand and entering. "Kate Vincini."

"Marianna Fox. But please, call me Minnie."

Kate laughed. "Great name."

"My father certainly thinks so." Mr Gustav Fox always introduced her as, 'a miny me' on account of their identical brown, almond-shaped eyes. And thus, after a time, she became known exclusively as Minnie.

"I hear you're taking 10, 11, and 12 English-Lit?" asked Kate.

"Yes."

"They're painful those years," she said conversationally, looking out the window across the south lawn. "I take 11 maths. Used to do 12 but they're too neurotic. I spend half my time being a therapist."

"It's the state of education these days," said Minnie, remembering her last role.

"They need to give us all personal assistants to help with the admin load," said Kate. "At least here we get a counsellor per year level. School board is considering adding another to keep up with the demand but I think it might be the thing to blow the budget."

Minnie hardly believed so. The school's Annual Report was evidence of the multi-million-dollar surplus the school generated and expanded yearly. Despite the costs of running the school, Mansfield Grammar was perfectly able to afford introducing more staff. She wished she had had this sort of assistance at her previous school, it might have saved her hours of administration and parental emails.

Moments later, Father Baldwin arrived with the rest of her bags. Grateful for his assistance and support, Minnie thanked him repeatedly as he left.

"If I didn't have service to prepare for..." he said apologetically, waving goodbye.

"Want a tour?" asked Kate.

"Don't you have classes?"

"Not until 4th Period," said Kate, walking quickly out of the bedroom.

Minnie followed. Kate was checking her smart-watch and putting on a parka. "I'm a fast walker," said Kate, leading the way out of the apartment. "It's a habit."

"I can keep up," said Minnie as she too was a fast walker.

"Have you seen the Head or did he send Father Baldwin?" Kate locked the apartment door.

"Father Baldwin," said Minnie.

Kate gave an empathetic sigh. "It's been an absolute hell since 'the death'."

"The *what*?" asked Minnie.

"Didn't they tell you?" asked Kate, eyebrows raised. She led Minnie down the hall, past the elevator, which Minnie assumed they'd be taking, through a heavy, intricately carved wooden door and down a flight of stairs leading outside to the gardens.

"Tell me what? Someone died?"

"Oh yes. Final day of last term. *Surely* it was mentioned in your interview," said Kate, looking at Minnie with disbelief. "Surely it falls under some 'disclosure' rule that they tell the incumbent teacher that a student killed themselves."

"Wait…" Minnie stopped walking and wrapped her scarf around her neck, bracing against the wind as the school bell rang. The students began to pour into the school buildings, heading back for afternoon classes.

"Stephen Graham," said Kate, holding back tears. "Hung himself. It was a horrible find."

"Does anyone know why?" Minnie was suspicious that nothing had been in the media. She was well connected in education circles and found it odd that no one had mentioned the suicide of a student. It was typical of a school to keep delicate and potentially embarrassing matters confidential, but a suicide at a school as prestigious as Mansfield Grammar would have made local or even state news.

"Faculty think the workload got to him," said Kate. "No one really knows … could be anything. Friends. Mental health? It was all kept quiet. What's even stranger is that Liu just upped and left over the holidays."

"Who is Liu?"

"Kane Liu. That's who you're replacing," said Kate. "Didn't they tell you *anything* in your interview?"

"I was told there was a twelve-month position and it was due to my predecessor taking a leave of absence," said Minnie, feeling no need to be covert about her interview.

Kate's eyebrows rose. "Well it's the truth – technically. Anyway, he taught Graham, which, if you ask me, smells to hell and high water."

"You're saying that Kane left the school on account of Stephen Graham's suicide?"

"I can't say for sure," said Kate. "But it's odd. I liked Kane and he was a top teacher. I've just always suspected the timing was odd. But don't spread that around. I've been in a few scraps with faculty who think I'm being a conspiracy theorist. Come on – I'll show you the classrooms and the office. Did they give you a map?"

"I got a box full of papers. There's probably one in there."

"Well, you might want to note some of this down," said Kate, leading her across the front grounds in front of the house where the students had used the space to relax and play games during lunchtime. Kate stopped and faced the wide expanse of the Victorian mansion. "Ok, so that is the residence of the 'single' staff apartments and to the right where that tower is are the staff offices and meeting rooms. We call it 'Main House'." She pointed to the similarly sized less-grand building to the right. "Refurbed servants quarters. VCE Building." She pointed to the building to a cream-rendered, modern extension to the left of Main House where a football field separated them. "Middle and Senior classrooms." She turned and pointed to the Victorian building behind them. "Juniors – 7s and 8s. Plus, rec hall, and orchestra hall." She pointed south eastward toward an alley of trees. "There's a church at the end of the lane. Anglican. Do you go?"

"If I'm on duty, I suppose." Tactful when it came to religion, Minnie remained professionally beige, preferring to keep herself to herself on the topic. Truthfully, if she never saw the inside of a church again, she would consider herself blessed.

"You'll have to do better than that for the Head. He'll gnaw your ear off about it."

"Something to look forward to," said Minnie. It dawned on her, quite suddenly, of how alone she felt. They were deep in the Victorian countryside, nestled between mountains, far from the city, and surrounded by beautiful, daunting buildings. The news of a sudden leave of absence and a death was a surprise to say the least. What was more, Kate did not seem the slightest bit emotional about the news. She was neither gentle nor sad in her delivery. Rather, she was matter-of-fact, which Minnie supposed was one way of being professional, even if it read as indifferent.

While observing the mountains that acted as a backdrop to this manicured oasis, Minnie wondered who had last ventured into the wilderness. They were not the mountains of ski resorts, nor were they dotted with small farmsteads, as seen in the mountain ranges a short drive to the west. These mountains were wild; as green and dense as the First Nations peoples had left them. As darkening silver clouds rolled closer toward them, Minnie wished to be inside by the fire. A small cluster of birds were gliding across the ranges. One broke away and headed toward the school, wings wide and fearless while riding the wind. With two purposeful flutters, it pushed its way across the grounds and settled, with practised familiarity, on the ornamental cross on the roof of the mansion. It was a cockatoo. They, like kookaburras, were not Minnie's favourite birds. They lacked the majesty of ravens and squawked obnoxiously. If they beheld instincts, this cockatoo certainly did because it settled its attention on Minnie and Kate while surveying the scenery from its stone post.

In a calculated effort to avoid the incoming rain, Kate thought the time was best spent walking Minnie through the staff offices. They were a series of small, well furnished rooms equipped with the latest technology and resources against the backdrop of a Victorian library. Senior students with a designated Study Period were dotted amongst the shelves and desks of the library, some fervently reading while others were whispering or napping against their books. Minnie appreciated seeing the students in tidy uniforms. However strict the uniform policies had been at her previous schools, none were reasonably adhered to by the students and even less so the dejected teachers who had tried in vain to demand the students take some pride in their appearance only to be blatantly ignored. Presently, the uniforms were pressed and tidy. When seated, the students draped their blazers on the backs of their chairs. A boy sitting at a long table with four others stood, closed his computer, rolled down his shirt sleeves, straightened his tie and put on his blazer before muttering his goodbyes to his friends.

"Demerits."

Minnie supposed her expression spoke louder than any vocalised question.

Kate went on. "Uniform policy. They don't look pristine cause they want to. Two warnings and then it's a demerit. Three demerits - parents get an email. Another violation within a 48 hour period - detention and parents sit in on a meeting."

"Seems dramatic," said Minnie, while wishing something similar had been enforced at her previous school.

"I don't waste my time enforcing it," she said, walking on. "Every-one uses the meeting rooms but we have these little nooks." She point-ed to small office spaces. "If you want a little privacy. Have they given you your computer?"

"Ah, no apparently I have to go to IT."

"We'll go there next," she said. "This is Jeff, our Head of Junior School."

Inside one of the nooks, a greying man surrounded by papers looked entrenched in his marking. The pinstriped shirt beneath his charcoal knitted jumper was unironed and the grey around his eyes indicated he was more than tired but potentially ill. Minnie's mother, Dawn, a holistic medicine practitioner had always warned that grey eyes were a warning sign of long-untreated ailments.

"Jeff," said Kate sharply.

Jeff's scruffy head snapped up. "Sorry," he said distractedly. "Fifty papers, you know how it is."

"This is Minnie Fox," said Kate. "She's replacing Kane."

"Oh, they told us you were coming. Jeff Rodgers." He extended a small hand that had a curiously angular pinkie finger.

"Minnie," she said, shaking it. "We seem to have distracted you. I'm so sorry."

"Not at all. It's good to be forced to stop. What school did you come from?"

"East Bridge Secondary," she said. "I'm so pleased to be here."

"It'll be a change," said Jeff, running a hand through hair that was overdue a haircut. "But don't let them intimidate you. These older kids. They think they know it all. Especially 12 Green."

That was Rob's homeroom. "I'm sure I'll win them over."

"I don't doubt you will," said Jeff. "Just mind the boys. They'll try to flatter you into a higher grade."

"I'm immune," said Minnie, trying not to take offense to the insinuation, however delicately it was put.

"Let's keep going. See you at dinner, Jeff," said Kate, already walking off. They headed through the staff room and Kate motioned to a group of women at the table. "Sandra Keys," indicating to a middle-aged woman whose auburn hair showed signs of greying, "... Judy English-", a short woman with a bob haircut and excessively decorated lanyard and, "Rachel Simonds," who was biting into a muffin. "Ladies, this is Miss Fox."

"Welcome," they chimed.

"They're in the wellbeing department," said Kate.

"I'll be your port of call," said Sandra. "I handle the Senior School students."

"It would be wonderful to meet then. If you have a spare moment..."

"I will email you a time on your school email," said Sandra, dunking another biscuit into her tea.

As Kate and Minnie walked away, she had the feeling that the three women were watching her closely. There was tension amongst the group. Had she overstepped by asking for a meeting? Was there a protocol she had missed? Perhaps she should have engaged in small talk? She glanced back; they were indeed watching. She offered a small smile and followed Kate further into the room where she would be introduced to a series of faculty members. From the other end of the staff room, a tall, bald man approaching his late forties emerged. He wore an impeccable navy suit and oxblood boots. A short beard and thick brows juxtaposed his shaved head.

"David," said Kate. "This is Minnie Fox. I'm giving her a tour of the school."

"Good of you," said David. "Welcome Miss Fox."

"I remember," said Minnie.

David Wókcik had been part of the panel that interviewed her and asked the most difficult questions. While she had been resentful, upon reflection during the drive back from the interview realised they had made her give depth to her answers, somehow making her candidacy more impressive to the whole panel.

What had been a fleeting smile evaporated, and he addressed Kate. "Did you reschedule your tutoring appointment with Kai Watanabe?"

"Kai asked for it to be rescheduled after his violin lesson at 4pm," said Kate. "I know it's out of scheduling times."

"Sandra knows?"

"Yes."

"This cannot keep happening. It eats into your time. Remind Watanabe all meetings are scheduled during free-periods in school hours, he is to see me."

As the Head of Senior School, David was Minnie's immediate superior and he did not, in that moment, look as though he would welcome a response.

"I was, in fact, coming to see you Miss Fox," said David. "I have your schedule and other administration documentation."

"Why don't I leave her with you, David?" asked Kate. "I have to rush to 4th Period."

"Thank you for showing me around, Kate," said Minnie.

Kate resumed her fast-paced walk out of the staffroom. Minnie smiled and took the file David held out.

"You will have a digital copy of everything," said David. "Let's go up to IT." He led the way back to the library, turning immediately up a flight of stairs to the left of the arches entry. The books on this level of the library seemed more precious somehow; more protected. There were leather-bound books, hard covers, and what seemed to be legal compendiums on the shelves. At the far end, a young woman with thick curly red-hair the texture of wool and bright red lipstick sat behind a sleek desk with three monitors.

"Lily, do you have Miss Fox's equipment ready?" David asked courteously.

Lily gave Minnie a big smile. "Hi, Miss Fox."

"Minnie," she said.

"Hi, Minnie. I do have all your gear here." She went to a nearby shelf and returned with a computer emblazoned bag with the school crest and name. "Ok, this is your tech. Computer, mouse if you want it – ear phones, internet dongle in case one of the storms knocks out the WIFI, charger and bag. You're lucky because you got a brand new Mac."

"New?"

"Well, Mr Liu didn't hand his in when he left. Still chasing that one up."

"Thank you, Lily," said Minnie, taking the bag.

"There's a post-note in there with all your passwords. If you have any trouble, I'm usually here till 6pm. My mobile number is on the note if there's a disaster."

"You thought of everything."

"This is an old school. Something always happens. Especially when we're expecting a storm."

"Storm?"

"First one of the winter season," said Lily. "Did you tell her about the ghosts, David?"

"Nonsense," said David. "Thank you, Lily. We won't keep you."

"Good to meet you, Minnie. Maybe I'll see you at dinner."

"That'll be good." Minnie followed David, carrying the hefty computer bag.

David took the time to show her the rest of the school, particularly the VCE building where she would teach her English and Literature classes. Minnie was astounded by the classroom that was now hers. It was in one of the original buildings and looked as though it might have served as a parlour or games room. Two paned windows allowed the dimming light to illuminate the deep green room. There were fifteen desks in five rows of three; she was unused to this as in her previous school, they practised a more collaborative classroom setting, grouping desks so the students could more readily study in groups. 'Pods' they were called, and she did not much like them. A smart-board spanned a large part of the far wall where the students desk faced, and a vintage teachers desk sat to the right.

It's magnificent, thought Minnie. *Dead Poets Society in living colour.*

During her teacher training, Minnie imagined teaching would be akin to the aesthetic and studious excellence as portrayed in such films and books as the Dead Poets Society and *The Secret History*. It was in her innocence and perhaps sheltered upbringing that she imagined life and adolescents would function in such an organised and respectful synergy. In reality, she had ended up teaching in schools that were left wanting for resources and studious pupils. Respect and reverence for education and teachers had disappeared with the new generation. Replaced with quick-facts, shorter study periods, lowered standards and the constant infringement of rising anxiety on student's ability to cope and show resilience, Minnie thought such movies were closer to works of fantasy than literary fiction.

"I cleaned out Mr Liu's desk of what I thought were his personal belongings," said David. "The resources..." He pointed to the small shelf beside the desk, "...belong to the school. You're free to use what you need. There are more in the teacher's resource room. If there is a resource we do not have that you need, email me and I will purchase it through the school account."

Another blessing of such a wealthy school. Requesting resources could be lengthy and often rejected due to funding shortages. The green desk chair was a retro, low-backed leather piece that she sensed had been a personal addition of Kane's. Schools were not in the habit of providing teachers with chairs that beheld either comfort or style, certainly not both. Minnie felt as though sitting in his chair was somehow disrespectful.

"Do you know if Kane plans to return after his time off?" asked Minnie.

"I could not divulge that information."

"Do you think I might organise for another chair?"

"Why?"

"This one seems to be his personal property."

"It can certainly be organised. In your interview, you said you were experienced in dealing with challenging student behaviour."

Having covered this line of questioning in her interview, she was surprised it was being brought up again. "One of my students stabbed themselves with a pair of scissors while I was reading Macbeth," said Minnie, veering clear of the textbook response from her interview.

David raised his eyebrows. "Not a fan of The Bard himself then?"

Minnie could not help but laugh. It felt silly and horrifying all at once. She could still see the fountainous blood gushing from Fin's hand and hitting another student in the eye.

"It's like a jet stream!" Sarah had cried.

"Ew, you're a vampire now!" screamed Noah, pointing to the boy who had just received the eye-full of blood. "Miss Fox, Justin's a vampire!"

Minnie wanted to implode the moment Emma Flanders had stood on her desk and screamed for all and sundry. In fact, Minnie could still hear the high-pitched pathetic squeal. It was then, while hastily wrapping Fin's gushing hand with her cardigan, ordering Justin to the nurses' office, calling on Will to run to the nurse and the Head, and begging the rest of the class to sit down calmly that she knew she had lost control. She would never live this down, never hear the end of it from parents, especially not Fin's parents. This was not a story she told in her interview. No, her 'evidence demonstrating her classroom management style' was taken from her 'happy' memories. All incidents were concluded well because she had always implemented 'department approved' procedures. When a troubled student stabs themself with scissors, department approved procedures do not seem to exist. There was no manual for when classrooms fell apart.

"Why do you ask?" said Minnie once they stopped laughing.

"These kids are a handful," said David. "Do not be misled by the fact that some of them look older. I'm not sure what's in the food these days but they all seem to mature faster now."

"I won't. I'm used to all kinds."

"I don't doubt it. It would be remiss of me though, if I didn't talk to you about 12 Green."

"What about them?"

"They've been off lately. Different. This year has been challenging for them."

"Because the boy died? I forgot his name, I'm sorry."

"Stephen Graham. He was in 12 Green."

"What was he like?"

"Odd," said David. "Quiet. Good student. Not popular, not un-popular. You'll see tomorrow what the class is like."

"Was there a clue as to what drove him to kill himself?"

"No, but on reflection... " David straightened his shoulders. "Well, it all becomes clear on reflection, doesn't it?"

"Do you think it had anything to do with Mr Liu's disappearance?"

"With all of my being, I hope not."

Chapter 2

The Students and the Faculty

M INNIE WOKE BEFORE DAWN following an evening of preparations. She felt woefully unprepared. The previous evening, Kate had offered her a glass of red wine to unwind; it remained untouched on her desk. Minnie, avoiding the usual headache that followed the drinking of red wine, opted for a bottle of tonic water to soothe her nervous stomach. Minnie left her apartment and made the journey to the senior school building, mug of coffee in hand. As she crossed the rain-glossed green, throngs of sleepy students stumbled to their nominated buildings. The school had, historically, been exclusive to boys, broadening its intake to include female students in the last two years. The ratio between boys and girls continued to be in favour of the boys, especially in senior school.

Minnie arrived at her classroom mere seconds before her students. She opened the door and waited, drawing curious looks from the arriving teenagers. They hesitated as to how to proceed. Spotting Rob amongst the confused students, she smiled. "Welcome everyone. I am Miss Fox and I am replacing Mr Liu." She looked to the closest student, a lanky African boy. "What is your name?"

"Adroa Okello."

"Hello, Adroa. Please take your seat."

"Charlie Humming, Miss," said the red headed boy beside him. "Pleased to make your acquaintance."

Minnie almost laughed but his eloquence made sense when she spotted the bow-tie with school colours rather than a school tie. "And yours. Please come in."

"Arnie Russo," said a bulky boy with ferocious acne.

"Connor O'Connor." Minnie thought his parents either had an awful sense of humour or little imagination to bless the poor boy with such a name.

Behind him, a shorter boy with an attempt at a moustache on his top lip approached with a paper in his hand. "Mr Liu told me to bring this at the end of last term, Miss Fox," he said. "I had an extension on my paper. He said he'd mark it for me. Since he's not here, will you?"

"What is your name?"

"Jimmy Fischer, Miss."

"Thank you," she said, motioning for him to add the paper to the pile of books in her straining arms. "I'll look at it."

Rob followed him into the classroom, giving Minnie his usual sheepish under-stare. "No fear. Ok," he said softly, taking a seat by the window next to Adroa Okello.

A group of four boys sauntered by and into the classroom without looking at her. Minnie recognised them, specifically the last one, as the group of boys who were vaping around the side of the school when she arrived. The remaining students, including a girl called Tabitha Myles, stopped to introduce themselves before entering. Minnie took a deep breath and held it as she put her books and computer bag on her desk. This technique allowed her to repress rising frustration long enough to speak without a quivering voice. She had learnt the procedure after being told her History lesson on the social norms of Chinese people during the Qing dynasty was 'so boring we're going to die' by a Year

10 girl in her first week of teaching. The memory of wanting to be swallowed by the ground played like a sting, but rather than collapse from the mortification, she took a deep breath, held it, pretending to have a technical issue with the presentation slide, and continued teaching with an even voice. 'Don't smile until Easter,' her mentor had told her. That way, the students could not break you. It worked for some, but not others. Students, especially Senior school students, were like truffle pigs; they smelt teacher fear from afar, especially private school students. They had a unique talent for making teachers feel as though they were their own employees and thus - results - however unearned in some respects, were expected.

Minnie approached the last and second last row, drawing the attention of the whole class. "You seemed in a hurry to come inside," she said cheerfully, mustering every ounce of mediocre acting talent. "What are your names?"

The boys stared at her.

"Are you nameless?"

The boy closest to her - the vaper - began to turn pink in the cheeks. He cleared his throat. "I'm Ralph Astley," he said as though expecting her to know the meaning behind his tone.

After a moments hesitation, the red-headed boy responded. "Harry Dormer."

"Lincoln Friers," said the other, quickly. He bowed his head as soon as she looked at him.

"Leo Garcia," said the final boy, his voice barely above a whisper.

"Well, Mr Astley, Mr Dormer, Mr Friers and Mr Garcia. You will be the first students to lead in our analysis of Sylvia Plaths collected poetry. Mr Astley, you have 'Daddy.' Mr Dormer you have 'Lady Lazarus.' Mr Friers you have 'Cut.' And Mr Garcia you have 'The Arrival of the Bee Box.'"

"What do you mean 'lead the analysis'?" asked Ralph, whose unusually straight eyebrows were set together.

"Well, in a moment I am going to explain to the class that you will all analyse a poem independently for its literary devices, themes and structure as homework and you will lead the class in discussing it."

"But that's your job," he retorted as though embarrassed to let her know.

The tension forced her chest to tighten but she was driven by the need to wipe the pomposity from his face and so looked at him directly. "I'm sure Mr Liu has taught you the rudimentary method in which to analyse text, Mr Astley? It's something you would have been equipped to do in Year 7. Or are you saying you do not feel confident in your skills to do so?" she asked, channelling her late husband's talent for redirecting commentary she did not agree with.

Ralph's high cheeks turned pinker; Minnie suspected from withheld rage. Clearly nobody had ever told this boy what he needed to hear. "Which poem?" he asked, though his lips barely moved.

"Daddy," said Minnie, holding his firm gaze. *Someone I'm sure you'll call to make a complaint.* "We all look forward to your notes."

As she returned to her desk, Minnie caught row after row of astounded expressions. She had become used to combating antagonistic students, especially those who saw the need to assert themselves as having sway over the class. Whether wealthy or from low economic backgrounds, disruptors had an identical drive: power. They would achieve it in most classes, grinding teachers down to the point of exhaustion and compliance, but they found a worthy opponent in Minnie; she had energy and sass to match where the occasion called. She had made one mistake in her teaching career - cowing to the loudest student in the class for the sake of peace - but never again would she allow it. While the four boys at the back swapped furious glances, she unpacked her bag and marked the roll on the school system.

"Kai Watanabe seems to be missing from class," she said, looking around the room. "Does anyone know if he is unwell?"

Nobody answered.

Typical, she thought and marked him as absent.

Without pushing for an answer, Minnie loaded the lesson slides on to the smart-board.

"Does everyone have the textbook? *Ariel* by Sylvia Plath."

The students nodded; some dove into their bags to pull the novel out. "I have small rules for my lessons. It is crucial that you are focused and engaged. This is *your* year. If you wish to do well in this class, ask questions. Speak up if you do not understand something, if you do not agree with something, if you're intrigued by something. Unlike the younger years, I'll allow laptop screens up, but if I find that you are playing games or shopping online during class time, there are consequences. They include writing class notes and revision notes by *hand*. If you want to triple your workload, getting caught gaming in class is the way to go. *Tomorrow*," she said, looking to the back of the room, "Ralph will jump start our close reading of 'Daddy.' While Ralph does that, I do expect questions and commentary from the class. We are not passive readers in my classroom. We are thinking and we are questioning. Does anyone have a question so far?"

Tabitha Myles raised her hand. "Will we all take a turn reading a poem, Miss Fox?"

"Yes. There are more of you than poems to get through so the longer poems can be split between two of you. But I'll send out a schedule for that tomorrow. If you have one in particular you would like to lead, let me know after class."

At the end of the hour, the group of four boys at the back were the first to leave, except Leo Garcia. Minnie noticed that as his friends swept out of the room, scowling and petulant, he took his time to pack his books and then looked at her for a long moment before leaving. There was a sadness to his face, a weight, as though he were carrying an emotional millstone.

Maybe he needs help with classwork, she thought. It was not unusual for students, especially boys, to pretend to understand content for the sake of sparing themselves the embarrassment of asking for help. It was a methodology she did not understand but she hardly understood adolescents anymore either. Leo must have thought better of approaching her for assistance, and before she could offer it, he was gone.

The following two lessons proceeded smoothly and she felt the students accepted her well. Ralph produced a decent analysis of the poem, and Minnie was pleasantly impressed. Perhaps he had always excelled academically, or perhaps he was determined not to embarrass himself in front of the class, nevertheless, she made sure to review his work positively and set his analysis as the benchmark from which they were expected to develop. The malicious spark in his eyes faded somewhat after that comment. Some asked after Mr Liu but she could only assure them he had to leave for personal reasons. It was not until that evening's faculty dinner that the topic was raised again, this time, with the tone of conspiracy that usually accompanied wine-fuelled conversation.

Dinner was a more formal affair than Minnie had anticipated. There were numerous tables set about the dining room, set for four or five, and drinks were being poured as the teachers milled. The marble fireplace was lit, at which two teachers in suits stood observing the flames. The deep burgundy walls were lined with portraits and photos large and small of the estate and its previous owners. They were stout, imposing looking figures with few appealing features. Minnie tucked her lanyard into her blazer pocket as she entered, nervously scanning the room for a familiar face. They would all become familiar eventually, but presently, most were strangers. David was the first to see her and parted from those in his company to draw her into the room.

"How was your day?"

"My smoothest one to date," she said.

"Drink?"

"Maybe a soda water," she said.

"You're a rare breed amongst teachers," he said, obliging. "If the job hasn't led you to the bottle then you've got another vice, surely." He peered at her expectantly through his glasses.

"Well, my husband..." Minnie stopped herself.

Explain this quickly and keep yourself together.

David's eyebrows shot up. "You're married, Miss Fox? Mrs, I should say."

"Yes." Minnie took a deep breath. The cold of the soda water glass was uncomfortable. "My husband died. I'm a widow."

"I'm terribly sorry. There was nothing in your paperwork."

No, not all details belong in paperwork.

"When people find out they feel sorry for me. They don't ask what happened, but I can tell they want to know. It's *deeply* uncomfortable. I'm thirty, David. No one expects a thirty-year-old to be a widow. They mean to be kind, but it just hurts. So I don't mention it. I'm just Miss Fox."

David gave her arm the briefest of squeezes. "Let's meet the staff."

It was a relief to meet and engage with faces she had seen fleetingly in the halls or the staffroom.

"Did you hear about the email?" Sandra Keys asked, dramatically lowering her voice so only Minnie, David, and her two companions, Principal Henry Waterstone and Edna Richardson, could hear. Minnie had met Henry on the evening of her arrival. His welcome was professional. Minnie considered him the type of man who was easily stressed. His receding hairline was surely partly the fault of the demands of spearheading an establishment such as a grammar school. Edna, the Head of Senior English, had called a faculty meeting and sent a singular email to Minnie that were both as blunt and to the point as her tone of voice. There was no doubt of her wealth of knowledge and successful academic outcomes but she was lacking in basic interpersonal skills. Most of her introductory phrases to Minnie began with, "Now I know you won't be familiar with this because you've come from a *government* school but..." Each time, Minnie received the jibe with a smile but she was sure there would come a time when that would not do and words would have to be exchanged.

"What email?" asked David.

"Didn't *everyone* get the email?" asked Sandra.

"Maybe it was just the English faculty?" said Henry.

"No, everyone got it."

"Are we going to hear about the contents of the email?" asked David.

Sandra frowned at him. "You must have got it, David. Your name was on the list of recipients. It's from Kane!"

"Kane Liu?" asked Minnie.

"Yes! Get your phone, David. You *must* have it."

David looked sincerely surprised as he searched through his phone.

"It says he left to clear his head after a stressful term. Says he's in Tasmania. I don't know if I believe it," said Edna.

"Is this the email?" Kate appeared at Minnie's shoulder, red wine in hand. "I emailed him back, no response."

Minnie could tell David was growing more confused as he read. Then, without comment, he put his phone in his pocket and smiled. "Let's not worry about all that now. Miss Fox deserves a warm welcome."

"He *is* on leave," said Henry, looking flummoxed by the discussion.

"Don't you think it's bullshit though? Come *on*! How does someone go from his success, his life to suddenly ending up in Tasmania on an apparent mental health break?" demanded Sandra.

"A boy died!" said Edna.

"It's beyond me, Sandra," said Henry. "If this is what I have been presented with and a teacher needs time off, what can I be expected to do?"

It was clear from the groups body language that they did indeed expect him to do *something* more than was being done. Minnie wondered what they expected him to be able to pass on – even if he did get in touch with Mr Liu, or know his whereabouts, did they expect Henry to invade his privacy? What was so unusual about leave?

Jeff Rodgers, Head of Junior school, approached the group, whisky in hand. He looked no better than he had the other day, pallid and worn out. "How were your first few days, Marianna?"

"Minnie, please," she said, blushing. "It was great. The students are really bright."

"They're not burnt out yet," he said good naturedly. "Give them three weeks and they won't be so keen."

"Did you have 12 Green today?" asked Sandra.

"Yes."

"How were they?"

"Fine."

"Did Kai Watanabe turn up to English?"

"No."

"We just had a catch-up session," said Kate. "For maths. He's going to be in classes tomorrow."

She was providing Kai with tutoring sessions to assist him in keeping up to date with the coursework he seemed to have missed, but he had not taken it upon himself to approach Minnie for such assistance. Being his English teacher, and English being the subject he had to pass in order to finish school, Minnie had voiced to Sandra only the previous day that Kai needed to contact her and come to class. Despite Sandra agreeing, she also continued to remind her that Kai had some emotional distress and needed time this term. Unfortunately, time was not on Kai's side nor did Minnie feel the need to provide time to a student who seemed to care so little about his own education.

In the short time before dinner was served, Minnie observed the room closely, drowning out the conversation occurring directly in front of her. The teachers were spread around in groups or pairs, entrenched in deep discussion on assorted topics. Two women, one in her thirties and the other in her late forties, were huddled in the far corner beneath a painting of one of the school's early founders in the late 1800s. The younger of the two showed the other something on her phone, something the older woman found so disturbing that her eyes widened, and she put her hand over the phone screen. In a flash, the younger put her phone in her pocket and exercised a pointed expression. The older woman looked around the room, disturbed, until her eyes fell on Minnie and those around her. She smiled at Minnie and waved; Minnie returned it and looked away, feeling as though she had inappropriately intruded on their privacy. Behind her, two men from the Humanities faculty were exchanging opinions on parental communication.

"You'd think they'd give it a week before they started asking for reports on their bloody children," said one man, drinking whisky on ice.

The other, a black-haired man who wore a fine gold necklace beneath his shirt, called Stephen Carrs, whom she had met briefly in the tearoom during lunch, agreed. "I've made standardised responses to copy and paste."

"There's no point even responding."

"New era, new rules, Wes," said Stephen. "Miss Fox – have you met Wes Dauphine?"

"Ah, the newest recruit to this chaos," said Wes, a portly man in his 40s, who instead of standing, extended his hand for her to shake. He had remarkably thin arms and legs for a man whose waistline told of a life of indulgences. He was pink-cheeked and the thinning hair on his head was haphazardly swept from his face. "Met everyone?"

"I'm steadily meeting everyone," she said, shaking his hand.

"So, you've taken over for Kane? I heard we hired a young teacher. You must have done well at your previous schools."

"I did as much as anyone," said Minnie. "Nothing remarkable."

"How are you finding it?" asked Stephen.

"Great, so far. It's different ... the history of this place alone is fascinating. I think I can settle in well."

"Remarkable history," said Wes. "Don't let anyone tell you otherwise."

"Why would they?"

"We have a few strange ideas floating around the place," said Stephen. "A few teachers want to see more 'diversity' without actually establishing what that diversity means."

Minnie nodded in understanding but wanted to avoid the topic. "Well, it seems there is plenty of diversity," she said, looking around at the various staff.

Wes laughed. "Not according to the hippies," he said, nodding to a group of four by the refreshments. "And it figures – Arts faculty."

"Come through and meet Jenny and Miren," said David, appearing beside her.

Jenny and Miren were the two women she had observed moments before. Jenny was the younger and had the look of a woman who was instantly trustworthy; Minnie felt at ease upon their exchange of 'hellos'. She was petite and dark-haired, dressed in neat pants and a patterned shirt. Miren, who looked pensive seconds before their arrival, smiled brightly and welcomed her to the school with a strong Scottish accent. "Settled in well?"

"Yes. Lots of unpacking to do though."

"It'll take you weeks," said Miren, readjusting the shoulders of her velvet, embroidered jacket. Her blonde hair, styled in a sophisticated long-bob, showed hints of grey at the temples. "I didn't get rid of my last box until six months in. Anything you need, I'm two doors up from you in the hall."

Minnie had noticed. There were a number of afternoons wherein she had return to her apartment, only to see the junior administrator bringing packages to Miren's apartment door. It was evident that Miren's wardrobe was extensive and expensive. Perhaps that was her treat to herself; an incredible wardrobe.

"Thank you," she said, smiling.

"I'm Jenny Rodgers. I'm the Dorm Leader for the Senior students. I also teach Middle School Art and ESL. My door is open if you need any resources," she said.

"Jenny and Jeff are married," said David, helping her make the connection with the names.

"We live in the cottage on the other side of the grounds," said Jenny. "It's a hike but we get privacy."

And gardening, Minnie thought upon seeing the dirt around Jenny's cuticles.

"How long have you taught here?" asked Minnie.

"Five years. It's a great school to settle into. Parents can be a little intense but that's what you get in the grammar system. I also run the Garden Club."

"Garden Club?"

"I take the students to the garden to help with planting and maintenance. Helps me to pass on some knowledge on how to care for the earth," she said gently.

"I think that's marvellous!"

"Helps those with anxiety."

"I imagine it would. Is it voluntary?"

"Yes. We average about 15 a week."

"That's a lot of hands!"

"You're looking for someone to take over the writing of the Botanical Encyclopedia, aren't you?" asked Miren. "Since Stephen..."

"Yes," said Jenny. "He was an incredible writer, Minnie. He was writing an encyclopedia of all the plants at the school – new and old. He was sketching them and everything. It's a great piece of work. But it's unfinished."

"Surely there's someone in the club who can continue the work," said Minnie.

"Not with his level of detail."

"If I notice anyone with the special skills you need, I'll pass on their name."

"Actually, I wanted to ask you David – the Grahams want to put it to the Board that a memorial be erected at the school," said Miren.

"When did you hear this?" asked David.

"The usual channels. It gets around."

"Hopefully no one suggests it's near the tree," said Jenny.

Minnie wondered if this was what the two had been discussing earlier. "Which tree?"

"The tree where he ... took his life," said Jenny. "It's not far from Main House. It's across the green. It's the maiden oak tree."

"It's called the maiden oak because the family that built the house planted it the first day they arrived," said Miren.

"Cause there weren't enough native trees in the area," said Jenny, unimpressed.

Minnie was disturbed by the notion that she may need to walk under and around a tree that had been the scaffold from which a young boy decided to end his life. "Is it common knowledge that's where he died?"

"Yeah. We watch it consistently, especially the groundskeeper and his team. In case of copycats," said Jenny.

"The students are being counselled," said Miren. "It's unlikely we'd have copycats. Stephen Graham was deeply disturbed, Minnie. Deeply. There was little anyone could do."

"He wasn't *that* disturbed," said Jenny. "He only started acting morose two weeks before end of term. Before that he seemed ... well, fine."

"We'll never know what caused the turn," said Miren.

"It's a lot of pressure for the wellbeing team," said Minnie. "I suppose there is a list of at-risk students available on the system?"

"Access the medical records of the students in your classes," said Jenny. "I don't think you have any at-risk."

"No," said David, supporting the statement. "Although Minnie does have 12 Green."

"That was Stephen's class," said Miren. "Some of the students might still be healing from the trauma."

"Can I ask who found him?" asked Minnie.

"Kai Watanabe," said David. "It's why we have had a few issues since. He fell behind in his lessons and there's been a concerted effort to get him back on track."

Minnie felt slightly guilty for being so firm on his returning to class. Having faced the bleakness of death, she knew the weight carried by those who witnessed it.

"Does he see a councillor?"

"Yes."

"Dinner is served!" called Sandra, waving for the room's attention.

With that, everyone moved slowly to their seats and enjoyed the first formal staff dinner of the second term. It was tradition for the teaching staff to bookend the terms by dining together. Minnie sat between Wes and Miren, awkwardly at first. The table also consisted of David and Kate. Around the room, on tables seating four or five, the staff began to eat and drink. Minnie settled into the discomfort of being the newest member of staff; the most disconnected from the flowing conversations between faculty who had years of challenges and accomplishments from which bonds had been cemented. Were it not for the visible power points and lighting, Minnie would have felt thoroughly transported back in time to the house's Victorian origins. The wallpaper was a deep maroon and flowery, blending in with the mahogany wood doorway, shelves and cornices. The paintings of the former inhabitants reminded Minnie that this had been their home once, their private dining room. She wondered if it ever occurred to them that the house would become a school, and that one hundred and fifty years after their deaths, people from around the world would congregate to eat together.

"It blows your mind if you think about it too much," said Wes, finishing his entrée of scallops.

"What does?" she asked, finally eating.

Wes nodded to the paintings. "Did they think their home would ever be open to the public? Or become a school? I doubt they thought much into the future. They couldn't possibly imagine their house would become what it has."

"Don't you wonder if their ghosts are here?"

"Paintings are like ghosts," he said agreeably. "These people... we wouldn't like them if they were around today. *He...*" said Wes, pointing to the portrait of a stern, weak-chinned young man in a dark suit, "used a lot of convict labour to build his fortune. The stones that built this mansion were cut by convicts. And his son, Reg," he pointed to the portrait behind them, "died at twenty-two. With three illegitimate children. One with an Indigenous woman, apparently."

"Is there evidence of his parentage to all those children?"

Wes laughed. "Nothing's proven with this sort of history. It's all rumour unless there's DNA. But, for all their bad behaviour, they funded hospitals and the women, including good Rose over there," he said, pointing to the portrait of a small-featured woman in blue satin, "did a lot for the community. She founded an orphanage. Her daughter became a doctor."

"You know a lot about them."

"I'm interested."

"When did the building become a school?"

"1880s," said Wes. "Ironically, they needed the money."

"We know where it went," said Miren, motioning to the opulent room. "Even the Millards had to run out of money at some point."

"The Millards?" asked Minnie.

"The family," said David. "The Millards of Oxford. That's what inspired them to turn it into a school. With their connections and wealth, they sold it as the finest education in the colonies. It proved wildly popular."

"It needs its own book," said Minnie.

"It's an amazing building."

"Needs a refurbishment," said Kate, finishing a radicchio salad. "The hot water in our building is shocking."

"We're on the haunted wing," said Miren, smiling mischievously.

Minnie laughed. "Is it a Grey Lady or a White Lady?"

"Why not all?" asked Wes good-naturedly.

"I have had more than a few reports of sightings," said David in a tone that suggested they should not reject the idea frivolously.

"From who?" asked Kate, suspicious.

"People you would not expect," said David, tapping her fingers on the edge of his napkin.

"Have you seen one?"

"No. But it would be too simple to reject the idea that something roams the grounds."

"Why don't you get your crystals out, Miren?" Kate asked teasingly.

Minnie observed Miren's eyebrow rise in silent contempt at Kate's question but wondered if Miren believed in ghosts and what her husband Jamie had dubbed 'the divine'.

"I'll ignore that," Miren said sharply.

"I do wonder what you see in those crystal balls of yours," said Kate, spearing a potato. "I bet you know all the secrets."

Wes clutched the top of his shirt and looked dramatically at Miren. "Not *all* the secrets," he said dramatically. "Can *nothing* be private?"

"*Childish*," said Miren, glaring at them both.

The three-course meal left Minnie feeling overindulged but satisfied. When she and Kate returned to their apartment, they parted ways sleepily.

Minnie woke drowsily just after midnight. A continuous and rapid knocking launched her adrenaline and she sat upright. Was there a fire? An intruder? She kicked off the blankets and stumbled to the door, blindly reaching for the doorknob. There was no smoke, nor was anyone on the other side of the door when she wrenched it open in preparation to flee the apartment. She stood in the threshold, still drowsy from sleep and stepped into the hallway; perhaps the knocker had gone into the lounge. She checked, then the kitchen, and looked to the front door; everything was still and dark except for a low light emanating from a sconce in the lounge.

Kate seemed not to have been roused by the knocking. Minnie returned to bed feeling silly; she must have dreamt the knocking. As she pulled the blankets over her shoulders and tucked them under her chin, she did not see the feet that passed her door, pausing briefly before continuing on their way.

Chapter 3

The Manuscript

THE WEATHER IN MANSFIELD worsened progressively. Short warm days turned into shorter and colder days. As more students chose to spend their lunch and free periods indoors, filling the library and recreational building, further staff were required for supervision. Minnie found herself with only fifteen minutes of free time in which to have lunch before supervising students in the library. Father Baldwin decided to walk with her. After a month, Minnie felt settled in the school, enough so that she had learnt the names of almost all the students, many of whom waved at her in the halls or in the yard. Kai Watanabe - sporting a buzzcut and morose countenance - appeared in the classroom most days but never spoke. His friendship group, she realised, was Adroa Okello and Rob. The three sat closest to the windows in front of the four boys, Ralph Astley, Henry Dormer, Lincoln Friers and Leo Garcia, who were slowly defrosting their attitudes toward Minnie. Despite her success in delivering the curriculum, she suspected she had not completely understood the nature of 12 Green. Something unsaid, or at minimum, undiscovered by the faculty lay intricately woven between certain members of this cohort. She had noticed the stolen side glances, the glares and ever so subtle shaking of heads were exchanged between them.

The faculty were as welcoming as could be expected but a sense of clipped formality persisted; Minnie suspected they thought some sort of injustice had been done through her appointment in the months since Kane's departure. She rose above it, mostly with Kate's assistance. She repeatedly reminded Minnie of the permanent nature of the school faculty and their apprehension at the sight of outsiders. It was a perspective Minnie neither liked nor understood.

"Mr Liu was *very* well liked and respected," said Father Baldwin in response to her mentioning the attitude of some of the staff. "His departure caught us all by surprise."

"Has anyone been able to contact him?" asked Minnie.

"No."

Minnie motioned for a student to remove his feet from the coffee table around which he and his friends sat. "He seems to have taken Stephen's death terribly hard."

"Kane did not specify why he needed leave, at least not to me. But I have assumed all along that Stephen's death was the reason. At least he has recognised the need for a rest ... for distance. It is more than I can say for some who clearly need the same."

"Lisa, please go to the nurse and have your temperature checked," said Minnie, pausing by a Year 10 student who looked ill with flu. "Diana, please ask if Miss Orange has some disinfectant wipes and see to this table," she added as Lisa walked away, hunched by her heavy book bag.

Father Baldwin nodded approvingly. "You cannot be too careful."

"Flu season is here," said Minnie. "Did you know Stephen well?"

"Not a willful church attendee," said Father Baldwin, lowering his voice. "Not many are these days. Seemed fine ... if not a bit ... bohemian in his approach to things."

Minnie struggled to align how anyone could carry on with a bohemian lifestyle in a modern private boarding school. She imagined he spent his days floating from class to class, knowing as much if not more than the teachers, all the while sporting a secret addiction to alcohol and cigarettes. If he was to keep with the lifestyle a vape would be too nouveau. *No,* she thought, shaking imaginary Stephen from her mindseye. That was for films.

Minnie paused; they were alone at the end of the library with no students within ear shot. "I think 12 Green are going to take a while to recover from his death. Did Stephen ever come to you wanting advice? Perhaps closer to when ... you know ..."

"If he did, I couldn't discuss it."

Minnie felt disappointed. "There must be more to Stephen's story. Someone knows something. This is a school, Father."

Father Baldwin looked approving of her statement. "And people talk."

"Even those who say they do not."

"In my experience, it has been those who attest to no such behaviour that are the most guilty of it."

"Everyone likes gossip."

"This shouldn't be gossip."

"*Everything* is gossip." Minnie spotted Rob in a reading booth with a girl from his year level. He looked both pleased and extremely sheepish. The girl was talking animatedly to Rob; flinging her highlighter as though using it as a prop before she turned back to Rob, whose eager eyes turned suddenly downward, and they laughed. The girl gently elbowed him, teasing him out of his bashful shell.

"Mr Wagner and Miss Atherton need to be reminded of school rules," said Father Baldwin in reference to what Minnie assumed was their proximity.

"Leave it to me," said Minnie who had no intention of doing any such thing. There were times to impose rules and other times to look away. There was no harm in their flirtation, in fact, she was shocked to see Rob sitting with a girl in public. He was the most shy boy she had ever met.

"Ah, you know young Wagner's mother?"

"Yes, I am friends with his mother. I have known Rob for many years. Mrs Wagner and I used to work together."

Father Baldwin raised his eyebrows and nodded in understanding.

The school bell rang. The students moved slowly from their repose, lifting their bags begrudgingly onto their shoulders and bidding their friends goodbye before shuffling to their classrooms.

Minnie had a free hour. Usually, this would be spent planning a lesson or suffering through admin, but she was prepared in advance. She planned to close her eyes for a time and rest. Upon returning to her apartment, she felt the prickle of an unnerving, familiar sensation. The cold turning of the stomach - a sensory response to danger - encouraged her to keep the front door open. Had she not become familiar with sharing an apartment with Kate, and thus expecting someone to be present, she would have sworn someone uninvited was there. On inspection, nothing had changed since the morning and the apartment was empty. Besides Kate's expanding collection of paperwork in the lounge, the apartment was clean and neat. The kitchen was pristine. Minnie considered putting her disquiet down to the still-new surroundings. That was, until she opened the door to her bedroom and saw a small stack of papers tied neatly with twine on the end of her bed. Beneath them was a full, worn out, cheap folder. Had Kate left her something? Minnie dropped her bag by the door, kicked off her shoes, and picked up the twine-wrapped papers.

It was a manuscript. *Beneath the Great Oak.*

There was no author, simply, 'He who is but matter.' Minnie was intrigued but also perplexed. She looked to the picture on her bedside table. "What do you think, darling?" she asked, as her husband looked back at her, smiling as they twirled on the dancefloor at their wedding. The beautiful moment was captured in perfect fortune; as Jamie danced with her, grinning and unkempt, the photographer marked the elation in their faces. It was her favourite photo and her most prized possession.

Enclosed in the folder was an assortment of papers; some handwritten, others typed, of schoolwork belonging to Stephen Graham. Minnie flicked through them. The papers were copies of writing tasks for Stephen and corrected by Kane. It seemed an ordinary collection of student work. Perhaps someone had mistakenly left the file.

Turning to the manuscript, Minnie pulled at the twine, releasing the loose leaf paper, and began to read. As she did, it became clear that while this was a story about a romance it was also erotic and deeply personal. This was crafted as an autobiographical story that curiously began at the school. Minnie flicked through the first few pages. It was well written and illustrated the writer's deep understanding and love for language. Was Stephen the author? It was a reasonable assumption, otherwise why include it with the other work? Why was it in her room? She turned it over; no post-it note, no message. She turned to the final page of the manuscript.

'I am but dust. There is no way, no light from the dense tomb that grips my flesh with barbs, ripping and ripping so that I am so stunned by the pain I am made placid in its grip. Goodbye sweet, Conqueror. Though you have lain waste with my love, I am, even in death, forever yours.'

Minnie looked away from the page and out the window to the great oak tree on the grounds. Had Stephen written this knowing he intended to take his own life? Was it a hint, perhaps, at the cause of his emotional struggle? The words did not read like adolescent infatuation or fleeting love that so touched all young people. The words were heavy and accurately translated the true burden of lost love. Had they been written by Plato or Wilde or even Poe, they might have been studied for their stratified meaning. A single tear ran down her cheek. She closed the manuscript and put it in her bedside table, unable to read further. Minnie took out her phone and thumbed to her video folder. She watched video after video of Jamie, soothed by his voice and laughter. As she fell asleep, releasing tears and allowing them to gently trickle into her hair, she clung to the voice in the video.

"This is a man's job," said the Jamie in the video, pouring over a set of assembly instructions in the lounge of their new home. "Give me... a day and a six pack of beers and this will be a sturdy bookcase." The Minnie in the video laughed, zooming in on his face as he studied the papers. His eyes flickered up to her; he grinned. "What are you doing, cheeky woman?" The video ended.

Minnie sobbed, bringing the phone to her heart. She pressed it there.

Chapter 4

The Body in the Kitchen Garden

"**G**ET UP!"

Minnie sat up so quickly she felt the immediate urge to throw up. Fumbling for her nightlight, she struck two items to the floor before the bedroom light turned on and blinded her. As her eyes adjusted, Minnie feebly ascertained Kate's outline in the doorway. She was dressed in workout wear and was flushed; she must have been running.

"What's happened?" she said hoarsely, aggravated at having been awakened so harshly.

"Someone's *dead*!"

What the fuck are the odds? "What?" Minnie swung herself out of bed and began to dress. "Who? A student?"

"I think... I think it was Sandra Keys!" She looked pinched with shock.

"Sandra? Are you sure?" Minnie zipped up her jacket and picked up her phone. There were two missed calls from David. "Are the boarding students in bed?"

"Yes. No one has disturbed them but we sent Jeff and Jenny to do a head count."

"How do you know what happened?"

"I found her! I… I think she's had a heart attack or something." Kate began to breathe rhythmically, consciously calming herself down.

"Jesus! Where?"

"By the kitchen garden! I was coming back from my run and she was just *there!*"

"This is crazy. Are you alright?" said Minnie, leading the way out.

"I think so."

Upon immediate exit of their apartment, it was clear word had got around. Faculty in various states of dress emerged from their apartments, crowding at the top of the hallway that led outside to the kitchen garden. Sandra's apartment door was closed. Nobody seemed to know what had occurred but were under the impression there was an intruder. Who or what had alerted them to such a thing was unclear.

"Do you know what's happened?" asked Miren, emerging beside Minnie in a silk, fur-lined dressing gown and velvet slippers.

Kate leaned in and whispered, "I think Sandra is dead."

"*Dead?*" Miren recoiled. She gave Kate a withering look and bolted toward the back door, pushing through the crowd without a word of apology.

Drawn by her attitude, Minnie followed, muttering, "Excuse me. Sorry. So sorry… Sorry… excuse me," as she collided with and slipped past her colleagues. She heard Miren gasp before returning hurriedly through to the hall. Miren took a moment, closing her eyes as though intending to wipe the image from her mind's eye.

"What happened?" demanded Stephen Carr. "Miren!"

"Someone… someone has died. Dear God. Someone call the police!"

When nobody seemed to be able to move, Minnie slipped by Miren and stepped outside. At the edge of the kitchen garden, David and the Principal, Henry, were using their mobile phone lights to observe a body. Even from where she stood, metres away, Minnie recognised Sandra's hair and clothes. She had seen Sandra in the hall many times in her bright blue slippers, bringing laundry back and forth, and there they lay, abandoned on the freshly turned soil beside her feet. Sandra looked to have fallen but her feet were caked with dirt, not simply at the sole but between her toes. Had she been walking barefoot in the soil?

Henry looked ashen and stressed; pinching the bridge of his nose as David spoke. Minnie looked in the opposite direction, toward the open grounds. Why was Sandra here? Minnie checked the time on her phone. It was 2.30am. It was incredibly late. She wondered if Sandra suffered from insomnia. After all, she suspected Kate did – why else would someone run in the middle of the night?

Wes appeared from around the corner; his robe barely closed around his wide stomach. Minnie watched him approach the scene, attempting to break into a jog. "I've called the police and parameds," he called to David and Henry. "Baldwin's gone to check the gates ... make sure they can get in." He looked up, acknowledging Minnie's presence. "Better stay there," he added. "The more people come around the more we contaminate any evidence."

Minnie nodded and returned inside to over a dozen expectant faces. "The paramedics have been called. I think we should cancel..."

"But was it Sandra?" demanded Kate, visibly aggrieved.

"I think so. I recognise her slippers."

A collective gasp filled the room; many wiped solemn tears from their eyes.

"Jesus Christ!" cried whispered from the back, crossing themselves.

"Must've been a heart attack or something," said Edna in disbelief. "Minnie, who's out there?"

"Henry and David," said Minnie. "Wes called the police."

"Why police?" asked Miren.

"Don't they always get called when someone dies? You do police and parameds," said Kate.

"I feel horrible that she would have been alone," said a small woman to the right of her. "We ... one of us couldv'e helped!"

Miren put a warm hand on the woman's shoulder.

"Who's with the boarding students?" asked Stephen from the back of the crowd.

"The Rodgers'," said Edna.

"Alright, well, let's cancel lessons for tomorrow but make sure the students stay in their dorms," said Stephen. "We can hold online tutorials from our offices."

"All teachers should communicate with their heads of department," said Edna, her voice imposing an authority. "I'll schedule a meeting for 7am. Watch your inboxes for a link. Can I get all home-room teachers on a call in the next five minutes so we can draw up a plan for the boarding and day students? Thanks!"

Returning to her apartment, Minnie debated whether or not to call Charlie and tell her to collect Rob. As a boarding student, he stayed at the school throughout the term and returned home fortnightly on weekends. Minnie knew there was a high likelihood that Charlie was awake at this time as she was a long-time sufferer of insomnia. It went against all professional duty and was an abject breach of the school's privacy for Minnie to call Charlie with information on Sandra's death before an official notice had been sent through from the Principal. Minnie sat on the edge of her bed, her finger hovering over the call button. Was Sandra's death an accident or murder? If it was the latter, firstly, why, and second, were other staff or students in danger? Had she, like Stephen Graham, killed herself? If so, how and why? More intriguingly, why in the kitchen garden? Was the location significant? What was Sandra doing up so late? She had clearly been up for a reason. The question was – *why*? Insomnia? Was she meeting someone? It would not be the first time she had known of teachers meeting secretly in the night.

Within half an hour, police and paramedics arrived and the school was consumed with anxiety, fear, accusations and palpable stress. The faculty were tense as they undertook the duties allocated to them by the heads of departments. It was decided that Henry, as Principal, should be responsible for focusing on Sandra and supporting the police in their duties, and the running of the school itself was delegated to David as Acting Assistant Principal.

The police had not sent enough officers to interview the whole faculty and thus interviews began at around 3.30am and continued well into the mid-morning, when it was finally made clear that Sandra's death did not 'look' like an accident but rather intentional.

"I don't know what that means," said Minnie to the police officer sitting across from her in the library.

While Officer Lara Holgate set herself to interviewing staff on the ground level of the library, her partner, an older man who looked less than impressed at being awake in the middle of the night, settled himself in one of the small nooks upstairs. Lara was only slightly older than Minnie, full bodied and sported a freshly cut blonde bob. While she wore no makeup, she did tint her eyelashes and her nails were short but manicured.

"Just walk me through your movements last night," said Officer Holgate without looking up from her notes.

Minnie recalled the events of the evening, pausing now and then to clarify any questions posed to her.

"And you're new to the school?"

"Yes."

"What made you come to Mansfield then?"

"I felt like a change," said Minnie, taking inspiration from the copious murder mystery programming she had consumed over the years.

"Care to elaborate?"

"Not really. I'm a teacher. There was a position. I applied. I was successful," she said simply and without malice.

"Right," said Officer Holgate. "Can you please check the notes here and ensure your contact details are correct?"

The officer turned the small notepad toward her.

Mrs Marianna Koppelman-Fox

0400 123 456

"Correct," said Minnie.

"Does your husband live with you on campus, Mrs Fox?"

"My husband has passed away," said Minnie.

The moment that passed allowed both women to observe an understanding. Minnie was an uninteresting widow with no deep connections to the school outside of being a teacher. She doubted she would hear from the police again.

At 6am, Minnie, who felt as though she had collided with a truck, and a wretched-looking David met in the empty staffroom. David's under-eye bags were made more prominent by the pallor of his skin. He was distraught by the events of the evening. Minnie put her two years as a barista to good use and fired up the milk frother as David leaned against the counter.

"Do you want some whisky in here?" she asked, joking.

Without flinching, or indeed blinking, David opened the cupboard above her head and pulled out a glass bottle marked as 'golden syrup'.

"Seriously?" Minnie laughed.

"It's a secret. Wes knows how to make a coffee count in faculty meetings," he said, placing it next to the machine.

"And no one has found it?"

"It's a miracle."

David stared into the distance as the machine squealed. Minnie patted the side of the milk jug until it was too hot to touch.

"Once we report this incident to the wider community, the school will be under scrutiny. *More* scrutiny."

"That's to be expected. The circumstances are unfortunate," said Minnie, handing him his coffee. "The police didn't say for certain that she didn't die of natural causes."

"The police haven't said much but I think I'm right in guessing they don't think it was a heart attack. I don't know how these things are supposed to work," said David. "The Board has called an emergency meeting and the school's lawyers are already on their way down."

"I think closing the school will be too much of an intrusion on the students," said Minnie. "What about the Year 12 exams?"

David fiddled with the coffee cup, staring defeatedly ahead. "Hence – this is a disaster. Not in the least for poor Sandra."

"Did you know her well?" Minnie finished making her own coffee and leaned against the counter.

"Yeah – even went to the same university. Sandra was great – really devoted to the students. She took it hard when Stephen Graham died. He was in her wellbeing portfolio."

"That's an interesting connection."

"In what way?"

"Well, I suppose it's intriguing that two people so closely connected die within weeks of one another."

"Same could be said of anyone here."

True, thought Minnie but she was beginning to find the situation unnerving.

"Was she married?"

"Nah – totally devoted to her work. She'd been here about ten years. It's so remote – who has the time to go into town and get to know the locals?"

"Did she get along with everyone? I've only known her a short ..." Minnie caught herself. "I only knew her for a short time but she seemed respected."

"When you work in a place this long, you can rub people the wrong way sometimes but Sandra never did. She was a good teacher... a good colleague."

"Special lattes?" asked Wes upon entering the staffroom. Watery-eyed and unshaven, he had clearly not slept. "If Edna ever schedules a 7am meeting again, I'll be up on murder charges."

Minnie shook her head, hiding a smile as she began making his coffee.

Wes sat down at the bench. "The police took Sandra away. At least the poor woman isn't lying in dirt anymore."

"We're closing the school for a week," said David. "The students will be picked up this afternoon."

"How are we managing the senior school workload?" asked Wes, scratching the stubble on his jelly-like cheek.

"Online. They'll have to do their exams on TechLearn," said David. "Classes are the same schedule. Middle and junior students come back Monday week. Set them a week's worth of tasks and upload to the system to get a 'satisfactory' or 'unsatisfactory'. I'll show you where to find some of the content we used during lockdowns. We need the time."

"Have you sent out the notice to parents?"

David nodded as he finished his coffee. "Those of us without a well-being group need to be on the extensions to answer parent questions. Ideally, we want all students with their parents by 6pm."

"That won't be a problem. I'm sure they're clamouring in their Range Rovers to pick up their little darlings," said Wes, taking the coffee Minnie offered him with a grateful nod. "Ok," he said before taking a sip. "What do we think the police will say?"

"What do you mean?" asked David.

"You're not serious?"

"I am."

Wes looked astounded. "Sandra. They'll ask for DNA if they think she's not died of natural causes."

"That's not for certain," said David, sipping his coffee.

"If she didn't die of natural causes, then we have to accept that there was an intruder on campus," said Minnie.

"Or..." Wes took a purposeful pause and sip.

"No," said David, definitively.

"You know I respect you mate, but you need to get a clue."

Minnie was astounded that David had not considered the prospect of someone at the school being responsible. It was an uncomfortable, or perhaps unfair conclusion, but it was not beyond the realm of reality. Wes, despite his lack of sensitivity, seemed to comprehend their reality more clearly than David. Perhaps it was exhaustion, shock or a mix of the two, but Minnie understood the situation clearly, why then, did David not?

At the end of the day, after seeing to the students, the staff settled in the dining room. They were broken; slumped, head-in-hands, and sitting stone-faced amongst armchairs and tables. Keeping students calm and parents' questions at bay had driven many of them beyond the point of explosion. Minnie passed her colleagues in the halls, the gardens, and the carpark multiple times throughout the day and shared fed up glances, eyerolls and muttering obscenities under their breath, most of which were followed by 'how many years till retirement?' and 'I didn't sign up for this shit.' As the newest member of staff, Minnie felt obligated to remain the most calm and supportive of her colleagues. By dinner time she was sporting a wild headache, aching shoulders, and a sore throat from her repeated and now perfectly practised speech to parents about child safety and having no information on the situation as it was a police matter.

"It's hit the news," said Kate, scrolling through her phone while resting her feet on another chair and nursing a half empty bottle of beer. "Prestigious Grammar school rocked again by death on campus," she read aloud when most of the room had turned their attention to her. "By now parents will be wondering if there is something seriously amiss with the private school which hosts 900 of the most privileged students in Victoria. It was made known today that a member of staff passed away on campus in the early hours of the morning. An official statement from the school announced an investigation was taking place. More to come."

"Well, that's not too bad," said Jenny Rodgers as she massaged her own neck.

Miren strode into the room; her silk Kimono billowing behind her. "Henry is meeting with the Board of Directors. This is a disaster."

"Why?" asked Kate, still sifting through news on her phone.

"Apparently, someone heard the police discussing whether it looked like Sandra was attacked," said Miren. "I don't think anyone can leave the campus."

"Attacked?" Jenny looked horrified. "Attacked for what? Why?"

"They cannot stop us from leaving campus," said Felicity, sitting across from Wes. "No one is under arrest."

"We can be cautioned not to leave the state," said Stephen Carrs, removing the heat pack from his forehead.

"But nobody knows *definitively* what happened," said Felicity, her eyes flashing as though daring anyone to oppose her. "For all we know, the poor woman... she *suffered a heart attack* and... and instead of mourning her the way we should, we're bullshitting with bullshit, *bullshit* conspiracies like this is a *bloody* episode of Poirot."

Felicity snatched the box of tissues offered by Jenny and dabbed her eyes, furiously pink in the neck and cheeks.

"She's right," said Jenny, pensively. "We shouldn't speculate. It's not kind."

Kate shot Minnie a look that was halfway between an eye roll and 'are they serious?' Minnie bit back a smile and shrugged.

Angela Greenwood, a Humanities teacher, sat in the armchair beside Minnie and closed her eyes. "I suggest everyone turns off their phones. I have 53 emails sitting in my inbox."

"I don't have email on my phone. Isn't it bad enough we're on call 24/7 here?" asked Miren, pouring herself a glass of wine. "I'm beginning to think the money isn't worth the stress in this job."

"It isn't," said Wes, with a deep barreling laugh.

Minnie observed a number of teachers in clusters around the room, many of whom seemed to be coming up with theories of their own. Without immediate answers from the police, it was only natural that the staff began to share information and conclude agendas and outcomes based on the limited facts presented. Hearsay was the backbone of many theories haphazardly woven together by those in conversation. Minnie found herself in the middle of a number of these conversations but never offered an opinion. Those who knew Sandra better were in more of a position to theorise as to why she was outside so late.

"Sandra wasn't a night owl," said Olivia Jeong, the office manager. "She hated the dark. She thought the property was haunted."

"Seriously?" asked Minnie as they left the staffroom.

"Everyone has something," she said empathetically. "Sandra was afraid of the dark."

"Well, she was out last night so clearly she pushed through her fear," said Minnie.

"But *why*?" said Olivia. "Sandra didn't even do overnight school camps and refused to be a den mother to the boarding kids because she's so scared of being on the grounds at night."

"Did she ever tell you why she thought the grounds were haunted?"

Olivia pointed to the painting of one of the original owners of the house as they wandered the main hall back to the office. It was of an impressive man with thick brows holding a pocket watch. The painting struck Minnie as unusual, but she could not think why. Why had the painter decided to capture such an unappealing expression? The man looked as though he were smelling something unpleasant or sneering. She had always tried not to judge people in paintings according to their expressions, deciding in the flicker of a moment whether they were good or bad, kind or ill tempered. It was unfair and disingenuous considering the painter had such a short time to capture their likeness.

"Jasper Millard. Hung himself on the grounds," said Olivia.

"That's horrible."

The surname was embossed under every portrait in the house. The Millard's were a powerful family in colonial Australia. They were not so important as to be titled, but important, or more accurately, wealthy enough to have become well known in high society both in Australia and abroad.

"Notice the time on his watch?"

"Two o'clock," said Minnie.

"That's the time he hung himself."

"Oh, was this painted posthumously?"

Olivia gave Minnie a serious look. "No."

Minnie side-eyed her colleague, unsure as to whether she was being subtly teased or told a genuine story. Evidence of its truth was non-existent and the details were remarkably worthy of a Shirely Jackson horror. "What a horrible coincidence."

"If you think it's a coincidence," said Olivia in a tone that suggested that she did not think it was any such thing. "Take it from me – Sandra had good reason to be scared of the dark. This place ... it messes with your brain."

Minnie left Olivia and her conspiracy at the office and continued to her rooms for some peace. She had a number of missed calls, mostly from Charlie. She responded with a text, promising to call soon. Before heading to bed, on impulse, Minnie opened her computer to check her emails. She was astounded when the top email in her inbox read from the school address of Kane Liu.

Chapter 5

The Melancholy of Kai Watanabe

IF KAI WATANABE WAS quiet before Sandra's death, there was little to no hope of communication with him now she had passed away. When her fifth attempt to raise concerns about his recalcitrance was met with bureaucratese, she recognised that she was expected to handle the situation without input from leadership. The only emotion the boy had demonstrated was a slight twitch in his high cheekbones when she mentioned the benefit that might come from having a meeting with his parents and the school. When he muttered a promise to attend classes in future, Minnie filed the notion of contacting his parents away for future leverage. Kai kept to his promise and was certainly present in the class but she soon gave up on any attempts to have him engage in class or answer emails, and by sheer exhaustion of will allowed him to simply exist in the room. She was in no danger of winning any pedagogical award. As Tabitha took her turn to read out her analysis of 'The Munich Mannequins' to the catatonic class, Minnie observed Kai as he stared out of the window; half slumped, drawing aimlessly on the corner of his notebook. Perhaps a meeting with his parents and a councillor was necessary; he was taking Sandra's death awfully hard.

After instructing the class to complete a thirty-minute written analysis of the poem, Minnie turned her attention, once again, to the email from Kane. Its timely arrival confirmed that while he was absent, the school was keeping him informed - where necessary - of events. How else would he know her name and email? It was reasonable to assume that Henry or David had responded to Kane's staff-wide email of the previous week and asked him to keep in touch with Minnie, seeing as she had taken over his classes. What was strange - or forgetful of them - was that neither had mentioned doing so.

Dear Miss Fox,

Apologies for not being able to meet you in person. If you need any resources for your classes, you can access my school server using my log-in details below.

Username: K-Liu

Password: Soliloquy

Regards,

K. Liu

Whatever instincts guided her, Minnie felt no need to inform anyone of the email. Her mother called it 'feminine intuition' but Minnie was less inclined to believe in power beyond what humans could see and hear, especially since losing her husband, and put her decision down to self preservation. Since Sandra's death, she had found herself engaging with colleagues less frequently. Their constant theories, hearsay rather, were tiresome. The staff were unhappy at having been interviewed by police, raging against leadership about the situation requiring they go 'above and beyond the scope of their contracts'. Forgivable behaviour but their theories - ranging from the lame to the absurd - encouraged her to avoid the staffroom as much as possible.

"Miss fox?"

Minnie blinked. The classroom was empty.

Kai stood in front of her desk; his dark brow furrowed with concern. "You didn't even move when the bell rang," he said.

"That's not professional of me, is it?" she said apologetically, closing her computer.

"It's the stress."

"Stress?"

"From the situation."

Minnie nodded. "Maybe. What can I do for you, Kai?"

"Ms Keys was my wellbeing support," he said, as though Minnie would understand his inference.

"Have you been reassigned to another wellbeing support officer?"

Kai scratched the back of his head so that the thick, black strands of his hair stood on end. "There's no point. I don't need one."

As intrigued as she was that he was conversing with her, especially considering her previous failures to get more than single-word responses, she wondered why he chose to discuss this with her rather than someone more senior, or even someone more familiar.

"It's part of your learning support. I know you and Ms Keys would have formed a bond, and you trusted her, but Mrs English and Mrs Simonds would be just as capable."

"Ms Key has my file."

"It can be forwarded to your next wellbeing mentor."

"Ms Keys knew things about me. Things I don't want shared."

Minnie shuffled her feet under the desk, crossing and uncrossing her legs at the ankles. She felt small under his focused stare and regretted her decision to remain seated while he stood at the desk.

"What can I help you with, Kai? Do you want your file kept confidential from your next wellbeing support officer?"

As Kai made to answer, the classroom door flew open and Kate strolled into the room, holding onto the handle. "Minnie, I thought we might – oh! Hello, Kai!"

Minnie was not startled by the unexpected intrusion, but made note of Kai's peculiar expression. His ears turned a noticeable shade of red.

"Tutoring?" asked Kate.

"Further reading," said Kai. "Thanks for the advice, Miss Fox."

He left before she could respond. Kate stepped aside, casting Minnie a sympathetic look as he left. "Good kid, lots of issues," she said. "Lunch?"

"I might just catch up on some planning. Sorry. Can we do dinner in the apartment? I'm not up for eating with everyone else tonight," said Minnie.

"Works for me," said Kate as she left.

After reading Kane's email again, she decided that what was needed and could possibly be attained was clarity. All she needed was evidence. She knocked once on the half-open door to Wes's office and entered, determined that she should find an answer. He was adding a healthy amount of whisky to his coffee. Unperturbed, he raised the travel-sized whisky bottle in offering before stowing it away in a drawer when she shook her head.

"You look done with this day," he said in greeting.

"The day, the week, the month," she agreed. "Do you know if any of the kids can track an email?"

"I'm sure they all can," he said, taking a healthy sip of coffee. "Little goblins can do anything except read a fucking book for more than a minute."

As tempted as she was to agree on the sorry state of the adolescent attention span, she pushed forward. "Anyone specific? Anyone who can keep information to themselves?"

Wes scratched his unshaven, portly chin. "What about Lily Orange? She is in IT."

"Can she keep things private?"

"She tries," said Wes, who did not seem wholly convinced by his own suggestion. "I'd hold off on involving a student in whatever machinations you're up to until you know it's not a breach of child safety, or whatever other fucking rules are imposed on us."

"So, Lily?"

"Lily. Why?"

"I need her to track an email."

"Who's it from?"

Minnie pulled out her computer. "Can you keep this to yourself for now?"

Wes opened his arms, smiling wistfully. "Who would I tell?"

"This school leaks like an old motor engine," said Minnie. "Don't think I don't know about Miren and Henry."

Wes laughed indulgently. "It's the stuff of nightmares."

Minnie showed Wes the email from Kane Liu. She waited for his exclamation of surprise, a moment of shock, but Wes responded to reading the email with a mere raising of eyebrows.

"How did he get your email address?"

"I wondered that. Easily explainable. David or Henry could have forwarded it. But why didn't they tell me? I'd have expected this. Otherwise ... is he still in the school system? Perhaps he could log in remotely and get my details?"

"No, he's blocked from the system."

"Clearly, he wasn't. Wait... if he's on leave, why would he be blocked?"

"The school would see him as not being on 'active' duty. They'd just block access to the system for privacy reasons."

Wes finished his whisky coffee. "You know, I'm not saying this to make you feel any kind of way... but Kane is a good guy. I don't pretend to know his motives for leaving so abruptly ... or why he didn't tell anyone, but I know he's a good guy. Just look at what he's written in the email. He's wanting to help."

"Leadership must know why he needed leave."

"Burn out. Happens all the time. Look at me..." he said, raising his empty coffee cup. "I'm sipping the Golden Hooch with the world's worst coffee to keep my last two brain cells going. This place will do more to me than a simple get-up-and-leave by the time it's done with me; I can tell you that."

"I have a few 'what ifs'?" Minnie was sure he could see the possibility.

"Which is why you want someone to track the email?" said Wes.

"Yes."

"It's a leap."

"You said it yourself - the school blocked him from the system."

"I say a lot of things."

"It's worth being sure."

"Why not just go to leadership and ask them?"

"Would you?"

Stalemate. Minnie found herself holding her breath.

"Ok," he said, leaning back in his chair and holding out both arms. "Ok, yes... sure." He slapped both hands on his desk. "Yes."

"Yes?"

"Yes. Lily. She's good. She does all my 'legal' movie downloads. For sure she'd know how to do this."

"Legal movie downloads?"

"I can't be bothered driving an hour into town to go to the movies, so Lily helps me," he said quickly. "Let's meet tonight. Here."

"It'll have to be late."

"What else do we have to do at a boarding school?"

~

Minnie ended her phone call with Charlie on a hopeful note despite her friend wanting details on how the school was handling Sandra's death. Over a week had passed since Sandra's passing and the students were well into the following school week, many recovering from having to complete assessments off campus. Minnie was bound by confidentiality, and could not repeat anything discussed in staff meetings, but she could assure Charlie that the school had returned to relatively normal function. Hardly a moment passed after the call ended, when a knock sounded at the apartment door. Rob stood in the hallway; he looked agitated.

"How did you get in here?"

Rob shifted uncomfortably. "I have to tell you something."

"Can we walk and talk?" asked Minnie, agitated and reaching for her jacket on the hook by the door. "You're not allowed in here. People will talk."

"Kinda why I need to talk."

Minnie was taken aback. "What do you mean?"

"Can we *go*?" he urged.

Rob looked over his shoulder and led the way down the residence halls and out the back door. The crisp air bit at Minnie's face and hands. She searched her jacket pockets in the hope that she had left her gloves in them. Rob was striding away from the building with haste; burrowing his face in the folds of his scarf to shield against the wind. Once they were far from Main House, passed the gardens and nearing the closed gates, Rob slowed down. The lampposts dotted around the grounds were their only source of light as the sun hid behind the mountains, signalling the end of the day. They were alone on the grounds, save the students with horses tending to their animals in the nearby barn. Every window in the surrounding buildings was lit. Figures of students and staff in various states of activity could be seen preparing for, beginning, or finishing tasks.

"Do you want to talk to me as a teacher, or your friend?" asked Minnie, observing his anxious state.

"My friend. I need to tell you a secret... but you can't tell mum."

Minnie wanted to highlight the unfairness of the demand, to reject the notion outright. She could not, in good faith, promise not to repeat something to Charlie, especially because it included her child. If Charlie ever discovered that Minnie kept information from her regarding Rob, the fallout would be catastrophic.

"*Promise.*"

Minnie was taken aback by the harshness of his tone. He looked desperate.

It was imperative she remained calm, to ease him into talking. "Tell me what's happened."

Rob's lip trembled; he held back tears. "It was a mistake. You understand, right?"

"What was a mistake?"

"No one intended it to happen. It just did! I think Stephen killed himself over it!"

"What? Over what?"

Rob's cheeks and ears were pink from the cold. He looked tormented. "There was this... this *understanding*... in the group. Everyone was curious. It was supposed to be harmless."

"What are you talking about?" Each phrase confused her more. "Which group? Curious about what?"

"There was a group of us – Stephen too. It was total curiosity."

Minnie wanted to shake him. Why was he speaking in riddles?

"Rob!"

Minnie and Rob looked toward the house, startled. Kate was approaching.

"I've been waiting in the library," she said, looking curiously from Minnie to Rob. "Didn't we have tutoring?"

"Right – sorry," he said, dejected. "Forgot the time."

"Wait..." Minnie was astounded by his change.

"Is anything wrong?" asked Kate.

"Nah, Lit question," said Rob. "Sorry, Miss Vincini."

Minnie wanted to tell Kate to wait for Rob in the library while they finished up but Rob had already begun walking back. She stood for a moment, angry that what had been so intense was suddenly dissipated. She debated whether to call Rob back and demand they finish their conversation, to send Kate away and cover the request with an excuse of acting in Rob's educational best interest. She felt trapped by Rob's sudden change and departure, and imposed upon by Kate who had seen no need to notice the privacy of the conversation and leave them be – tutoring session or not.

"Absent minded, all of them," Kate said to Minnie and they all walked back to the main property. "Why am I always chasing after these bloody kids?"

Minnie observed Rob in silence, following his lead. He had gone from overtly anxious to calm so quickly she was concerned for his mental state. Rob had always been a private person, rarely emotional, and shy. If he knew something about Stephen's death she wanted to be told. If he was involved in something dangerous, perhaps illegal, she wanted to be told. She was bound by Reporting Laws related to child safety, but the lines were blurred in this instance. Was she duty-bound to press the issue? *What is the group? And what was supposed to be harmless?* She needed to write this down before she forgot. Minnie watched them head toward the library. Kate gave her a half-hearted wave goodbye before reminding Rob of his obligations to keep appointments.

It would be almost midnight before Wes messaged Minnie to meet him in the library. Minnie snuck from the apartment, ever grateful that Kate slept with a white-noise machine on high, and slinked to the library using the light from her phone to light the way. Lily smiled excitedly; her round face illuminated by the harsh light of the three monitors. Her signature red lipstick had faded throughout the day, and her mass of red hair was tied back haphazardly.

"Let's do this," said Wes, lowering his portly self into a swivel chair by the desk. "I'm so curious about this mystery I can't stand it."

"Can you sign-in here?" asked Lily, nudging the keyboard toward Minnie.

"You know this cannot be discussed," said Minnie, hesitating.

Lily nodded earnestly. "I can keep secrets."

Minnie wanted to say it was counterintuitive to trust a barely-twenty year old student with staffing secrets, but her options were limited. If she was going to try to confirm unequivocally that Kane was in Tasmania then she needed help. Lily peered at her through her thick-rimmed glasses, bright-eyed and as innocently earnest as a child. Once Minnie entered her security details, Lily was away. She typed quickly, said nothing, and observed the three screens as needed. She looked manic, hypnotised by her work.

After twenty tense, silent minutes, the sound of the clicking keyboard ceased, and both Minnie and Wes sat up from their doze with instant expectations. Lily looked concerned. She was looking from the first to the third screen, back and forth.

"*What*?" Wes demanded. "Did you track it?"

"Well, yes – but the IP address makes no sense."

"Why?" asked Minnie.

"The fucks an IP address?" said Wes.

"It's an Internet Protocol address. Think of it as a special address for your computer or phone."

"But the internet is the internet," said Wes.

"What do you mean?" asked Lily.

"The internet…" he said, waving his arms around. "It's everywhere. How does it have an address?"

Lily looked both amused and shocked. "Ok, I'm not even going to make fun of you right now. All you need to know is that every device has an IP address. Your computer, your phone – it is a signature. It's how I can go on the internet and find where a specific thing – like this email – was sent from."

"Did you find it?" asked Minnie, ignoring Wes's increasingly confused expression.

"Yes – it's *here*."

Wes rubbed his temples. "I've never felt so stupid. *Two* post-graduate degrees and I'm the dumbest in the room right now."

"What's here?" asked Minnie.

"Mr Liu's computer!" said Lily.

"What?"

Lily waved them over. Once behind her, Lily showed them her screens. The first screen had Minnie's email open on a web browser, the second showed a black background with a myriad of writing, and the third screen showed a browser with a map.

"Ok, so I pulled the email data and ran it through a few programs. All that's relevant to you is that the IP address that sent this email is on the school grounds."

"Meaning?"

"The device that sent it is on the grounds."

"Right now?"

"Right now."

"So Kane is *here*?" asked Wes, pointing to the map on the third screen.

"That's not what I said," said Lily.

"The computer is here," said Minnie, finally understanding.

"Correct. Want to know something else?"

"Yes."

"I tracked his phone IP. That's here too."

"Where? Can you tell us which room? Building maybe?"

"No. Sorry."

"How do you know his phone IP?" asked Wes.

"Mr Liu used to come to me for help with tech too," said Lily. "This is just weird. Why would his phone and computer be here? Did he leave them behind?"

"Maybe he never left," said Wes.

Minnie and Lily looked to him with expressions of disbelief.

"I'm *voicing* what we all *need* to be thinking," said Wes defensively. "Kane all-of-a-sudden decides to go on leave and no one hears from him since. Kane loves this school and loves his job."

"What are you saying? He's hiding in the school and sending emails?" asked Minnie.

"I don't know what I'm saying. I'm just trying to come up with answers. I'm losing more hair than I can afford right now," he said, running a thick hand over his thinning hair.

"Did you hear the rumour?" asked Lily, sheepishly.

"What rumour? There are a thousand rumours."

"The one about Mr Liu and the Year 12 theatre boys," said Lily.

"You better not be going what I think you're going with this," said Wes, his little eyes flashing.

Lily blushed. "I didn't say I believe it... it's just been repeated," she muttered.

"What rumour?" asked Minnie.

"Ah some bullshit about Kane having it off with the Year 12 theatre kids," said Wes. "It's absolute *crap*."

"It does explain why he left in a hurry," said Lily. "You can't deny it *might* be."

"*Do not repeat that horseshit,*" said Wes. "That's how people get *ruined.*"

"But what if it's true?" Lilly pressed.

Wes scoffed. "Where's the evidence? Find me *one* witness or one victim. Listen Lily, if the person telling you the rumour isn't happy to put their name to the words, don't believe what they tell you. It's far braver to stand in witness than to stand in the shadows and make up stories."

While Minnie thought Wes's anger was misplaced on Lily, she agreed wholeheartedly. Rumours in schools were daily occurrences and it was up to the shrewd and the tight-lipped to stop the rumour in its tracks by not repeating it. Minnie did not deny for a moment that where there was smoke there was fire, and rumours, like folktales, had real origins, but they were hardly ever what was expected. If someone, or multiple people, was spreading false rumours of Mr Liu's behaviour toward the students, that may explain why he left in a hurry. Was it perhaps the shame of the accusation that caused him to take leave? Was this likely why leadership were so tightlipped? *And did this have anything to do with the group Rob had mentioned*? She sincerely hoped not because if it did, it lent more weight to the rumours surrounding Kane.

"No one has said this to me," said Minnie.

Lily's eyebrows rose. "Really?"

"No one."

"That's odd," said Lily, closing the computer down. "It was Kate who told me."

Wes rolled his eyes. "Fucking classic."

Chapter 6

The Nude Photo Scandal

EXCLUSIVE SCHOOL TEACHER'S DEATH ruled 'suspected homicide'.

"As usual," said Wes after reading the newspaper headline, "these bottom-feeders cannot structure a proper sentence."

"As offensive as the syntax is, should we not be distressed by the content of the headline?"

They were alone in the dining room, enjoying precious few moments of serenity. Soon, their colleagues would join them, sleepily and distractedly, for mere mouthfuls of coffee and toast before shuffling to their offices to prepare for the day.

"Naturally, we're not animals," he muttered, scanning the article. "Fuck this was written with crayon. Don't journalists have any flare anymore? It's like reading the taste equivalent of bran!"

"How are we expected to react in front of the students?" said Minnie. "I don't know if I can make sense of it."

"Who'd want to kill, Sandra? And *why*?"

"And was it an intruder or someone on staff?" It felt like the more pressing question.

"This is going to be an absolutely shit day," said Miren, entering in an emerald wool suit.

"Lots of emails due to the article?" asked Minnie.

"Ah the emails can burn for all I care," said Miren, while sorting her coffee and toast. "I've just read that my friend and colleague of ten years was murdered. How can I come to terms – how can *anyone* – come to terms and teach effectively at the same time? The higher ups won't hear a word about us taking a day for grief. They've made the councillors available to us for an hour or so but nothing else."

Wes looked perplexed. "You thought the school would approve a day of leave?"

Miren glared at him and joined their table. "Shut up."

"It's a *business*. They don't give a crap about us. We're cogs in the wheel, Miren."

"We're *people*," she said, flicking a linen napkin across her lap.

"You know, you have *some* sway over the higher ups, Miren," he said pointedly.

"I'll pour this over you, you fucking walrus," she said acidly, pausing before taking a sip of coffee.

Minnie pretended to be engrossed in the article on her phone, but she suspected Wes was referring to Miren's not-so-secret relationship with the Principal, Henry Waterstone.

Wes raised his hands in a show of regret. "That's on me – I know how you feel about us talking about your private life. And despite the fact that *everyone* knows, I won't mention it again. Or the fact that you can convince Hippy-Henry to give us a long weekend with the power of your ..."

"Watch it!" Miren warned.

"... *womanhood*."

"You fucking disgrace," she said, laughing.

"I'm a sicko."

"I'm sorry about him," Miren said to Minnie. "He has no respect."

"Ah, he's alright," said Minnie.

The week that followed saw the school, on edge by the misfortune that seemed to have plagued them for months, begin to resemble an unremarkable institution of education. The polish and pride of Mansfield Grammar was fading, replaced by anxiety and suspicion, falling standards and lax repercussions. Following the revelation that Mr Liu's computer and phone were on the school premises, Minnie and Wes met nightly to discuss the possibilities of finding it. It concluded in a close call, when, two nights after the discovery, they set out to search Mr Liu's apartment. They moved quietly and quickly, without lights, through the wood-panelled halls of Main House, up to the third floor. The teacher's residences were in the same location; only Boarding Masters and couples lived outside of Main House.

The apartment, situated one level above Minnie's in what was the old servants quarters, was unlocked. Wes and Minnie shared a look of disbelief as the door swung open upon their turning the handle. "Well, stealing this was a waste of time," said Wes, holding up an old key with a tag that read 'L3A2'. The air was stale; clearly the rooms had been closed and empty a while. Minnie was tempted to open a window as she was in the habit of airing her rooms daily. It took but a few moments of surface inspection to realise the apartment was empty.

"It's emptier than empty," said Wes, opening and closing cupboard doors.

"Walls and floor," she said in agreement.

Wes, visibly deflated, was leading the way out when the distinct, heartstopping sound of approaching footsteps. Minnie had no intention of being caught by the person in the neighbouring apartment. They turned off their phone lights, held their breath, and waited. Oddly, the footsteps were slow and purposeful. Wes looked to Minnie, his brow creased; through the dim light of the moon, she saw beads of sweat across his forehead. She held his gaze and then looked pur-posefully down at the shadows on the floor, visible beneath the gap at the base of the door. Wes followed her line of vision. Someone stood outside the door. They stared at the shadow, silently imploring for intervention from a higher power. Whether their appeals were heard or not, Minnie would never know, but the moment the shadow turned and departed, she released her breath and rested her hands on her knees.

"Edna," said Wes, breathing out in a whisper.

"How do you know?"

"The woman bathes in Chanel No. 5."

Once on the second floor, they came face-to-face with Kate. She met them with raised eyebrows. "Ghost hunting?" she asked sarcastically.

"Don't turn your nose up to things you don't understand," said Wes with contrived playfulness.

"Where have you been?" asked Minnie.

"Tutoring," said Kate with a helpless sigh. "Watanabe really isn't making progress. I'm going to have to email his parents."

"I'll leave it here then," said Wes. "Night, ladies."

Kate and Minnie walked back to their apartment. "Just be mindful with Wes," said Kate, unlocking the door. "Take some of what he says with a grain of salt."

Minnie felt her phone vibrate in the back pocket of her jeans. She did not need to look at it to know it was Wes messaging to comment on their close call.

"Oh?"

"Bit of a know-it-all."

That was undeniable but what was also true was that he was keep-ing the secret of the mystery of Kane's email. "Tea?" asked Minnie, heading for the kettle.

"Sure." Kate unzipped her jacket and flung it in her room.

"You have scratch marks on your back," said Minnie, concerned.

Kate looked startled. As was human habit, she attempted to look over her shoulder at her own back. She patted her left shoulder blade with her right hand. "Oh, yes... I had a really bad itch when I was running."

"Must have been!" said Minnie, turning back casually to get the tea from the cupboard. She did not feel it necessary to point out that her back looked like the result of falling into a bramblebush.

"So, how have you settled in?" she asked, emerging from her room while pulling a jumper on.

"Oh, great! The classes are going well. I don't know if I can handle the death of another faculty member though," said Minnie. "Herbal or black?"

"Herbal for me," said Kate. "Peppermint, if we have it."

"Insomnia?"

"Since I was a kid," said Kate. "The running helps but I'm wired differently."

They settled on the couch. All around them, stacks of papers and books signalled the need to work; whether marking, planning or admin, a teacher's workload was constant. Minnie had little to no intention of working that night. She was edgy from almost being caught in Kane's apartment, and even more on edge at having no answers to the many questions that, with each action she took, insisted on multiplying.

"This is nice," said Kate. "We haven't even had time to sit and talk, have we? It all just gets in the way, doesn't it?"

"Yes, it does." Minnie returned to the couch with cake.

"Can I ask you something?"

"Sure." Minnie took a bite but a tingle of apprehension whipped at her nerves. Did Kate suspect her and Wes of having come from Kane's apartment?

"Are you married?"

Minnie looked at her; Kate nodded to her left hand and reached out to touch the blue sapphire on her engagement ring. Kate's finger brushed the precious gem. "I was," Minnie found herself saying, admiring as the light reflected off the blue. Kate's hand retreated; Minnie straightened the bands as a way to buy time and push down the tightness in her throat that signalled tears. "I'm a widow."

It was to Minnie's great surprise that Kate smiled. "I knew there was a reason for why someone like you would come to this far-away place."

"Someone like me?"

Kate nodded. "Young, smart... clearly accomplished. Why would you come here?"

"Maybe I did want somewhere quiet," said Minnie. "Somewhere to ..."

"Heal?" Kate suggested.

It was Minnie's turn to smile. The moment her mouth turned, it broke the seal and the familiar flood of tears cascaded down her cheeks. Kate reached out, gripping her hand.

"Hey," she said softly. "I'm sorry. I shouldn't have asked. It was insensitive."

"You don't heal," said Minnie, wiping her cheeks. "There's no such thing."

A long moment of silence passed wherein each sipped their tea, sitting uncomfortably in the weight of emotion. The pressure in her chest would take hours to pass, as always. She pulled her phone from her pocket and showed Kate the photo of her and Jamie.

Kate smiled. "He looks kind."

"He was. Very." Minnie smiled at the photo as though the Jamie in the image could see her. Sometimes, in her extreme moments of loneliness, she imagined it might be true; that he was there somehow.

"How long ago?"

"Six months," said Minnie. "One day. One ordinary day. Then it turned extraordinary. I couldn't do anything afterward. The school offered me a week of grief leave."

"A week?"

"Five days to be specific." Minnie got up to get more cake. When she returned, she brought the whole half she'd stolen from the dining room.

"The system really looks after us," Kate said sarcastically.

"I left."

Kate frowned.

"My first day back after Jamie died," said Minnie. "I was in my classroom... then I couldn't speak. It was like God – or *whatever* is out in the universe – took away my mind, and my voice. All I remember is picking up my bag and walking out of the school."

"Where did you go?"

"The mountains," said Minnie, nodding toward Mount Buller. The undulating wilderness that acted as the backdrop of the school. "Jamie loved the mountains. So, I went there."

"You went there to die," said Kate.

Minnie locked eyes with her. In that moment, she felt naked in her own truth. She had never admitted it to anyone, least of all herself. She had gone to the cabin they had frequented so often. Perhaps it had been to remind herself of the happiness they had shared, perhaps it was to act as a blanket of comfort in her pain. As she sat in front of the fireplace, staring into the flames, she longed to reach out and feel her husband, even if it was on her way to heaven. Death had made her question the existence of other worlds as a way to hold on to the hope that they might be reunited. No religion had ever been part of her life but when Jamie had ripped from her, she was forced to question her beliefs. In her sanity, she knew that death was final but in her grief, Jamie was waiting for her on the other side.

"I went there to die," she admitted. What she did not admit was that the school had filed a formal complaint with the states teachers association for 'severe unprofessional conduct'. Unable to reconcile that a teacher in grief could not complete their duties so quickly after losing a spouse, the school had suggested an investigation and the temporary suspension of her teaching licence. Minnie, unable to think straight, called her brother, a lawyer, and had him handle the paperwork and negotiations while she came to terms with her loss in the mountains. She was glad she followed his advice and saw a therapist, for it was his letter, confirming she had suffered a breakdown, that saved her the hassle of dealing with the bureaucracy.

Kate blinked away tears. "I need something stronger than tea now," she said, making for the kitchen.

Minnie kissed her wedding rings, as was her habit.

Kate returned with a bottle of brandy. "Drink before dinner?"

Minnie laughed. "I've spoiled mine," she said, nodding to the cake on her fork. "What brought you here?" She sensed Kate's hesitation. "It's only fair. I shared my secret. Now you share yours."

"I have lots of secrets," said Kate, handing her the brandy. "I came here for the community. It's small. It's routine. It's work."

Minnie agreed. "Yes, it is."

"Sometimes I think about how old this place is and I imagine the lives of the people in it... the original owners," she said, looking around as though observing a museum's galleries. "It's what drew me here. I got sick of public schools and their blank, square box build-ings. Sometimes you have to go beyond the 'functional', you know? You need to *look* at beautiful things. Beautiful architecture, beautiful scenery, beautiful people."

It was certainly something Minnie could appreciate.

"Are you from Victoria?"

"Queensland," said Kate. "Fucking Gold Coast. The only thing that place inspired in me is fitness. Actually, I lie. It inspired me to fucking escape."

"No surf and sun for you then."

"No way. I'll take the mountains any day of the week."

"Can I ask you something then? In the spirit of getting to know one another?"

"Go ahead."

"Why do you think Kane left?"

Kate sighed and poured herself another brandy. "You won't like my answer."

"Oh?"

"I don't like to speak about people who aren't here to defend themselves but Kane isn't the saintly man everyone makes him out to be," said Kate. "I'm sorry, but he just isn't. Everyone here likes to think of him as this dedicated teacher and do-anything-to-help colleague but we are all aware of the rumours. Leadership doesn't talk about it much because of confidentiality but the rumours are there."

"Which rumours?"

"Oh, that Kane likes to be *close* to some of the students. No one's gone as far as to accuse him of anything *specifically* indecent but once the word is out..." Kate shrugged. "Anyway. That's why I think he left. I think something was about to come out that he didn't want made public."

"Where do you think he is?"

"Bottom of a well for all I know," she said nonchalantly. "Apparently he's in Tasmania."

"What about Stephen Graham?"

"What about him?"

"What was he like?"

Kate's expression settled into one of wistful sorrow. "He was a good kid. He had friends but he kept to himself. No one could have seen it coming."

"No one?"

"I don't know what he told his mentor. I suppose Sandra was the only person who'd know but she's gone now."

"What do you think happened to her?"

"I think she crossed someone she shouldn't have," said Kate.

"In the school?"

"No," said Kate, shaking her head. "Sandra used to help in town. Volunteer, you know?"

"Is it possible someone became interested in her? Maybe a little obsessed?"

"Maybe. Nothing can be off the table with this kind of thing."

"I think it's far more likely that Sandra was seeing someone in secret," said Minnie. "I've watched enough crime shows to know these things are usually the result of a relationship breakdown."

"True," said Kate, twirling her brandy glass thoughtfully in her palm. "I don't think anyone in here could hurt another person."

Minnie nodded but in reality, she did not know whether to consider Kate naïve or a liar. The police, though no closer to catching a culprit at present than they were the night of Sandra's death, were thorough in their investigation of the grounds and security cameras. No one knew what the police had uncovered so far but it hung over their heads like a circling albatross. When would the police visit next? Would it be to collect more evidence or to arrest someone?

In the dining room, dinner had hardly been served before an uncomfortable wave of murmurings enveloped the room. Slowly, with nudging and encouragement, colleagues were telling one another to check their emails. Like dominos, their expressions morphed from curious to horrified, followed almost immediately by their beseeching of the person beside them to check their emails. David and Minnie, latecomers to the dining room and still serving themselves, noticed the copycat actions of the staff, and without asking, checked their own phones. Surely enough, there it was. In capital letters, the subject line of the email read – *NSFW*. The sender's email address was also titled anonymous.

"NSFW?" questioned David, opening the message.

"Not safe for work," Minnie clarified, looking at his screen.

There was no text in the email, simply a link. The file was a JPEG and Minnie understood it to be a photo. As various exclamations had erupted from around the room, she understood before David moved to open the file that it was either offensive or confusing or both. As it would turn out, it was both. There was a cropped photo of a naked woman lying on her back. She seemed to be mid-copulation with a man whose face was also cropped from the photo. There was something unclear about the image. It seemed, to Minnie anyway, that the image was not the original. It was a picture of the original image but she could not tell with certainty. With the ready availability of filters, the slightly grainy and overly contrasted image could be original and simply adapted.

"Jesus Christ!" whispered David.

Minnie leaned closer and immediately jerked back. "Oh my God."

"Who the fucks sending porn on the school server?" blasted Wes.

Minnie, in unison with the staff, looked across the room to his laughing face.

"We're all going to fucking jail if these people are even a day under-age," he said, tilting his head to observe the photo more closely.

"I'm sorry," said Edna. "Is this a hoax? Should we be calling the authorities?"

"You need to call a *lawyer*," said Wes. "Please let this be staff because we are all *fucked* if these are students."

"Do you really think so?" asked Miren. "In all seriousness? Should we be getting support?"

"Could it be from a film?" asked Minnie in hope. "Maybe it's a screenshot from a movie?"

"Can everyone just calm down?" called David.

"It's probably ripped from a porn site," said Wes. "Everyone chill out."

"Never in my life..." Edna turned her phone upside down, visibly disgusted.

"Really?" Wes teased. "We're not in the Victorian-era, Edna. We're all adults - don't tell me you've never seen a nude. Jesus Christ..."

Edna's cheeks burned pink. Kate was busily zooming in and out of the image. Minnie did not feel the need to open the message; at this point, there was nothing to gain. Rather, she seemed to be the only cool head in the room. As David removed his glasses to wipe the sweat from his nose, Henry bounded into the dining room, obviously in search of his deputy. An eruption of complaints and demands were projected toward him. Minnie suspected his instant regret at having come at all. Her phone vibrated, indicating a text message.

Rob: *Can you meet me now? It's urgent.*

Minnie glanced around at the outraged faculty and slinked from the room.

Library. Two minutes.

The library was not yet closed for the evening. Nobody would suspect her meeting a student there for any reason other than to study. As she made the journey, she bumped into teaching and support staff, all of whom wanted to stop to discuss the image. "Henry's in the dining room," she said to each one. "I don't know what's going on."

Rob was waiting in an alcove in the classics section of the library. Lily was not at her desk in the IT area. Less than a dozen students across Middle and Senior years were present, all on the ground floor. They were in various states of stress; some sat unreasonably close to their computer screens, seemingly in an attempt to understand the work more readily through proximity, while others were consuming copious amounts of sugar when the coast was clear. Judy English, a wellbeing and Science teacher, was on library duty and treated the 'no eating' rule like a legal edict. She was observing, in a hawkish manner, two Middle Years students as they practised for a test using flashcards and dived into their bags for sweets when an answer was given correctly. It never ceased to amaze Minnie; the lengths students would go to in order to break a rule.

"Did you see the photo?" was Robs greeting once she got to the top of the stairs.

"Do you know who it is? Do you know who took it?"

"No one took it."

"Clearly someone did," said Minnie.

"It's a *screenshot*," he hissed, red in the face.

"Rob – have you been crying? *You tell me what is going on this instant.*"

Rob broke. "I don't know who sent it. But I know who it is."

"Both people? The man and the woman?"

Rob nodded, wiping his face. "It's Stephen."

"What?"

"It's him."

"How do you know?"

"I saw the video."

"The *video*? You mean someone filmed this?" That made sense.

"They did it. Stephen and…"

"And *who*?"

"I can't… I can't…" Rob sat down, trembling. "I can't say."

"You can't seem to look me in the face either," she said sternly. "Who is the woman? Is it a student? A teacher? Someone from town? An employee of the school?"

Rob wiped his face and leaned back in the alcove, resting his head against the wall. "This wasn't supposed to get out."

"Answer my question. Who is the woman?"

"If I tell you, you'll run away like Mr Liu."

"Run away?"

"That's why he left. He found out. Couldn't handle it. He found out about Stephen."

"Rob, did Mr Liu ever go to leadership with this? Do you know if he ever told the Principal or his wellbeing mentor?"

Rob shrugged. "If he did, I never found out."

"Is this the first time you ever heard of Stephen having a relationship at school?"

"No."

"Did he know he was being videotaped?"

"Yes."

"Is it … is it like an initiation thing? Some gross kind of … performance that needs to be on camera in order for everyone to be accountable?" At this point she felt as though she was simply spitting words, piecing together anything she had heard about secret society's hoping that something encouraged a reaction.

"I've already said too much."

"You've told me nothing that helps me except that a dead boy's nudes are being circulated amongst the staff. Is this another student? I have to report this to the police. Do you understand? We don't have privacy privileges."

"What do you mean?"

"I have to report any and all suspicions of child abuse," said Minnie, feeling a familiar burning sensation in her left ear. When she was particularly emotionally distressed, her ear would begin to tingle and burn, turning steadily red.

"Stephen was willing. This isn't abuse."

"Yes, it is – he was a minor. Is the woman or girl in the photo also a minor?"

"I can't say."

"You're fucking kidding me." Minnie was flat angry now. "This is what you were trying to tell me the other day. Isn't it? Do you know who sent this photo?"

"What's the email address?"

"It says anonymous," said Minnie.

"There's no such thing," said Rob.

Minnie handed him her phone open to the email app. "That's what it says. Do you know who might have sent it?"

"A number of people," said Rob, scrolling. "You haven't opened it."

"I don't need to see it on my own device. Do you know who? How is it any number of people might have sent it?"

"People know about this," said Rob, returning her phone. "A select group. The group I was telling you about. Stephen wasn't shy."

"No? Because all accounts I've had of his character have been that he was shy," said Minnie, more convinced that this was an initiation of some kind. *Hazing,* she thought, *that's what they call it in America.*

"Not everyone knew him well," said Rob.

"Do you think he killed himself over this?" asked Minnie. "Do you think someone was bribing him with the video? Maybe this photo?"

"He definitely killed himself over this," said Rob. "But it has nothing to do with the video or the photo."

"I don't understand."

"He killed himself over her," said Rob.

Minnie remembered the manuscript. '*Goodbye sweet, Conqueror. Though you have lain waste with my love, I am, even in death, forever yours.*' Had it been his parting goodbye? Was the origin of the story born from this tryst? *Though you have lain waste with my love...*

"Had she left him?" asked Minnie.

Rob nodded. "Moved on. He couldn't handle it."

Minnie took her phone back, feeling disgusted and dirty that such content was on the same device where she stored her most precious memories. Rob was distraught; his right leg bounced up and down and he sat with his head in his hands. Minnie knelt down and placed her hands on his.

"Who else knows that you know this is Stephen?"

"Just the crew," he mumbled tearfully. "I think it's one of them. I think one of them released the screenshot."

"Can I ask why this has upset you so much?"

There were two reasons she could think of but she needed his confirmation. Either he was saddened on Stephen's behalf, for his memory, or he knew this was the beginning of something big.

"There are more," he said.

"Of Stephen?"

"Of different people."

Minnie's heart sank. "Rob…"

"Don't ask me."

Minnie's hands tightened on his. "Rob, please… don't tell me there are photos or videos of you."

There was no response except the sobs. Rob's shoulders shook and his hands moved to cover his face, shielding himself from her bewildered expression. Torn between her mandatory duty to report 'knowledge of the existence of inappropriate material of a child' and her instinct to shield Rob from scolding and investigation, she sat with him as he cried, feeling greatly the need to cry herself. Whether he knew others had participated in these videos or had engaged in them himself, the issue for her was still the same. Someone out there knew of their existence and had released a screenshot to the staff. *Why?* Revenge? Power? Was this linked to Sandra's death? By Rob's own admission Kane knew of the images and may have left because of them. Was this some sort of initiation ceremony? *Who are the crew he keeps mentioning? Did Kane mention the images to anyone? Human Resources? The Principal? Did he leave a clear reason for wanting to take long service leave on such short notice?*

Rob said nothing more but nodded distractedly when she asked if they could speak again in the morning. Minnie sat in the nook a while longer after Rob's departure. She weighed the pros and cons of each action and outcome in her mind, beginning with whether or not to see Henry and Human Resources immediately. If she did, she would have to reveal that she knew the identity of the boy in the photo and that there were possibly other images and video in the hands of Rob's illusive 'crew'. This alone would create an explosion of controversy and horror within the school. The more she thought on the topic, the more she was convinced that everything was connected. Stephen's death, Kane's departure, Sandra's death, and now the image. What was sure was that someone at the school circulated this image to start something, but what? *What if I go straight to Henry to tell what I know and find myself in danger?* She needed to figure out the core of this conspiracy before going to anyone else. It was enough that Wes knew of the email. He had proven himself capable of keeping a secret, but she did not trust that he did not have a motive for doing so. At present, the only person she could trust was Charlie. Unable to break Rob's trust in her, and strategically deciding she needed him to remain open to speaking with her, she did not call Charlie. Rather, someone else was needed who could act without releasing her identity as a source.

Chapter 7

The Body at the Gate

OFFICER LARA HOLGATE WAS the detective in charge of investigating Sandra's 'suspected homicide'. She had been the officer to interview Minnie on the morning of the discovery. It was with great apprehension that Minnie called Lara at Mansfield Police Station at midnight the evening of what became known amongst the staff as 'the nude picture scandal'. Kate, who had spent most of the evening in silence, left soon after they returned to their apartment to 'run off the disgust,' as she put it. Minnie could not blame her. While sitting cross-legged on her Pilates mat, she waited impatiently to be connected through to Officer Holgate's mobile number. It took little to convince the station that she had information relating to the death of Sandra Keys and only felt comfortable speaking to the officer-in-charge.

"Hello?"

"Officer Holgate?"

"Who is this?"

"It's Marianna Fox," said Minnie. "From Mansfield Grammar School. I'm sorry to call so late."

"Fortunately, I'm a night person, Mrs Fox. How can I help you?"

"Actually, I hoped I might help you."

"Oh? Do you have information that could assist the case?"

"I have important information though I am not convinced of how it fits with your case. But I need to stress the importance of my needing anonymity."

"Why?"

"It involves a student and I think you can investigate this without using my name."

"At some point, I will need a statement from you. That statement will have your name on it."

"I'm sure it will all be fine, after the fact," said Minnie.

"What has occurred?"

"I think you'll get a call from Henry Waterstone presently relating to this. But I have further information that I hope will assist you." Minnie launched into the explanation of the nude photo, how it came to be known, Rob's confession, and the small nuggets of information relating to the 'crew'. When she heard Kate returning to the apartment, she turned her music speaker on, placed it by the wall, and played classical music so as to muffle her voice through the wall. She did not want to be overheard.

"Why did this student call on you?"

"I have known him for over ten years. I'm friends with his mother."

"Does the mother know?"

"No."

"Just to confirm – Rob Wagner told you that he knew with certainty that the boy in the photo..."

"The screenshot," Minnie corrected her.

"... the screenshot – was Stephen Graham."

"Correct."

"But he did not reveal the identity of the female in the image."

"Correct."

"I understand you've promised to keep Rob's information to yourself, but I am obligated to interview him. This is a serious accusation. Without knowing the identity of the female in the image we could be looking at child porn distribution or sexual misconduct with a minor."

"I know that."

"Can I ask why you've called me rather than going to your principal and following policy?"

Minnie looked at the flame of the candle on her bedside table, absent-mindedly pushing at the cuticles on her toes. "To be honest, I think someone at this school knows more than they're saying. I think these deaths – Stephen and Sandra – are linked. I also think Mr Liu left because he must have found out. All I am trying to do at this point of time is avoid becoming another body while trying to do my job."

"As the picture was distributed to all staff, the police will become involved in that matter. That's another department. It's likely the Principal has contacted them already."

"I think so. But I think I'm right."

"About?"

"Everything being connected."

"Have you ever heard from Mr Liu?"

"Yes. I received an email from him recently – about a week or so ago – offering assistance with resources if I needed them."

"Right," said Officer Holgate, who sounded as though she was writing. "What was the email address?"

"His school address."

"Do you have the exact date?"

"No, but I can find it."

"By tomorrow, please."

"If Mr Liu knew that this kind of content was in existence, I don't know why he didn't tell the authorities. I can't figure out why he just left."

"That's for me to figure out. There are a number of inquiries we can make. I will be at the school first thing."

"Will you interview, Rob?"

"I have to. He will need a parent or guardian. But I will organise that myself."

Minnie remained awake through the night. Insomnia, her nemesis, gripped her mind with barbed hands and refused to let go. *Find the answers*, it demanded. *Ask the right questions.* She drifted, briefly, at the height of the night, as the rain assaulted Mansfield with the ferocity of thunder, but the storm that broke her sweet relief brought her back to reality. She rose from the bed, grateful for the dim glow of the candles around the room, and pushed the curtains back to observe the rain. The window was thick with condensation and with a swipe of her sleeve, the misty mountains of the distance were revealed. She peered closer and pressed her nose to the glass, cupping her hands around her temples in order to eliminate the light of the room, and saw the Maiden Oak moving in waves with the wind.

The ancient sounds of the woods sang with the thunder. The gentle grumble in the distance signalled the great explosion that was set to land in and around the flat plains of the estate. Minnie veered back as the windows shook on their hinges. When the latest flick of lightening illuminated the grounds, Minnie was drawn once more to peer outside. In the far distance, emerging from beyond the oak, a figure trudged through the heavy rain. *Who would be out there in this weather?*

When dawn seemed close, Minnie, resigned to the fact she would go without sleep, dressed and found Kate in the kitchen preparing coffee.

"Couldn't sleep either?" she asked.

"No. Thanks to the storm."

Kate's usually bright and pink-cheeked complexion was as pale and grey as the morning light. Her wealth of curly hair was damp from her shower and braided into a thick, loose plait. She appeared solemn, thoughtful, but depressingly so.

"Are you alright?"

Kate shook her head, holding back tears. She continued making coffee; pulling a second cup from the shelf. "It's a bit too much," she said, raising a shaky hand to pour the coffee. "Leadership are just *useless*. All these shit events keep happening and it seems like everyone is just walking through them like they don't matter!"

Minnie could not agree more.

"That photo really shook me, you know? It was *disgusting*. And I know you must be horrified because you left when everyone was arcing up."

"It was a lot," said Minnie, feeling no need to reveal why she had truly left. "Did Henry say when he'd be contacting the authorities?"

"He called last night," said Kate, putting two heaped teaspoons of sugar in her coffee. Minnie waved 'no' when she offered to put some in hers.

So two police departments will come today. Minnie took the coffee as offered, grateful to have something warm and caffeinated.

"I know it's not the right weather. But do you want to go for a walk?" asked Kate. "I feel claustrophobic in here."

"Sure," said Minnie, wanting to do anything but leave the apartment on this frosty Saturday morning. Guilted by Kate's teary expression, sleepily, she pulled on her coat, wrapped a scarf around her neck, slipped on a knitted hat, stuffed gloves into her pocket and carried her coffee mug outside. Down the wood-panelled halls wherein portraits and photos of the original family looked down on those who wandered, they neared the back stairs that led out toward the kitchen gardens. One of the housekeepers was busily cleaning.

Kate was distracted, agitated. She led Minnie outside and followed the rocky path that wrapped around to the front of the Main House. They went east, toward the church. The grass was slick with rain and glistened in the early light of the dawn. The sound of crunching rocks irritated Minnie's sleep deprived mind so much so that she moved to walk on the grass to soften the sound. There it was. Irritation. With sleep deprivation, Minnie was no use to anyone. Jamie would have insisted she remain on the couch and doze through the day, avoiding caffeine. "No matter how tired you get," he would insist, laying the television remote on her lap. *You always knew what to do*, thought Minnie as she urged her tired legs to continue on.

"Have you been by the gardens around the church?"

"No," Minnie admitted, grateful for the slower pace.

"Oh, good. It might be nice to take a lap around there."

The open gardens met a more heavily wooded area. The inter-twined trees had grown in such a way that they created an arched grove, leading them toward the chapel beyond the lane. Branches of various proportions lay in a wild array on the ground, victims of the storm. An Australian blackwood seemed to have been viciously knocked about by the wind and was leaning into a number of other tall trees beside it. Minnie watched it cautiously, anxious it should not suddenly decide to tumble on her the moment she passed. Steam emerged in abstract waves from their mugs, urging sips at various intervals of their quiet journey. Hints of dawn sun peeked through the night curtain. Kate slowed her stride, squinting ahead while holding her coffee cup to her chest. Minnie paused beside her and followed her line of sight. At first, she doubted her own eyes. It was not yet light enough to trust what she thought she was seeing. Their breathing deepened – partly due to the bitter cold, and partly due to their mutual accelerating anxiety – and almost at once, they realised what despicable horror was enacted before them.

The white chapel was built in the traditional long shape and had three pointed windows along the length of each side. It was illuminated clearly in the dawn light as it was situated at the end of the tree-lined archway. The smaller entry house had a heavy, wooden door that was, conspicuously, open. The chapel was surrounded by a picket fence, at the head of which was a sturdy, tall, gate door of at least eight-feet. It was at this gate, with rising nausea, that Minnie and Kate stood, having thrown their coffee mugs aside and run forth, with hands over their mouths and viewed Jenny Rodgers' body hanging.

"What the *fuck*?" Kate decried hoarsely.

"Jesus Christ," said Minnie, closing her eyes. She turned away.

"She's been here all fucking night!"

"How can you tell?"

"She's soaked through!"

Minnie remembered seeing someone walking in the rain. Had it been Jenny? She pulled out her phone, trembling. "There's no *fucking reception here*!"

"Go. Run back and get help. I'll stay with her."

"You sure?" asked Minnie, holding down the urge to vomit and unable to look back.

"I'm sure. Go!"

Minnie bolted down the road. She passed two of the groundsmen, Phil and Rick, who were carrying chainsaws and tree pruners. "Don't let any students pass this point. There's been a horrible accident."

"With a tree?" asked Phil, pulling his half-finished cigarette from his mouth.

"No. Someone's died. Just don't let them past."

"What?" demanded Rick, lowering the wheelbarrow. "Are you serious?"

"Just don't go there!" Minnie continued running. By the time she got to Main House, four police officers, including Officer Holgate were arriving at the entrance. "Hey!" she called, waving frantically. "Officer Holgate!"

David and Henry appeared at the stone steps, emerging from the entryway. The police turned to her, all with hardened expressions. Whatever their attitude was toward the situation, she hardly cared as she found it within herself to push the final few hundred meters and heave a great gulp of air at the completion of her journey. Henry, looking slightly perturbed, began to invite the police inside.

"Now wait a minute!" Unwilling to be ignored for the sake of removing the police from the line of vision of students and staff who may be emerging from their dorms and apartments, Minnie's tone drew everyone's attention. "We've found Jenny at the chapel."

"And?" asked Henry. "The police are here on serious business, Miss Fox."

You asshole. "I think Jenny being dead is serious business, don't you, Henry?"

That caused a shuffle and straightening amongst the group. Henry looked astounded.

David stepped forward. "Dead?"

"Lead the way, Mrs Fox," said Officer Holgate.

"The chapel. Kate's with her now."

As staff began to emerge, making their way to their weekend dorm-supervising duties or simply taking a morning stroll, the sight of four police officers, the Principle and Acting Vice Principle following Minnie up the garden path toward the chapel drew many stares.

Introductions were made on the move. Officer Holgate, the most familiar with the teachers due to her being in charge of Sandra Keys' homicide inquiry, introduced the other officers while keeping up with Minnie's stride.

"This is Officer Clarke," she said, indicating to the greying man on her right. "Officer Clarke and I are working together on Ms Keys homicide. Officer Chen," indicating to the policeman directly behind her, and then to the woman beside David, "and Officer Russo, have come to investigate your call regarding the photo sent to staff."

"Thanks for coming out," said Henry. "Henry Waterstone, and this is our Acting Vice Principal, David Wójcik."

Minnie could not have cared less for the names of the police officers. She would know them soon enough when, undoubtedly, they would question her exhaustively. When they reached the point where she had last left the gardeners, Minnie saw they had abandoned the wheelbarrow and their gear. Naturally, curiosity would have encouraged them to see what she had described and she anticipated finding them with Kate. Surely, moments later, with the morning in full bloom, she led the group down the tree-lined path to where Kate was being comforted by Phil, visibly crying, and Rick stood with his head in his hands. Minnie paused mere feet from the others, unable to go further. It was enough to see the raw nature of death once, but to see it again, so close and with time to observe the details of a corpse, was horrendous. She hardly registered Henry and David's exclamations of shock.

Officer Chen spoke into the two-way radio at his shoulder. "Central – we've been alerted to a body at dispatch location. Female. Late-thirties."

"Received. Ambulance on their way. Can you confirm the status of the female?"

"Female is deceased."

"Will advise when forensics are on their way," was the garbled response.

Once he collected himself, David stood beside Minnie with his hands on his hips. "This is a nightmare. We will have to find Jeff," he said, pulling out his phone.

"That's not the way," said Minnie, twirling her wedding band. "No one should find out that their spouse is dead over the phone."

"Can't you bring her down," Kate asked, wiping her face. "This isn't right!"

"We understand, Miss," said Officer Chen. "Procedure requires that nothing on the scene is touched until it's been seen by forensics."

"But she's just..." Kate waved her arm up and down, crying again.

While Henry busily answered all questions posed to him by Officer Holgate, Rick, Phil and Kate were being questioned by Officers Russo, Clarke and Chen. On observation, Henry was stressed, and asked more than once why they could not bring Jenny's body down from where it hung. He turned, unable to look at Jenny's body. Kate was sobbing, wiping the stream of tears with her sleeve as she answered Officer Chen's delicately posed questions. By the time Officer Russo was finished with Rick, he was on his third cigarette.

"You'll all need to be available to sign your official statements," said Officer Clarke, pocketing his notebook some twenty minutes later.

"We'll let you get back to your jobs," said Officer Holgate. "Henry, I suggest acting with pure discretion."

"This is central – ambulance ETA is ten minutes," called a voice from Officer Holgate's walkie talkie.

"We'll escort you back to the school," said Officer Clarke.

"I'll take Mrs Fox's statement," said Officer Holgate, indicating that she should remain behind.

"Gracious God!"

Everyone turned; Father Baldwin was racing down the road, followed by a number of staff and students. The police moved quickly, stopping him and the group in its tracks. Minnie did not see how this would do any good. It would have been clear even at their distance that someone was hanging from the gate. Father Baldwin looked from the body to Minnie, to Henry, to Officer Russo who was the first to reach and stop them from coming further. It seemed the staff came to their senses before Father Baldwin and ushered the students away rather forcefully.

"Will you be alright?" asked David.

Minnie nodded, wishing greatly that Jamie were with her. "I'll be fine."

"What do you think happened?"

"I have no idea. We just found her like this."

"If you ask me," said Rick, pausing beside them, "this took more than one person."

"Why?" asked David.

"Hanging people isn't easy," said Rick, lighting another cigarette. "That took effort. Whoever did this wanted her dead, for sure."

"She may have suicided," David suggested.

"Rick, put out that cigarette!" demanded Henry. "These grounds are non-smoking and you're in front of students. It's against policy!"

"I don't see anything in my contract that states I might see a dead body on school grounds," Rick bit back. "The situation calls for a ciggie, mate."

Minnie appreciated Rick's attitude. As much as she disliked smoking, she had begun to dislike Henry just as much. Deciding that his peace of mind was more important than another round with the principal, Rick motioned to Phil and they departed. They were stopped by Officer Russo who reminded them of their need to give a formal statement.

A shiver ran down Minnie's spine, though she tried to suppress it. Something was going terribly wrong. It was bubbling beneath the surface, though neither she nor anyone else could see it. Minnie was convinced, now, with this death, that what was transpiring was connected: Stephen's suicide, Kane's leave, Sandra's and now Jenny's deaths. She wondered how long it would take the police to realise and to answer the ever-expanding list of questions. New to Minnie's list were: *What did Jenny know? Was she killed and if so, why? Was she somehow connected to the photo?* Minnie was new to the school and the most out of her depth with regards to knowing the staff and students. What she knew for certain, at this point, was that she had two options: resign and leave immediately, or remain and trust no one.

~

Three hours, a series of emails, and an emotional staff meeting later, Officers Holgate and Clarke appeared at her classroom door to interview her. It had been a relief to be away from everyone for a while. She had watched, standing aside on the stone steps of Main House, as Jeff Rodgers disintegrated at the news of his wife's death. While she was in awe at the swift and supportive way in which the staff worked together to organise the students, she could not help but wonder if leadership were more concerned with protecting the reputation of the school above the fact that deaths - likely multiple homicides - had occurred. The staff meeting was more concerned with ensuring the staff responded similarly to inquiries from parents and pupils, that no one contacted or responded to the media, and that they utilised the mental health support services as needed with full support of the school. A memorial service would be held the following week. The staff, too stunned or perhaps aggrieved to speak, were silent as Henry made his way through the agenda as outlined in the email. Olivia, the office manager, asked rather bluntly why no one was mentioning the high possibility of Sandra's and Jenny's deaths being homicides and what would be done to protect the rest of the staff? She was rebuffed in the most unequivocal manner using professional jargon that anyone in the room had ever witnessed.

"At present, no one has alerted any member of leadership of the potential of homicide so speculation is not recommended," said Henry. "If anyone has queries or concerns, they are to be raised *only* with myself or David, so we avoid unnecessary rumours."

This authoritative pronouncement naturally fell on deaf ears. The lie was so blatant it brought the room to temporary silence. Sandra's death was widely being reported as a homicide.

Presently, Minnie quickly closed the document in which she was outlining her list of unanswered questions, when Officer Clarke preceded Officer Holgate and motioned to two chairs at the desks in the front row.

"Go for it," she said, watching the older man swing the chairs in front of her desk.

Officer Holgate looked curiously around the room. "This is quite an office," she said admiringly, resting French-manicured hands on her hips.

"Nothing like the classrooms I was in growing up," said Officer Clarke with a smile that wrinkled his whole face.

"Not part of the one percent then, Bill?" asked Officer Holgate, looking out of one of the arched windows.

Officer Clarke laughed, pulling out a notebook. "No such luck there."

"How can I assist?" asked Minnie, acutely aware of the guns at their waists.

"Let's start with the photo," said Officer Holgate, taking the seat beside her colleague. "Any ideas on who the girl is?"

"None," said Minnie. "I'm only new here. I don't know everyone well."

"And last night you called Officer Holgate to tell her the male is Stephen Graham?" asked Officer Clarke.

"Yes. You see, Rob was distressed."

"We'll have to speak with him," said Officer Clarke.

"We might hold off on that for the moment," said Officer Holgate, pointedly. "There's more to bring to the table. How did Rob know it was Stephen?"

"Apparently Stephen told him. This is a child protection issue in my opinion, more than anything else," said Minnie.

"The female is likely another student," said Officer Clarke.

"There are ten girls total in senior year," said Minnie. "It shouldn't be hard to narrow it down if it is."

"Do you know anything about local girls? Teens who might sneak up here?" asked Officer Clarke.

"Definitely a possibility," said Minnie. "Rob never mentioned it."

"We've spoken to Rob's parents," said Officer Holgate. "They don't want their son questioned without them. They're on their way."

"Good."

"Is there anything else you can tell us?"

"It's all I know."

"Has Mr Liu contacted you since the email?"

"No."

"We've attempted to get in contact with him. No response," said Officer Holgate.

"Maybe Tasmanian reception is sketchy."

"Tasmania?" asked Officer Clarke.

"He's in Tasmania."

"How do you know?"

"Everyone does. That's what I was told. He's on leave in Tasmania."

Minnie assumed Officer Holgate was making note to follow up with Henry.

"Can you walk us through your morning up to finding Mrs Rodgers' body?" asked Officer Clarke.

As Minnie gave her testimony, including Kate's distress at the photos and their journey toward the church, various expressions flickered over Officer Holgate's face. She was a fit woman, built like an amateur bodybuilder; her face was chiselled and her skin showed signs of long-term stress. Minnie could not tell whether she considered the events to be mundane or odd, but the moment wherein she raised her eyebrows – when Minnie mentioned that Kate suggested they walk toward the church – she sensed Officer Holgate was pressed with suspicion.

"Why the church? Where do you usually walk?" she asked.

"I don't, really," said Minnie. "Kate just wanted to give me a tour. It was innocent enough. She knows the school well."

"How did Ms Vincini seem to you when you found the body?"

"Horrified. We both were."

"Do you know of any reason for why anyone would want to harm Mrs Rogers?"

"No – but there was something odd," said Minnie, remembering the first staff dinner. She recounted how she had seen Jenny showing Miren something on her phone that left them both uneasy. "I could be wrong. Maybe it was just a rude message from a student or something in the paper. I don't know. But they both seemed really secretive about it."

"Miren…?"

"Sorensen," said Minnie.

"Are you happy for us to mention your name with this information?" asked Officer Clarke.

"I'd rather you didn't," said Minnie, watching as he rested his notepad against his portly stomach, his pen scribbling away. "I'm new here. I don't need enemies. Also," she added, remembering the figure in the rain, "I saw someone outside last night. Just before I called you."

"Can you identify them?"

"No, but they were definitely there."

"Any identifiable features? Colour of clothing? Height, maybe?" asked Officer Clarke.

"I think they *might* have been wearing a raincoat but it was truly too dark to see."

"I'll follow this up," he muttered, noting it down.

"You mentioned that you think the deaths are connected," said Officer Holgate. "Can you elaborate?"

"Well, Sandra was Stephen's wellbeing mentor. That means, she is his 'go to' person for all social and emotional concerns. Jenny taught Middle School Art but she was also a Boarding Mistress. She would have known the movements all around the boarding buildings. While she didn't teach the seniors, she would have had them through her care the last year or two years ago. She knew Stephen. I'm not saying I'm right, but what if that screenshot isn't from a video made last year, but the year before... or earlier. If Jenny was aware of it – *if* – then someone would have good reason for harming her."

There was a pause. Both Officers seemed to be contemplating her theory.

"Do you have a suspicion of who else might be involved in those videos?"

"No," said Minnie. *Not yet.*

~

"I've been holding back the hoards," Wes announced.

"The whores?" asked Rachel Simmonds, clearly mishearing.

"Hoards. Ho-a-rds," said Wes, as though teaching phonetics.

"Has anyone seen Jeff?" asked Edna.

Minnie was busily making coffee at the sideboard while the staff poured into the dining room. Henry had called a staff meeting for 4pm. Slowly, begrudgingly, the staff arrived. The usual hum of light chatter was replaced by edgy murmurs that had a unified theme of 'resignation'. After a day of emails, phone calls, supporting students, consoling staff, and a tense exchange with Charlie and Michael when they arrived to support Rob through his testimony, Minnie was ready to pack her bags and leave for an island holiday. Preferably an island with no phone reception. Despite rules around professional conduct, everyone was day drinking, and the rumours of how Jenny ended up dead were more vicious than those surrounding Sandra. The staff, unable to go another moment without answers from the police, were accusing some boys in Year 12 on account of their being 'big enough to pull her up and hang her' and that one of their secret groups 'needed to keep her quiet'. These theories were swiftly rebuked by others, especially Judy and Rachel, both wellbeing mentors for senior students. "If you have evidence of a 'secret group' you need to tell us," Judy warned those busily accusing the students of wrongdoing. Two staff, Kelly Pinkler and Tess Lo, resigned that morning with immediate effect. "They forgo any benefits," said Lily as she recounted to Minnie what she had heard of the situation. "They're leaving tonight."

"Fair enough," said Minnie, noting to herself that any so-called 'benefits' fell hideously short when the risk of being murdered was growing daily.

"I'm half tempted to do the same," said Lily. "Especially knowing what I know about Kane's computer," she added pointedly.

"You haven't told anyone?"

"No! *Do I look like I want to be found dead*?" she had whispered dramatically.

"Where's the union?" demanded Angela Greenwood of the Humanities department.

"Oh don't start," Edna snapped.

"Start what?" Angela retorted. "We're entitled to union representation at a time like this!"

"Someone should be on their way," said Stephen Carrs. "I called this morning."

"Thank God," said Angela.

Minnie agreed, believing that Edna's chignon was pulled too tight and thus affecting her faculties.

"What's the union going to do?" demanded Edna, bristling.

"More than you," said Kate, taking her seat beside Minnie by the window. "While we're on it – don't you feel somewhat ashamed for telling Miren to 'toughen up'?"

Juicy, thought Minnie. The barely-restrained expression of delight on Wes's face told of his mirroring feelings.

Edna's expression hardened. "You shouldn't listen in on other people's conversations."

"You shouldn't be such a callous bitch when someone's just died."

"That's it! I'll be speaking to Henry about your language! This is abuse in the workplace!"

"Don't bother! The unions coming – take it up with them! I'm sure anyone gives a shit considering two of our colleagues are on fucking ice right now!" Kate shouted. "Get some perspective!"

Wes stood up and waved Kate down while guiding Edna to a seat. "Come on now... we're all feeling edgy. Let's not break ranks."

Edna plonked herself tearily into the chair by the far wall and slammed her diary on the table. An unsettled hush fell upon the room. Kate rested her forehead in a trembling hand.

"Are you ok?" asked Minnie.

"Yeah," said Kate, "just done with all of this."

As more staff arrived, including Miren and – to everyone's surprise – Jeff, Minnie was busily exchanging texts with Charlie. They had finished speaking with the police and would wait for her to be finished in the staff meeting and see her before they left for Melbourne. Minnie felt guilty for involving them but by the wording in Charlie's texts, she was more confused than angry. She wanted to take Rob home.

Henry arrived fifteen tense minutes later, followed by David. Both carried their diaries and solemn expressions. The room fell quiet. Olivia entered and closed the doors, sitting herself in the only spare chair by the coffee bar. It was unusual for Olivia to leave the front desk. Minnie noted her tense demeanour; she looked to have been crying.

"Ok, so," began Henry, "before we begin, I'd like to take a moment to say to Jeff that we are all broken by the events of today. Jenny was a powerhouse and a crucial member of this school community. I wish I had the mental strength to say more but to be honest it seems hollow, for now."

Jeff was nodding, tearily.

"To everyone else, this has been the most difficult few weeks for this school and for me as a principal. We've had to consult with the School Board, again. The police... parents."

"Haven't we all?" asked Angela.

"Exactly," said Kate. "We've all done it tough today."

"Yes," said Henry, whose veil of calm was growing thinner. "We're working with the best," he continued. "Without you, the school would not be functioning. It is imperative that we continue as a unified force for the sake of the students."

"What's being done for us?" asked Angela.

"In what way?"

"Our mental health? What's being done?"

Henry seemed truly brought to confusion by the question. As dozens of pairs of eyes, all of which held the same eager expressions, turned to him and David, the principal and the deputy took a moment to look at one another.

"Shall I note this for the union?" Angela pressed, pushing her green-tortoise shell glasses up her nose. "That our principal didn't take into account the mental health of the staff?"

Henry floated his hands as though trying to calm down a nippy swan. "It's a delicate balance."

"You're about to get some resignations," said Felicity, whose small stature did not match the zest of her statement. If she had been indignant the week of Sandra's death, she presently held the expression of a fed-up television judge. "This is why we called the union."

"We have to prioritise the students."

"Do we?" asked Felicity as the tension in the room thickened to the point where several staff shifted in their seats. Minnie turned in her chair so that with minimum effort, she could pivot between looking from Henry and David to Felicity. "As far as I see it, there is no school without teachers. So what are you doing to support us? We've done our job today. In case you hadn't noticed. You were able to meet with the Board and parents, and the schools designated PR person, because we did work outside of our *contractual* obligations. We've spoken to police now more times than we care to remember. We are doing more than our job but it seems yours and the Board's focus is on keeping the school running."

"Seconded!" called Angela.

"I wonder if you'll say the same thing for the memory of the next dead teacher," said Felicity. "*Condolences.*"

"Now that's not fair," said Miren.

"It is," said Felicity. "I know we don't always see eye to eye, Miren. But this is ridiculous. You have to agree – no matter what the *personal* circumstances are. I want to know what is going to be done for *us*. We, the teachers. We lost two friends. We haven't even been given time to grieve! *Get back to work*! That's what they're saying. That's literally what this meeting is for - sorry this is a sad time, get back to work. I have my letter of resignation written up. All it needs is a signature."

Minnie could not help but sit in awe of Felicity. This small, tightly-wound woman was saying what they all wanted to know. What was being done to support them?

"What do you request?" asked Henry, and David flipped his diary open.

"Request?" asked Wes. "Are you serious?"

"What would you like?" asked David, stepping forward as the room began to buzz. "What can we do to support you?"

"Let's start with therapy," said Wes. "The bill needs to be covered by the school!"

"Support staff so we can take time off," said Angela.

Minnie knew there was no chance of that occurring. Aside from imploding the schools budget, support staff would be difficult to find (especially where two murders, allegedly, had just occurred), and senior school teachers were preparing students for exams. They would not be given leave. The only way Minnie saw the suggestion working was if temporary staff were hired to carry out boarding duties, allowing the classroom teachers with those duties more time to regroup.

"What about security?" asked Olivia. Judging by the expression on her face, Minnie suspected she had suggested this beforehand and been rejected.

"Good idea," said Wes. "Where's the security?"

The question brought Minnie to wonder if anything had been seen on the security cameras. She noted the question in her phone and added: *Who's reviewed the footage?* Mansfield Grammar had dozens of security cameras, both inside and on the grounds. Henry was busily promising to 'look into' the suggestions being made by the increasingly prickly staff. Minnie, no stranger to the lies and deceits of school principals, considered the likelihood that Henry had not reviewed any security footage. It was doubtful. If she was a principal, it would have been the second action she took, following calling the police. Had Henry seen the security footage from the garden? If so, was it likely he'd have seen the killing? Was the camera angled in such a way that Sandra's death was visible to the authorities? No one had been arrested or questioned so intently that pressure was felt by any one person, so Minnie assumed that police were either holding their cards close to their chest or had no ideas at present. Either way, she wanted to know if video footage existed. She glanced at Lily who was vigorously biting her thumb nail as Henry informed them of the Boards decision to keep the school open.

An hour later, Minnie was waving Charlie and Michael goodbye in the carpark. She had convinced them not to take Rob with them, promising to check in on him often during the day. Michael, furious that his son had been questioned by police, was firm in his exchange with Rob while they said their goodbyes.

"Any *bullshit*... if I find out that you were involved in any of this *fucking bullshit*, you're pulled from this school and all activities," Michael threatened.

"This is only because he could identify the boy in the photo, Mick," said Minnie. "That's all. Rob isn't involved."

"I still don't understand why you didn't tell us," said Charlie, dabbing her cheeks.

Rob, who had the decency to look ashamed, shrugged at his mother. "Dunno."

"What do you think, Minnie?" asked Michael, exasperated. "Do you think the schools got a handle on this?"

"God no. How many murders and photo scandals do you think schools handle on a daily basis?" said Minnie. "There's no manual for this. But I'll look after Rob. He's got me."

Rob glanced at her from under his fringe. The corner of his mouth lifted ever so slightly. Minnie knew how grateful he was that she had not revealed any more of his testimony, neither to the police nor his parents. She felt the sickening pang of guilt in her chest. Lying was not her strongest gift but what she had neglected to tell everyone was not the information that needed revealing, yet. Only time would reveal if her actions were worthy or miscalculated.

Chapter 8

The Necessity of Conviction

"**N**one of it makes sense," said Minnie, staring at the mindmap on her computer.

On a shared document, an intricate weave of names and interconnecting lines, beside which a series of questions were listed, performed the role of assisting her in making sense of her thoughts. The stark glow of the computer screen contrasted the warming glow of the assorted candles. Minnie kept the heavy curtains open, allowing the shadows of the trees to dance on the walls as they swayed and heaved with the wind.

"No, it doesn't." Charlie's voice emerged from Minnie's earphones. Her face hovered on the side of the screen, peering from her end at the document as though proximity would make the puzzle suddenly click together. She had long since succumbed to her sore eyes and pulled out a pair of brightly coloured glasses, but by habit continued to peer over them rather than through them when reading aloud. "The only thing that I see is that both Sandra and Jenny were in wellbeing positions."

"Well... Jenny was a Dorm Mother not a wellbeing mentor but I see what you mean. Both positions of trust," said Minnie.

"What does this have to do with the photo? Do you think they're linked?"

"I think so," said Minnie, uncertain. "Maybe they saw something."

"We know that it was Stephen in the photo but not who the girl is?"

"Thanks to Rob, yes."

"I still can't believe he was aware that Stephen was sleeping with someone and didn't say anything," said Charlie, rubbing her eyes.

"That's not unbelievable," said Minnie. *What's unbelievable is that he wasn't the only one*, she thought. "Teenagers have always been the same."

"Did you see the photo?"

"Yes. Unfortunately."

"Do you recognise the girl?"

"No, there's no face."

"Describe it to me."

"Why?"

"I want to understand why *that* photo was sent. Were they posing? Like a selfie? Was it staged?"

"No, to me it looks like a screenshot of a video," said Minnie after giving a brief description of what she remembered of the image. She refused to open it, unable to look at the image of a dead teenager in an intimate moment.

"So, you don't think someone was behind the camera?"

"We can't know that for certain," said Minnie. "But it could be why Stephen killed himself."

"Because he was aware the video might come out? Do you think someone might have blackmailed him?"

"It's all plausible," she said, typing the question on their already extensive list.

"Why do you have question one in red?" asked Charlie. "*Where is Kane Liu?*"

"I don't think Kane is where people think he is," said Minnie.

"Why? The man seemed to need time off. Henry said he went to Tasmania on leave."

"No one can get in touch with him," said Minnie.

"Off grid?"

"Might be...there's something else," said Minnie, going on to explain about the email and utilising Lily to help track the location of the computer.

"Jesus Christ! Are you trying to become a detective? Isn't what she did illegal?"

"I'm sure it might be," said Minnie. "But everyone gets a little cagey when talking about Kane and I think the fact that his computer is on the school grounds is evidence pointing to my theory being correct."

"But the computer is the schools property. Naturally he left it behind and you can find it."

"Then who sent the email from his email address?"

"Anyone could have."

"But why? The email was about him - if we go with your thoughts...and Kane left the computer... a, the school would have flagged this openly when the email was sent around, b, it would mean someone wrote an email pretending to be him."

"I'd wager if someone sent an email pretending to be him then Kane has been pushed out."

Minnie remembered Rob's words in the alcove. "That's why he left. He found out. Couldn't handle it. He found out about Stephen." Rob had been clear in that moment. Observing the mindmap, Minnie followed the multiple lines leading out of the bubble with Kane's name. He was connected to everything, whether through evidence or theory, everything linked back to him.

"What are you going to do?"

"Keep digging."

"What's your theory?"

Minnie sighed. "I think it's all about the photo. Someone on the teaching staff knows the truth about the video and I think it might have been Sandra. She was Stephen's wellbeing mentor and knew that Stephen was on shaky grounds, mentally. I think she knew about the video before Stephen killed himself and was planning to speak on it. Whoever killed her -"

"But no one is sure it was a homicide."

"- wanted to keep her quiet. No, we've heard nothing but that doesn't mean it's not being investigated as such. The woman didn't just drop dead in a veggie patch at 2am."

"Why not?"

"For one thing, one of my colleagues was very clear about Sandra being afraid of the dark. Why would she be out at 2am?"

"Maybe she was meeting someone?"

Minnie added the question to the list. "Who?" she added, typing.

"Have you gone to the Principal with this?"

"God no."

"Why not?"

"He's a puppet for the board," said Minnie. "The man didn't even want to get therapy for the teaching staff. He essentially told us to get back to work. Besides, he'd think I'm crazy."

"Figures."

"How did he seem on the parent conference?"

"To me? Shaken up. The man was essentially reading off a teleprompter."

"What did he say about Jenny?"

"Very little," said Charlie. "I think he did a shit job of trying to make us feel like the school was in good hands."

Minnie rubbed her temples. "It's all just ghastly. First Sandra, now Jenny. No one think's Jeff will stay on after this."

"Minnie, if you think there's something off, why are you staying there? *If* they were homicides, and only *if*, then isn't it better you leave?"

"And do what? Besides, I'm not involved - if someone is doing this, if Jenny didn't kill herself and Sandra didn't die of a heart attack, there's a reason."

"Do you think Rob is in danger?"

"No," said Minnie, though she was certain he knew more about the situation than he let on. She was determined he should reveal his information as soon as possible.

Before retiring for the night, having consulted with her list of questions one more time after hanging up with Charlie, Minnie typed, *Who are the 'crew'?*

~

By the end of the day's classes, Minnie was struck by the need to remove herself from the school. The autumn seemed to have called winter early and Mansfield was ensconced in blustery and rainy weather. She walked briskly from the school, past the barns in which the horses were being looked after by some senior students, toward the woods, while considering the pieces of the puzzle before her. Teachers were reporting a spike in anxiety amongst the students that was so high that classes were at half capacity most of the week, requiring Dorm Leaders to be present in the student lodgings throughout the day and night so as to supervise. Fifteen students, mostly juniors, had gone home with their parents. It was not unusual for teaching staff to witness unhappy parents accosting Olivia at the front desk. Henry or David were often called to assist in placating them, but the clientele at Mansfield Grammar was not used to being told to rein themselves in and act according to the Behaviour Policy. The Monday morning following Jenny's death, Minnie had witnessed a particularly irate mother in the lobby promising to go to the media when Henry explained that nobody could speak on the deaths while they were under investigation. The mother, who wore a large faux-fur coat over what fashion influencers were calling 'sport luxe', wound down the window of her luxury four-wheel drive as she drove away.

"We will be pulling all donations until further notice, *Mr Waterstone*," she called.

Minnie had felt little sympathy as Henry shielded his face from the dust and gravel that shot from beneath the tyres. He was worn and defeated.

Making her way up a wooded hill, Minnie pulled the hood of her raincoat higher on her head and pushed herself to walk faster. She needed to feel the strain in her legs, to breathe heavily, to think of something other than the pieces of a messy puzzle that no one seemed interested in exploring. Humans were incredibly resistant to trauma. They were too close to the event in the timeline to return to normality, but as Wes put it, "In a few weeks, it'll be a crazy story. In a few years, it'll come up over dinner and someone will just say, 'Yeah, wild times', and keep eating." After about a kilometre of walking, watching only her feet so as to avoid twisting an ankle on the jagged rocks and slippery ground, she looked up and noticed something moving in the bushland to her right. She paused, squinting through the rain and watched as two then three and ultimately six figures emerged from the trees. Minnie took cover behind a wide trunk and watched as they walked in pairs down the hill toward the school. By their movements and height, she could tell they were all boys - students. Minnie was particularly drawn to the tallest of the group; he was being spoken to rather loudly by the boy beside him.

"... and then just shut the fuck up! That's all we need to do! Listen to me, Wagner - if I find out you've blabbed to Miss Foxy ..."

"Don't call her that!" Rob removed the hood of his coat and rounded on his friend.

"Oh fuck you," said the other boy.

Minnie realised it was Ralph Astley. The boy was shorter than Rob but stronger, a clear sportsman.

"Getting defensive over a teacher, Waggy Boy?" Ralph continued as Rob moved to continue walking. "You're the weak link in this crew, Waggy. I'll be watching."

"You need to chill out," said one of the four boys who had paused to wait for Rob and Ralph.

Minnie squinted, leaning forward. It was Leo Garcia.

The boy who had been leading the group back moved to stand with Rob. It was Kai Watanabe. He was almost as tall as Rob and the simple act of moving to stand with him seemed to encourage the others, especially Ralph to keep walking and cease the clear animosity that was felt toward him. The two exchanged words in low voices and after Kai gave Rob a pat on the shoulder, they resumed their walk.

The other two boys, Harry Dormer and Lincoln Friers, while not clearly in her line of sight, were obvious to Minnie. She taught them four days out of five and had grown accustomed to the sight of them. This group was rarely out of one another's company. It had not been clear to her that Kai had been part of this group, nor that Rob had been close with them either. They must have had the final teaching period off because they seemed to have been in the woods for a while. *What are you all doing here?* It did not seem likely this area was within their permitted bounds. She would clarify this with Kate.

Pushing herself further along, the woods seemed to grow thicker. After reaching the next peak, she found a gap in the trees and was able to look back toward the school. The school grounds and a vast amount of the lands were visible and, despite the rainfall, were clear to her. Main House and its adjacent additions on either side and opposite, the gardens, the maiden oak tree, the football pitch and the barn. The weather had forced everyone inside for the time being but people emerged outside from time to time, slinking under umbrellas or using their jackets to cover their heads in vain as they moved swiftly from one location to another. No one person was identifiable from where she stood, but she could discern student from teacher. She focused, for a moment, on the maiden oak tree. Imperious in the space with its thick branches and auburn leaves, Minnie suddenly wondered from which branch Stephen had decided to take his life. What was significant about the tree? What had driven him to die in such a manner? Why not poison, or a gun? The tree was in the middle of open space to the west of Main House, visible from her bedroom window. Based on the position of the staff bedrooms, and the student lodgings in the building across the grass, the position of the tree was an assurance that he would be seen, that he would be found early. Had he wanted to make a statement? If so, what was it? And to whom?

That night, as the staff congregated for dinner, Officers Holgate and Clarke appeared. They were out of uniform and carried two duffle bags each. The dining room fell to a hush.

"What the...?" muttered Wes.

Minnie and Officer Holgate, shared a glance from across the room. Henry moved to stand by the two police officers, shaking their hands in turn.

"If I could get everyone's attention for a moment," he called, raising both hands in the air as though summoning the attention of a crowd.

"Fucking joker," Angela mumbled from the table behind Minnie and Wes.

"It's a wonder he still has a job, to be honest," said Kate, also from the table behind Minnie.

Miren, whose secret relationship with the Principal was anything but a secret, looked over her shoulder disapprovingly to Kate and Angela . She pushed up the sleeves of her cashmere jumper, all the while shaking her head, before returning her attention to the head of the room.

"Officers Holgate and Clarke will be setting up a *temporary* office here at Mansfield Grammar in order to continue their investigation," said Henry, clutching and unclutching his hands as he spoke. "They will be on the ground floor in the original drawing room so for the time being, parent visits will be conducted in the student lodge. I'll leave the organisation of that with the Dorm Leaders, if I may."

"No worries, we have nothing else to do," Angela muttered, heaving a great sigh.

Wes raised his hand. "Investigating what?"

"We are continuing our investigation into Sandra Keys' death," said Officer Holgate when Henry motioned for her to answer.

"So it wasn't a heart attack, or...?"

"We just want a clearer picture of what's going on," Kate added to Wes's question.

"There isn't a lot we can share," said Officer Holgate. "What I can say is we are exploring all options at this point and being here allows us to follow through on certain evidence with more expediency."

"So is it a murder inquiry or not?" Wes pushed.

"This is all *very* disconcerting," said Edna, turning to David, who stood up front and to the left of the room beneath a painting of an English notable on a grey horse. "Are the parent's aware that police will be staying at the school? Are we being observed in our classes? Are we being questioned further?"

"Potentially anything could be asked of us," said David. "Except classroom interruptions."

"Well then as the union representative I must call the union. We cannot be expected to be answering questions at all hours and be followed around the school. Is a member or members of staff suspected of involvement, Officers?" Despite the fact that Edna had not endeared herself to Minnie nor shown herself to be anything but a difficult colleague and uptight, Minnie completely agreed. What were the terms of engagement? Why had a union representative not been called?

"What we are here to do has nothing to do with your work responsibilities," said Officer Clarke.

"We are here to investigate a suspicious death," said Officer Holgate. "I'm afraid that's as far as we can go in our explanation at this point in time. If anyone has any questions, please do come and see us. We are sorry to have interrupted your dinner."

Minnie and Wes shared a glance. *Suspicious.*

Fifteen minutes later, as the staff ate and drank by firelight, Lily appeared at Wes and Minnie's table with a plate and a curious expression.

"I've been thinking," said Lily, sitting beside Minnie.

"Not too hard," teased Wes.

"About the ... the thing from the other week," said Lily. "I checked it again today. It's still here."

"Why did you check it again?" asked Minnie.

"It was more curiosity. I wondered if someone might have abandoned the computer. If so, likely, the computer would be flat by now. Out of battery, you know? But it isn't. I could still see the IP address and location. It must be charged."

"And it's somewhere on the grounds," added Minnie.

Lily nodded.

"But that means someone's charging it," said Wes, appearing disquieted.

Lily nodded, plunging her fork into a baked potato.

Minnie and Wes shared a look. "Someone would have seen him by now," said Minnie, answering Wes's unverbalised question before he had a chance. "Unless he has a full functioning secret house somewhere, it's impossible."

"It's not, though," Lily pressed, whispering. "Half of what he'd need is easily stealable from around the school."

"What would be the benefit of Kane going rogue at school? What does he get from saying 'I'm on leave' then secretly staying?" asked Minnie, unable to believe someone would hide in plain sight for months. "What would induce someone to do that?"

"What if someone else has the computer?" asked Wes, lowering his voice significantly.

There was a pause wherein the three took a moment to reflect. The moment - a second of suspended time wherein all theories were possible to Minnie - was broken when Kate slid onto the empty chair at their table and demanded, "What's got you three so tense?"

"Them," Wes deflected smoothly, indicating to the two police officers dining with Henry, Miren and David.

Kate nodded. "Painful."

"We should just do as they ask," said Lily. "What's the harm?"

"They should just close the school," said Kate, tapping her fingers on the table in a rhythm that made sense only to her. Minnie wished she would stop.

"Need a smoke?" asked Wes.

Kate paused in her tapping and smiled. "Behind the shed?"

"Only place they won't see the smoke," he said, throwing his napkin down on the table as he made to get up.

"Who's 'they'?" asked Minnie.

"CCTV," said Kate. "They're everywhere. Behind the garden shed is one of the only places without a camera."

"You're going to smoke behind a shed?" It was the least appealing task Minnie could imagine undertaking at present.

"I don't usually," said Kate, rising with a sigh. "But... stress levels..."

On the way back to her apartment, following several unhappy staff out of the dining room, Minnie noticed the police officers moving into their new office on the ground floor. Climbing the stairs with purposeful ease, she considered the new development. Knowing nothing about police protocol outside of what she had seen on Midsomer Murders and the odd episode of an overproduced American police drama, Minnie considered that time indeed - as told by Officer Clarke - was the reason for setting up an office at the school, but she was wise enough to suspect more consequential reasoning was behind the decision. Sandra's and Jenny's deaths were being treated as homicides, that much was obvious. The police were careful not to confirm or deny any theories; which infuriated some and confused others amongst the staff.

The following morning, minutes before her Literature class, Minnie was busily stacking the students practise SAC exams (School Assessed Coursework) on her desk when a soft knock on the door stole her focus.

"Come in," she called, consulting her classlist and counting the booklets.

It was Ralph Astley. While his presence caused her instant annoyance, she waved him in and was quite surprised to see him enter with hesitance rather than his usual haughty stride. Raph was amongst her least favourite students and she had grown to severely dislike the entitlement with which he approached learning and interacting with teachers.

"What can I help you with, Ralph?" she asked, bracing herself for the practised self-importance.

"Just thought I'd come before class to ask if there's anything you think I need to do to lift my grade in this exam, Miss," he said.

"For English or Lit?" she asked.

"Both, I suppose."

"Studying wouldn't hurt," she said, moving around her desk to pick up another box. "It's a practice exam today, Ralph. You'll need to study my feedback closely and apply it to the actual exam next week."

"Do you think you'd be able to go through the feedback with me?"

Minnie dropped the box on the desk with force, irritated; he looked flushed.

"Come on, Miss," he said, smiling ruefully.

Instinctively, Minnie stepped back when he stepped forward.

"Can't you read feedback, Ralph? You don't need me to spoon feed you the answers."

"Other teachers do it."

"That's their prerogative. We have tutors on staff if you need to consult," she said. "I'm happy to *clarify* something you might not understand but I cannot assist you where I do not assist the rest of the class. That's not equitable."

Ralph held her graze for a moment. Minnie's stomach turned again, this time, because what he was doing was absolutely clear. Students like Ralph were rarely, if ever, rejected. They certainly were not rejected because of equity.

"You know, Miss, there are a few staff who work ... *closely* ... with their students," he said, stepping forward again.

Minnie was grateful for the desk between them. She attempted to breathe deeply through the tightening in her chest but she had no such luck. She struggled, intimidated by the height of him and his unrelenting stare, to breathe normally. *Closely?*

"They get good results, Miss Fox," he said, holding her gaze. "*Very* good results. Certain senior students appreciate the ... *input*, if you follow my drift."

"I'm afraid I don't," she said firmly, withholding the urge to add, "you fucking rat."

"There are benefits to being accommodating when asked to be," he said. "I'm happy to do extra work ... at any time that suits. Grades, and all that."

Minnie was perplexed and driven to thank all deities that came to mind when Kai appeared at the door. The teenager narrowed his eyes at the sight of Ralph and stepped inside, adding to the already elevated tension.

"Can we come in, Miss?" he asked, hesitating. "There's a few of us here."

Minnie nodded and Ralph gave her a genuine smile before taking his usual seat in the back of the class. The tension dissipated as the class filed in, removing scarves and blazers as the heat of the room brought relief from the bitter weather outside. Kai said something to Rob as they took their seats by the window; Rob's head turned sharply to Ralph who winked back, smirking. Rob, ears burning red, began sorting his desk.

Minnie clenched and unclenched her hands, breathing deeply for three intervals, unseen by the students as they settled at their desks. She pushed down tears of frustration and sought to busy her hands. *Should've punched him,* she thought. It was by stroke of good fortune that the class did not require her to lecture outside of providing the rules for the practice exam. Her voice would not have carried and her nerves were ready to snap.

"Let's get going," she said, handing out the booklets. "Take one and pass it on to the person behind you," she instructed the four students in the first row.

Five minutes later, Minnie launched the timer on the smartboard clock at the front of the room, and returned to her desk. Nineteen heads were down, frantically reading the front page of the exam booklet and hastily examining their notes. Nineteen out of twenty students. Unfortunately, Minnie glanced at the back row where Ralph had not begun reading. He smiled at her, unseen by the rest of the class, but by the hidden smirks on the faces of Harry Dormer and Lincoln Friers, who sat either side of him, something was at play that she did not understand.

Chapter 9

Dark Deeds

THE STORM WAS PARTICULARLY rageful on Wednesday evening. The lights flickered on and off in the lounge and hallway, a constant reminder that the varying strength of the power-boards around the building were in need of replacing. Weighted by the feeling of being watched and conspired against since the awkward exchange with Ralph Astley, Minnie retreated from socialising with her colleagues in order to collect her thoughts and decided to spend the evening in her bedroom. The police had not contacted her and went about their business with a degree of discretion that, were it not for their presence in the dining room for breakfast and dinner, she would have forgotten they were there. There were mentions here and there of staff being questioned, and Minnie observed Henry and David walking the perimeter of the Main House with Officer's Holgate and Clarke, pointing at the security cameras.

"Surely there is something on the cameras," Kate had commented over lunch.

"I doubt they even work," said Angela, stabbing her panna cotta with a spoon.

"Who said?"

"With this school's budget, they definitely work," Minnie had said.

"With this school's principal, it's a wonder we have hot water," Angela retorted but refused to say more.

As hail thrashed the grounds, Minnie sat slumped in the armchair by the window, flicking through the photos of Jamie. This was one of the few occasions in which her habitual need for organisation and preparedness paid dividends. All photos of Jamie were carefully stored on her phone in a folder labelled with his name. If the 4862 photos were printed, each would have a faded corner, a physical mark of her finger flipping the pages, for the times that she swiped through this album since his death were innumerable. She lamented the amount of photos, wishing daily that she had taken the time to photograph him more. She wished she had been more diligent in recording more videos; of interviewing him when the mood struck her. Life kept them busy. Her six years with him had only allowed for the 4862 photos in her phone, a few thousand from his own phone, most of which were of her, and an album of photos from his childhood, gifted to her by his mother on their wedding day. It seemed inconceivable and drove her to tearful lament whenever she remembered that all she had of her husband was a wedding ring, a few thousand photos, and memories. She paused, lingering on a particularly hilarious photo in which Jamie was emerging from a lake, having fallen in when the fish on the end of his line slipped free. Whether purposeful or not, nobody in their group knew, as he protested throughout the night that he had indeed intended to chase the fish into the water. Minnie had captured him emerging, triumphant and red in the cheeks, from the water in his red shorts holding the slippery fish high in the air as though showing off an Olympic medal. The photos that followed were of their friends around the campfire, laughing and drinking, posing awkwardly but flushed with humour and joy.

Wiping her face clean of tears, she put her phone away and her thoughts instantly turned to the unopened photo in her inbox. The 'nude photo scandal' as it had been titled by staff, continued to grip their attention. More than half the staff had engaged legal representation, terrified that they would be found in some way complicit in sharing illegal content. Minnie, unwilling to look at the photo on her own device, was more interested in Lily's reminder of the status of Kane's phone and computer. She had added numerous questions regarding the phone and computer to her growing list, including:

(32) How is the battery still running?

(33) Where is the computer? Where is the phone? (Same location?)

(34) Is Kane on the premises?

Last she had looked through Kane's empty apartment, accompanied by Wes, nothing was found. Granted, they had little time to look thoroughly but the apartment had been clearly vacated. The detectives in her favourite crime drama's usually required a second look and always revealed a key clue that only the DCI could link to the killer. She glanced at the clock on her bedside table. It was five minutes to midnight and she was wide awake. Judging by the sound of the guided meditation emerging from her room, Kate was in and likely not to emerge for the rest of the evening. Minnie took a torch from beneath the kitchen sink, put her shoes on by the door and slinked out, careful to close the door quietly so as not to alert the other apartments of movement. Neighbours, whether in a house or apartment, were remarkably nosey and she was in no mood to explain herself to anybody. To her right, the small window at the end of the landing showed pelting rain and the low purr of the wind sent a shiver up her spine. If ghosts were real, this was the sort of evening in which they would appear. She skipped over the loose floorboard in the hallway, and made her way up a short flight of stairs to the third floor, the old servants quarters, where Kane's apartment remained unoccupied.

The intention was to find a sign of occupancy or technology. The door had a charming original handle which was placed lower on the door than modern handles. She tried it, hoping that as it had a few weeks ago been unlocked, it would continue to be. Intriguingly, it was not. Someone must have been to check. The lock was easy to pick. Jamie had taught her years ago as a way of showing off at a party. He had unpicked the lock of a friend's pool house with a hairpin when they had sought somewhere private. Even in his intoxicated but playful state, his hands had been steady when tripping the lock, and his victorious smile the last domino to her resistance.

Minnie slipped into the apartment as soon as she heard the lock release, conscious of the potential for the old hinges to squeak. Armed with the torch, she set to work and searched each room for a sign of life. It was empty. This was of benefit to Minnie as it minimised the number of places she needed to search. She ran her hands over and under window and door frames, inside the kitchen cupboards, and under the bathroom sink. Nothing. Deflated, Minnie sat by the door in the empty front room. She was no policewoman, and almost certain that Officers Holgate and Clarke had been through the apartment recently, but it was clear that nothing was present in the apartment. Not even a ghost. It seemed more than likely that Kane was simply away in Tasmania, as was stated by the school, and had no reception with which to answer the schools inquiries. The apartment had been completely packed, indicating that Kane's departure was permanent. Otherwise, why pack an entire apartment? It was completely bare; not even a sponge was left behind.

Odd.

Minnie flipped the torch, her eyes darting left and right, from the kitchen to the bedroom. In her thirty years, she had moved properties three times and each time, something had been left behind. An old mop, cleaning products, an old coffee table, clothes hangers - *something* had always been left behind. Unless Kane was frugal, in that he did not want to pay for anything new and took *all* his possessions, or meticulous, in that he packed everything and disposed of what he did not intend to keep properly, something was always undoubtedly left behind.

Why is it empty if he is only on leave?

She typed the question into her phone and highlighted it in bold. When she looked up from her phone, one of the floorboards caught her eye. Raised ever so slightly, it was the floorboard under the window directly ahead. Upon closer inspection, a kind of notch had been driven into the bottom left corner of the board closest to her body. She cast the torchlight on the floorboard. It was a definite and smooth groove. Despite knowing she had no screwdriver or scissors on her person, she patted her pockets in the ridiculous hope that she had somehow packed the perfect tool needed to lift an 18th century floorboard. Rather, all she had was the hairpin. Placing all her hope on this small, flimsy tool, she lowered the arched end into the groove and found, with great relief, that it slipped through perfectly and while leveraging the floorboard on the pin she could pry the rest of it up with her fingers.

"Go me," she whispered to herself.

Interestingly, one board did not lift. Four boards seemed to have been recut and shortened at some point in the property's history so that a lid of 30cm x 30cm approximately, was created and hidden perfectly when lowered. Minnie flashed a light into the secret compartment. It was empty but for a single corner of paper at the base of the shallow bay. Something had been hidden here. Dust lined only the edge of the compartment corners. Whether this space was original or recently created she could not tell, but what was clear by the lack of dust within the entire space was that it had been recently emptied. Was it emptied when Kane went on leave or afterward? She added that to her list of questions.

At this point in the detective shows, the DCI would be inspired and link all the pieces of the puzzle, confident that they had their murderer. Minnie, meanwhile, felt no such confidence.

After she closed the apartment, hoping no one would notice that the lock was not in place, she made her way down the short flight of stairs back to the second floor and came face to face with Miren. Dressed in a deep-blue velvet robe and matching slippers, Miren slipped a small tube of hand cream into her pocket and began rubbing it along her fingers, her expression one of mild surprise. Minnie's stomach gave a lurch; she had been waiting.

"Find anything interesting?" asked Miren.

"I heard a noise, so I went to see what was going on," said Minnie.

"So did I - and here you are."

They stood in mutual silence for a moment.

"You're not the first person I've heard roaming around up there," said Miren, breaking the stand off.

"Who else?"

"Not sure. That's why I decided to come up and check. There must be gold hidden in Kane's apartment."

"Do you know it's empty?"

Miren's eyebrows shot up. "I saw movers, yes. How empty?"

"There's nothing in there. How many times have you heard noise from the apartment?"

"Four... maybe five times. Want to move? Sick of Kate already, are you?"

"No."

"Then why were you in there?"

"I have my reasons."

"Do those reasons have anything to do with the email? Or the photo?"

"What?"

Miren shrugged. "It's only logical. I've wondered about the email myself."

"What about it?"

"Would you be emailing the school while on leave?"

"No."

"There you go. And we've heard nothing since."

"Maybe he's corresponded with Henry?"

Miren gave a wry smile. "I'm quite sure he hasn't."

"What do you think, then?"

"I have some thoughts, suspicions. But I'll keep them to myself."

"I'll do the same then."

Miren looked approving. "Wise."

"Have the police spoken to you?"

"More than I deem necessary."

"Do you think they believe both Sandra and Jenny were killed?"

"It's the only explanation for why they're here. Why - what do you think?"

"They would only be here if they think someone else might be killed," said Minnie. "The excuse of commuting between here and town is a charade, if you ask me."

"That means they know more than they're letting on. They must have a suspect in mind."

"Who would act with police in the building?"

"Desperate people always find a way."

"You think whoever did this is desperate?"

"Evidence is being exposed."

"What evidence? There's nothing connecting the two."

Miren looked surprised. "I thought you had put a few more pieces together, Minnie. Seems you need to look a bit closer."

"At what?"

"I always suspected that students were involved in this. Whether directly or indirectly. It's curious to me that the class Kane, Sandra and Jenny all had in common, one way or another, is 12 Green."

That was a piece of information Minnie had not yet considered. "Speaking of them, I have a question for you. Do you know if any of the teachers here tutor their own students?"

"It's not often done - but catch up sessions in the library might be approved if it's in consultation with the department head. We have tutors on staff if they need extra assistance."

"I've been told this is common practice."

"By whom?"

"I'd prefer not to say."

"If someone is trying to pressure you, then you must speak to David or Henry. Is Edna pushing this on the English department? She's been known to work her team hard to keep on top of national results. Say no, Minnie."

"No, it's not Edna. I don't think she is keen on my being in the classroom, let alone doing extra teaching duties."

Miren laughed. "She's a tough nut to crack. She's cold, definitely. It must be difficult to be nearing the end of your career and seeing brighter, younger professionals coming through. It's human nature. Don't take it personally."

"I'll do my best," said Minnie, who intended to continue to take personal offence.

With that, they parted ways with the unspoken understanding that the conversation was not to be repeated.

The following morning, as Minnie and Father Baldwin walked through the icy, glimmering gardens on morning yard duty, she spotted two students from her senior English class sneaking out from behind the now notorious maiden oak tree.

Minnie tugged her sunglasses halfway down her nose, hoping that what she had seen was a mere error due to the dark lenses and lack of sleep. "Leo and Tabitha," she called, waving them down.

"Far too cold and early to be sneaking about," said Father Baldwin disapprovingly.

"It's not what you think," said Minnie. This was a third confiscation she would make that week alone.

The two students approached; both looked decently ashamed. With her blonde ponytail swinging, Tabitha followed Leo.

"Hand them over," said Minnie, holding her hand out.

They hesitated, glancing at one another.

"Don't try," Minnie warned. "Hand them over *now* or I'll have you turn out your bags and pockets. Your choice."

"But it was just *once*," said Tabitha, begrudgingly handing over a small silver bit of plastic that looked like a USB.

Leo gave up a blue one. "I'm sorry, Miss."

"I'm disappointed. I would not have guessed that *you* both would be vaping at school."

Both students turned pink in the cheeks.

"I'm sure you have refills in your dorms."

Tabitha opened her mouth to argue but Minnie shot her a look. Between being short on sleep and out on an icy morning yard duty, she was out of patience and certainly out of grace. "I'd like all your refills in my office by the time class begins. If not, I'll inform your wellbeing teachers and set detention. Am I clear?"

"Yes," they muttered.

"This stuff is poison. It rots your brains and it's horrifically addictive," she said firmly, pushing her sunglasses back up. "Do either of you need health counselling? Are you addicted?"

"No, Miss Fox," Tabitha said quickly.

"I believe I can sort it out," said Leo. "Sorry again - we'll get you the refills."

"Off you go to breakfast," she said, dismissing them.

Father Baldwin sighed as she pocketed the vapes. "It's an on-going battle. If it's not one illegal substance, it's another."

"Yes, well - everyone needs to do better to make sure this doesn't get into their hands."

"Quite brazen, weren't they?"

"They were at an angle that they wouldn't be seen from Main House, or the student buildings," she said as they neared the tree. From this position, facing the manor, she could see hers and Kate's bedroom windows on the second floor. If she stood behind the tree, she would not be seen, but in front of the tree, she would be in full view. Something about this was significant but she was still quite sleepy and could not place why.

Father Baldwin stood a few feet away.

"Shall we go back? Our replacement will cross over with us in a few moments," she said, noting the position of the tree in the notes on her phone.

"Yes."

"Is everything alright?"

"I just don't feel good about being so close to it," said Father Baldwin, looking thoughtfully at the students emerging from their lodgings. "I saw him, you know. When he was found. I got there before his body was cut down. That was the branch." He pointed to the thickest and nearest branch as Minnie crossed beneath it.

A shiver ran up her spine. "That must have been horrific."

"It truly was. Death is not how we imagine it, Minnie. It looks so... final, in reality."

Of that, Minnie was completely aware. Having watched her husband die in a hospital bed, Minnie was astutely and unfortunately aware of what death looked and felt like.

Father Baldwin walked the rest of the way with a wistful, sad expression. Minnie felt it would be rude if she interrupted his thoughts, so she walked along in silence. The sun beyond the cotton clouds was unusually bright and sought to melt the frost that blanketed the school and its grounds. A thin layer of ice made the grass glimmer like emeralds. Two of the groundskeepers, Wilfred and his apprentice Sharon, identifiable by the toolbelts that hung off their heavy-duty cargo pants, were attempting to scrape the ice from the windows at the front of the house; the rest would be left to nature but appearances were essential and where there might be guests, ice or no ice, the school was to be pristine.

"What do you make of sin, Miss Fox?" he asked a moment later.

Minnie spotted Rob and a pretty girl from his year level walking across the grass toward the dining hall. It was the first time in a number of weeks that he was smiling. It was an interesting moment in universal alignment, that Father Baldwin should pose the question when she knew that Rob was aware of secret sin and hesitant to betray the sinners.

"What kind?"

"Sins against God. Moral sin."

The universe did not want her to have a quiet morning. "Well, Father, in my opinion..." Minnie paused, observing the older man closely. "Lying is a sin, yet it may be done for the benefit of others. It would make the act of lying a necessary sin. I would hope that God could distinguish between the two."

Father Baldwin nodded. "If it was posed to you that a sin was suspected to have been committed. No such honour as a sin such as lying to save another... but a true act of unfathomable evil - do you trust in God's ultimate law?"

Minnie laughed. "God's law? Father, do they not teach you the answer to this question at seminary school?"

"I am curious of your opinion. As a trusted figure with no religious ties."

"Father, has someone put you in a difficult position?"

"I'm not sure yet," he said, squinting in the distance.

"Unfathomable evil?" she mused. "I do not think there is much that's unfathomable, considering the types of movies around today. I would say, if you know something you must turn to the police. *Do* you know something? About Sandra or Jenny's deaths?"

"No, not ... not in that way." Father Baldwin's brow creased and he resumed walking. "One can never be truly sure."

"Have you spoken to Henry about your suspicions?"

"I don't put much stock in our principal," he said with a sigh. "It is not my place to comment on the capability of people in the school - quite frankly I consider teachers to be commendable people, but Henry has always struck me as a man who's short on most of the qualities needed to run such a historic and important establishment."

That's quite the burn, thought Minnie.

"Then you should go to the police. The smallest piece of information might help," she urged.

"I will. You've convinced me."

The man is easily convinced. "Now, can I ask you something? Have you heard of teachers providing extra tutoring to students outside of class?"

A series of expressions crossed Father Baldwin's face, triggering a twitch in his left eye. "It would not be usual. There are tutors for that. Has the request been put to you?"

"We may not be in a confessional but I am holding you to the same parameters," said Minnie. "Yes, it was. In an uncomfortable manner too."

"By a colleague or a student?"

Minnie side eyed him. "You tell me your details, and I'll tell you mine."

"Touché. I have not seen many teachers take time for their students for tutoring - but it is not *not* done. Kate kindly tutors some of her students - lots of them need extra support in senior year. She has been quite a support to Kai Watanabe, even Stephen Graham used to seek support from time to time. I know David used to support the science students occasionally. The tutors on staff are perfectly equipped to help and that way you are not sacrificing your time. *But* I know that some students prefer their own teacher and if that teacher is inclined to help, then why not? Are you inclined to take the time to tutor your student?"

"No. I directed them to one of the tutors," Minnie said rather more bluntly than intended.

"Good. Good."

As they neared the stone steps outside of Main House, Officer Holgate emerged. She was out of uniform and looked worn out. Her appearance would have drawn judgemental looks from the staff, all of whom prided themselves on their presentation, and it was a requirement of all teachers and support staff to be dressed in professional and tailored clothes. Officer Holgate looked as though her days were long and her nights longer. Her cropped, blonde hair was tied back, she wore no makeup, and the dark circles around her eyes were evidence of the hours being invested in the cases.

"Minnie," she said, smiling tiredly at them both. "Good morning."

"Morning. Have you met Father Baldwin?"

"I believe my colleague, Officer Clarke, interviewed you?"

"Correct." Father Baldwin pushed his glasses up his narrow nose. "Actually, where can I find him?"

"Dining room."

"See you later," he said, excusing himself.

"He is exactly what I expect a priest to be," said Officer Holgate. "Are they all like that?"

"Probably. He's not even old, really. Just talks like he is. Were you looking for me?"

"Yes. I need to interview Robert Wagner again. I have a letter from his mother saying she gives permission for you to be in the room acting in the position of 'responsible adult'."

"Is that legal?"

"It's on paper."

"Can I know what you want to interview him about?"

"The picture."

"Again?"

"Again. When suits you?"

"I have a free period now. It needs to be done by 10am. I have a class." Minnie was not happy to lose a precious free hour; an hour in which a number of duties needed to be completed, including marking and answering emails.

"Let's go. I'm sure Rob won't mind missing his first class of the day," said Officer Holgate, leading the way inside.

"Clearly you haven't been to a school during exam week," said Minnie. "No one misses class. Not even if they're sick."

"Different to my school," said Officer Holgate, approaching Olivia at the front desk. "Would you please call Robert Wagner and have him come to the office?"

Olivia acted as asked. While on the phone to the dining hall, where all students were expected to be eating breakfast, she cast a firm look at Minnie that spoke of her resentfulness at being asked to action requests of police. Whether Olivia did not like working outside her professional parameters or simply did not like the police, it was not clear. Minnie gave a non-committal smile in return, observing that Olivia's lime-green acrylic nails matched her pant-suit. *Certainly bold, Jesus Christ.*

"He will be here shortly," she said and her smile dropped the moment Officer Holgate turned her back with a brief word of thanks.

Officer Holgate led Minnie into the old drawing room, which, for the purpose of expediting the investigation, had become a sleeping quarters and office, all in one. Gone were the furnishings of the room that acted as a family visiting space, including sofas and small tables. They were replaced with a large wooden table with two computers, a camera and stacks of folders, two chairs, a whiteboard (curiously flipped over so the blank side was visible) and two camp beds. Officer Holgate opened the drawn curtains.

"You keep everything pretty closed away," said Minnie.

"You never know who will walk in. We work with the curtains closed, mostly. Please, sit." She pointed to the chair at which the camera was facing. She added another chair next to it, which Minnie assumed would be for Rob.

"This is intimidating," said Minnie, thinking out loud.

"It's just a chat," said Officer Holgate. "

Five minutes later, Rob's lanky figure emerged. He hesitated when Officer Holgate called him in. "Sit next to Miss Fox, please."

"Ok," he muttered. "Can I just leave my bag here?"

"By the door is fine."

Rob looked at Minnie with a familiar perplexed expression. "Do you know...?" he began whispering.

"Not to worry, Mr Wagner," said Officer Holgate, cutting him off. "Just focus on me. Mrs Fox's here in the capacity of 'responsible adult' because your parents couldn't make it to be in the interview today. They've signed a document -" She pushed a piece of paper across the table with a digital signature for them to see, "allowing for Mrs Fox to sit in with you for questioning today. She's here as a personal support, not as your teacher. Do you understand this?"

Rob looked to Minnie. "Yes."

"Do we have to sign anything?" asked Minnie, noting that the document outlined the role of 'responsible adult' was strictly for the present day, as was stipulated by the date.

"You do," said Officer Holgate. "Next to Mr and Mrs Wagner's signature there."

Minnie took the pen she offered and quickly signed and dated the document.

"Good, now - I'll begin." She pressed the record button on the camera and consulted the computer screen for a moment. "Is your name Robert Alexander Wagner?"

"Yes."

"And Mrs Marianna Koppelman-Fox?"

"Yes."

"For the sake of the recording, Mrs Fox has been interviewed previously in relation to this case, as has Mr Wagner. All summary details are available on the previous recordings. Mr Wagner I wanted to revisit the topic of our last interview - do you remember that?"

Rob nodded.

"Do you remember we discussed the photo that was sent around to staff? The photo in which you identified Stephen Graham as the male in the image?"

"Yes."

"Now, I want to confirm that you were aware of the photo's existence before it was shared with staff anonymously?"

"Yes."

"Were you aware that it had been shared on that day to staff?"

"Yes."

Minnie's stomach flipped.

"How?"

"What?"

"How were you aware it had been shared?"

Rob halted. "Um..."

"Did *you* send this photo to the college staff, Mr Wagner?"

"No!"

"Do you know the identity of the person who did?"

"No," he protested, going pink in the ears.

Minnie glanced at him; she remembered the night the photo was shared. He had messaged her the moment the image had arrived in their inbox. He had been overwrought about the image before she arrived at the library at his request. How had it not occurred to her to ask how he knew of its existence before now? She kicked herself for being so absentminded.

"Mr Wagner…"

"Rob," he said, looking at the table.

"Rob," said Officer Holgate, unperturbed. "Did you send the photo?"

"No."

Officer Holgate continued to gaze at his bowed head for a long minute. By the glint in her eye, Minnie began to wonder if she could read minds. Could those grey eyes penetrate truth and sift through lies? "I'll ask again and I remind you that it is against the law to lie to police, especially when being questioned - do you know *who* sent the photo to the staff?"

"I can't say."

Minnie uncrossed and recrossed her legs, agitated.

"Are you covering for someone, Rob? Trying to keep someone from getting in trouble?" pushed Officer Holgate, adopting a softer tone.

Rob did not respond and continued to stare at the desk. The urge to halt the proceedings was on the precipice of being vocalised. Minnie wanted to hug him, to shield him from the questioning that was making him curl into himself, as though attempting to disappear. Sadly, there was nowhere to go, especially with a camera pointed directly at his face.

"Why don't we look more closely at the picture then?" Officer Holgate pulled a copy of the photo from the nearest folder on the table.

Rob was rubbing his eyes; when he pulled back, rubbing his hands agitatedly on his pants, Minnie saw the remnants of tears. Her heart panged.

"You confirmed in our last interview that the male in this photo is Stephan Graham," said Officer Holgate.

"Yes."

"But you do not know the identity of the female."

"I can't say for sure."

"Can't because you don't know, or can't because you won't?"

Rob's eyes flicked to hers with uncharacteristic defiance. "I'm not saying anything more than I've said."

"Rob, I need to clarify the identity of the person in the image because I want to confirm whether what occurred when this image was taken was a crime or not."

"It's not."

"So the people in this image are the same age? They consented to being photographed?"

Rob looked to Minnie. "I'm not saying anything else."

"Rob, how many people know about this image?" asked Minnie, attempting to be as gentle as possible.

"A few," he said.

"Who?" asked Officer Holgate.

"Not saying."

"Rob, look at me - the people who know... are they dangerous?" asked Minnie.

Officer Holgate allowed the questioning; seemingly, she understood that Minnie could get more out of Rob. Her sharp grey eyes remained steadfast on Rob, acting as live lie-detectors.

Rob hesitated. "Nah."

"Would they react badly if they knew you were here talking to police?"

"Anyone would."

"The female in the photo - she wouldn't want people knowing it's her, right?" Minnie tried to appeal to his sensitivity.

Rob nodded.

"If it's a student, or perhaps a girl from town - maybe Stephen had a secret girlfriend? Do you think she knows her photo has been sent around?" asked Minnie.

Officer Holgate raised her eyebrows but did not seem to wholly disapprove of the question.

Rob shrugged. "Dunno."

"Do you know if this is the only photo with Stephen in an intimate situation?"

"It's not."

"How do you know?"

"Well, cause it's filmed. This is a screenshot. If you take shots of the whole video, there would be loads of pics."

Logical. "Are there other videos?"

Rob shrugged.

"Did Stephen tell you about this video?"

"Think so..."

Officer Holgate made to speak, but Minnie was quicker. "Do you think Stephen thought it was exciting?"

"Yeah."

"So he might have mentioned it to you once or twice?"

"Stephen... was confident about all that," Rob said slowly, choosing his words carefully.

That was hard to believe, considering the feedback she had received about him as well as seeing his picture. The boy was not what her mother would tactfully describe as being 'no Paul Newman'. The lanky young man had the look of an overworked clerk, with dishevelled sandy hair and teeth that needed braces, Stephen had not yet grown into himself. Therefore, aside from the disgraceful idea of judging a growing youth for his appearance, Minnie could not imagine there were throngs of other teenagers waiting for his attention.

"Would you say you had a good relationship with Stephen?" asked Officer Holgate, and Minnie understood her freedom to ask questions was over.

"Sure."

"Were you friends?"

"Sure."

"Did you hang out?"

"Sometimes."

"How often?"

"Well, we saw each other every day."

"Just in class and around school or in down time too?"

"Depends. I have a girlfriend," said Rob, blushing ever deeper. "Stephen had his own stuff going on?"

Really? Minnie was impressed. She doubted Charlie knew about this new girlfriend.

"Like what?"

"Writing. He was writing all the time."

"Trying to become a writer?" asked Officer Holgate, making a note.

"I think so. Maybe a journalist or something. He talked to Mr Liu about it a lot."

Minnie noted that for her journal.

"How do you feel about the photo coming out?"

"Not good."

"Bit unfair isn't it? His privacy being invaded like that."

"Yeah."

"You mentioned you have a girlfriend?"

"Yes. Sarah."

"Sarah," said Officer Holgate, smiling. "Did Stephen have a girlfriend?"

"Can't be sure - but maybe. There aren't many girls in our year level."

"You'd only date girls in your own year level?"

Rob gave a look that implied it was obvious. "Otherwise it's gross."

Officer Holgate laughed. "Yes, it would be. If Stephen had a girl-friend at school, do you think people would know?"

"Maybe," said Rob. "Some people keep to themselves. Some groups don't talk to other groups - so if they secretly date, nobody knows."

"How can they date if it's a secret?"

"People find ways."

"Tell me about these groups. Who doesn't talk?"

"I don't care much. I'm mates with whoever."

"Do you think some of the students break off into groups based on what the parents do for a living?"

"Maybe."

"Was Stephen popular at school?"

"There's no popular here," said Rob.

"In any school, there are popular students - aren't there?"

"It's different here."

"How?"

"People don't bother each other. Stuff goes on... but no one cares if you want to be popular. If you stand out too much, it annoys people."

"So being popular is... unpopular?"

"You stick with your group and you don't act too loud," said Rob with finality.

"So who is in your group of friends, Rob?"

"Kai, Charlie, Adroa, Lincoln, Leo... Chill people."

"Do you have surnames for these students?" Officer Holgate asked Minnie who nodded in the affirmative. "Do you think any of them have seen this photo?" she asked Rob.

Rob shrugged.

"Has anyone in your friendship group mentioned this image?"

Rob shook his head.

Minnie glanced at her watch. Officer Holgate took the hint and ended the interview.

"You've been a good help, Rob. Thank you."

"Sure. Can I go now?"

"Yes."

Chapter 10

No One is Innocent

"It's been five days, and no one's been arrested."

Minnie and Wes sat on opposite ends of the sofa in her apartment, exhausted from the week of exams and fighting the beginnings of winter colds. Wes had arrived at her door, armed with brandy and a cheeseboard, sometime after dinner. After commenting on the absurd number of lit candles in the apartment, he served the brandy (insisting that his French grandmother swore by it as a tonic for all ailments) and they settled in for a number of hours on the couch, exhausted in both body, mind and soul. The fireplace, which by Kate's own admission was never used before Minnie moved into the apartment, was crackling healthily, serving as a relaxing soundscape.

"They have bupkis," said Minnie, borrowing from her mothers linguistic repertoire.

"At least no one else has been killed," said Wes with sarcastic optimism.

It was tasteless but Minnie could not help but laugh.

"Do you think anyone's considered the possibility that Sandra died of natural causes and Jenny just hung herself?" he added, readjusting himself into a more upright position. "I mean, let's consider it."

"What are we considering with half a bottle of brandy in us?"

"I get my best ideas when I'm a bit drunk," he said as though his reasoning were fullproof.

"Ok." She anticipated that his explanation was bound to be mostly hilarity with an element of reason.

"Neither were well - Sandra physically, and Jenny mentally. Maybe Sandra's death tipped Jenny over the edge?"

"It's possible."

"But you're not buying it."

"No."

"You're right, it's dumb. And the computer and phone are still live?"

"Lily checked yesterday."

"And you have no intention of mentioning this to the police?"

"Not yet."

"It could be considered obstruction of justice."

"You could argue that."

"So what's our angle? What are we going to do? I'm kind of getting restless waiting for the police," he said.

"Me too." She was itching to actively pursue the truth.

"Then let's do it," said Wes, sitting up fully.

Minnie blew her nose for the third time that hour. The cold was settling in. "How? What can we do?"

"Let's start making inquiries of our own. People talk to us - we're talkative. Let's see if anyone takes some bait."

"What's the bait?"

"The photo."

It seemed the most logical. "What's the angle? Suspicion? Disgust? Do we just act like we want to gossip?"

"That's how I get information. Here's a bit... I was talking to Jeff the other day while he was packing up his house, and he said Jenny had been acting odd for a few weeks."

"Well, that can lend to the theory that she killed herself," said Minnie.

Wes shook his head. "Jeff said Jenny was convinced of something that wasn't real."

"Like a ghost?"

"Maybe. He said she was convinced she'd seen something 'unreal' in the woods one night," said Wes as though this was evidence enough.

"Unreal? That's what he said?"

"That's what he said," Wes affirmed.

"Ok." Minnie added the question to the list on her phone. "Did he say when Jenny saw this 'unreal' thing in the woods?" She imagined a werewolf prowling the grounds, stalking teachers and students who dared walk alone at night.

"No, but he said Jenny's mood took a bad turn when Stephen died."

"Because she had been his Dorm Leader?"

"Correct."

"And Sandra was Stephen's wellbeing mentor."

"And Kane was Stephen's English teacher," Wes added. "Come *on*, there has to be something other than Stephen linking these deaths!"

"Kanes not dead."

"But he is on leave and I'm willing to bet money that he's not just on leave - that man ran-the-fuck-*away*."

"Tell me about this rumour around him."

Wes rolled his eyes. "So gross - Kane isn't like that. *I get it* - before you say it - we don't know what goes on in people's minds, but Kane is just a good guy. I'm not surprised he left his stuff behind and got the fuck out of here. Kane is a straight shooter and if he even suspects that something is off at this school, he's likely to be *the* whistle-blower."

"Are you good friends?"

"I mean I think... I hope."

"Then why didn't he leave you a way to contact him?"

Wes ran a pudgy hand over his hair. He took a tissue from the box on the coffee table and patted his beading forehead. "I'm not going to lie, I'm a bit cut up about it. I have his number, we're buds but he's left his phone behind. *Somewhere.* I tried calling to check up on the guy and he never answers. Now we know why."

Minnie wondered if Wes had been particularly hurt by Kane's absence and defended his character at all occasions because he had a personal vested interest.

"It hurts anyway," she said gently. "It's ok to be hurt."

"I thought we were better than that. Maybe I didn't make it clear enough to him that... we're friends at a level that he can trust me. I mean, I don't know. We could just be making shit up and he's literally in Bali or something living large."

Minnie smiled, patting his arm. "Where do we even begin?"

"Stephen," said Wes. "I think everything links back to him."

Minnie was inclined to agree. "Shall we look at his records?" Minnie collected her computer and resumed her seat.

"Suppose there might be something interesting there," he said, pouring himself another brandy.

Within minutes, they were scrolling through Stephen's school records, including academic and pastoral. Some of the pastoral records were hidden behind a password, marked as 'Pastoral Access Only' while others were marked as 'General Access'.

"Must have been seeing a psychologist or there's serious stuff in the locked records," said Wes. "Only Sandra would have been able to access them."

"What about his wellbeing mentor before Sandra?" Minnie noticed his pastoral records went back five years.

"David used to be the wellbeing mentor for middle schoolers," said Wes. "He might know something. He's not done pastoral work for years now."

"I don't blame him," said Minnie. "I never liked it."

"It's a shit gig," said Wes. "I did it one year - still recovering," he said, raising his brandy glass.

"Try doing it at an underfunded public school," she retorted. Wes grimaced.

"Here's a note from Jenny," said Minnie, clicking the title, 'Five Incident Points'.

'This is a note to support the deduction of five incident points from Stephen Graham. He was found outside of his Residence after house-hours for the third time in two weeks. Following two warnings from myself and one from Mr Liu, it is deemed the best course of action. I will follow up with Stephen tomorrow.

Addition: Spoke with Stephen about respecting school rules re: lock-out times. Stephen was remorseful and understood the point of the rules.'

'House-hours' were from 9pm - 6am wherein no student could leave their residence building.

"When was this?" asked Wes.

Minnie read the date next to the note. "November 30th, 2021."

"Almost the end of school last year," Wes mused.

"I haven't noticed students wandering around at night," said Minnie.

"The smart ones know where to go," said Wes. "I think they go to the woods. Some of the seniors slip off to the stables."

"Ew."

"Anywhere will do for teens, no matter how rich they are."

"What about cameras?"

"They don't cover every inch of the grounds."

"Where do they cover?"

"Not 100% sure ... all the gates, halls, front offices ..."

All places one would expect.

"Maybe that's what the police have been doing this week. Reviewing tapes. What do you know of Stephen's family? Are they part of the super rich?"

"I don't think so," said Wes, as though the thought was a useful consideration. "They didn't seem as... up themselves as some of the other parents do. I think they're dentists... maybe surgeons? I can't remember — it came up at his funeral. It's vague to me now."

Kate returned to the apartment in a flurry. Dressed, as always when not teaching, in exercise clothes, she threw her work bag by the coat rack.

"The police are holding Father Baldwin," she said, kicking off her runners.

"What?"

Minnie and Wes sat up, shocked.

"Apparently he knows something about Stephen," said Kate; her face windswept and her eyes bright. "The police have said that he and Jeff are both persons of interest."

"What's a person of interest?" asked Wes.

"Jeff? Jenny's husband?" Minnie wondered aloud. "How can that be?"

"I don't know! This is what Olivia told me - just now!" said Kate. "Can I have some?" She pointed to the brandy.

Wes poured her a glass. "Tell us exactly what Olivia told you."

"You're a gossip whore - thanks," she said, taking the glass.

"You just walked in and told us that two of the nicest people on campus are 'persons of interest' in these deaths," said Wes. "*Speak!*"

"Well, Olivia said that the police have been looking at all of us closely. *Everybody.* Father Baldwin went to them a few days ago and gave a statement about something - no one knows what..."

Sin, thought Minnie, remembering what Father Baldwin had asked her on their morning yard duty. He had gone to find Officer Clarke and reveal a suspicion. How had it ended with his being labelled a 'person of interest'?

"... and then Olivia said that this morning they needed to interview him again. Then she said Jeff has been top of their list of suspects from the beginning. Apparently most cases of homicide are committed by a domestic partner," said Kate, her manner growing more frantic. She moved to stand in front of the fireplace.

"Homicide? So it's official?" asked Minnie.

"Apparently the police will be making an official statement tomorrow morning," said Kate.

"Wait a minute ..." Wes looked positively combustible. "What if they were having an affair?"

"Who? Sandra and Jeff?" asked Kate.

"No - basic. Boring. Sandra and Jenny."

"And Jeff killed them both?" asked Minnie.

"I believe that," said Kate.

"It's steep..."

"It's more than plausible," said Wes.

"But Father B...?" Minnie fell silent. *Sin.*

"Maybe he saw them."

"Well, well," said Kate, sipping her brandy. "A couple of dykes."

Then what did Jenny see in the woods, thought Minnie.

By the time morning arrived, all staff were aware of the developments in the investigation. They congregated earlier than usual in the dining room, anxious and defensive. Half the staff were either yet to finish dressing for their lessons or had completely given up the pretence of caring about their appearance and arrived for breakfast in clothes from the day before or dressed so casually it was unprofessional. Most staff were sporting grey circles around their eyes, and while this was not unusual during the exam periods, which they were presently enduring, the stress was heavier. Minnie and Wes were keen to listen to conversations around the room and therefore parted ways and took to opposite sides, listening closely and speaking only when spoken to.

Even Edna, who usually avoided speaking to Minnie, was not shy in voicing her feelings while she and Judy English were buttering toast at the buffet. Her greying hair was twisted in its usual chignon, though unusually, there was a blue pen sticking out of it. Minnie understood the pen was there as a sign that she must have risen at dawn to begin marking papers. Ever the martyr, she spoke aloud but not to Minnie, directing her words to Judy, who had been a close friend of Sandra's and was busily expressing her hope that the police would give them answers soon.

"They better be announcing their departure from the school," Edna said flippantly, choosing the smallest scone on the pile and slamming it on her plate. "I'm sick of feeling like I'm under constant surveillance."

"How many times have you been interviewed?" Judy asked sympathetically.

"*Three*," said Edna. "You'd think I was a suspect!"

"We've all been interviewed three times," said Minnie, feeling ungracious and needing to point out Edna's commonality with the rest of the staff.

Edna scoffed. "Doesn't make it right."

"*I* heard they sent police to Tasmania looking for Kane," said Angela Greenwood, appearing behind Minnie holding a coffee and croissant. She looked - like the rest of the staff - as though she had been up all night. "Mind putting a dollop of the strawberry jam on for me?" she asked Minnie, nodding to the plate in her hand.

"Why would they *send* police instead of asking Tasmanian police to go to his house?" asked Minnie, obliging.

Angela shrugged. "Rumour has it - they don't think he's in Tassie."

"Why?"

"No evidence. No flights, no reservations - his bank cards haven't been active for a couple of months," said Angela.

"How do you know this?" demanded Edna, clearly keen to know more.

"They like to talk in the kitchen garden," said Angela, looking proud of herself. "Very naive of them to think no one else would be there."

"And what made you hang out in the kitchen garden?" asked Edna.

"I like fresh tomatoes," Angela responded before leaving to join Felicity at a table near the back of the room.

Minnie and Judy sat together with Kate and Miren. They were behind the sports and health science teachers. *Nice people*, Minnie thought, but she could not understand how, despite the cold, they only wore shorts. There were six on the phys-ed and health team, all men, who wore wind-jackets emblazoned with the school emblem and ran every morning as a team. Minnie had seen them numerous times when she went to open the curtains each morning. She often wondered why Kate did not join them.

Wes caught Minnie's eye from across the room. 'Good?' he mouthed.

She nodded, taking a sip of her coffee.

"Are you alright, Kate?" asked Judy. "Not eating?"

"No," said Kate, twirling an empty coffee cup. "No, I don't have much of an appetite."

"You look like you've lost weight."

"Do I?"

"Must be all the running," said Miren, cutting into a blueberry muffin.

"Must be," Kate responded. "Actually, maybe I will have something. The toast smells good."

Minnie watched her go. Kate had not looked tense when they left the apartment. She paused at the buffet table, her back to the room, and seemed to be taking a deep breath.

"Minnie," muttered Miren in a low voice, lifting her teacup to her lips. "I wonder if you could meet me today. Discreetly."

While the urge to raise her eyebrows was high, Minnie merely nodded. She was intrigued. "Sure."

Officers Holgate and Clarke arrived with Henry and David, the latter of whom avoided eye contact with everyone and stood with his hands clasped in front. Henry seemed to have given up all pretence of order and control, appearing out of his usual tailored suit and visibly exhausted. Miren crossed her arms, leaning back in her chair. A hush fell upon the room; David took a step back when it was obvious they had taken centre stage.

"Firstly, we want to express our gratitude for your support and professionalism at this time," Officer Holgate began. "We do appreciate how difficult this has been. I hoped to clarify some points this morning - mostly to avoid rumours that I'm sure have been circulating." She cleared her throat, pulling out a small notepad. "Firstly, due to recent evidence, we can confirm that both inquiries into the deaths of Ms Sandra Keys and Mrs Jenny Rodgers are for homicide."

The atmosphere grew dense; tense and frightened. No one spoke but many staff shuffled in their chairs and either gasped or put their hands to their hearts. Kate, still standing by the buffet table, wiped a tear from her cheek.

"Due to this development, we will require fingerprint and DNA submissions from all staff," Officer Holgate continued.

As though of one mind, Minnie and Wes shared a look. The room exploded into low murmurs of protest.

"What happens if we say no?" asked Andrew Cohen, one of the phys-ed teachers.

"Shouldn't they only take DNA from people they think are suspects?" asked Edna.

"I'm calling my lawyer," said Stephen Carrs, rising from his seat.

"Before you do," said Officer Clarke, raising a hand, "let us finish."

"This is an absolute outrage," said Stephen. "You've taken us for absolute *fucking mugs*!" he shouted at Henry. "All of you."

"This is not ideal," said Henry.

David continued to look at the ground though his expression mirrored the discontent of the staff. Minnie wondered what particularly he seemed to oppose. Had there been an argument between Henry and David? Had they cooperated with the police or did they resent their presence? It was difficult to pinpoint one person at which to point anger. The police were doing their job. Henry and David were - seemingly - doing theirs. Communication was severely lacking. Multiple staff had resigned in the last week alone. The Board of Directors was less communicative than Henry.

"*Not ideal*?" Stephen looked around the room, laughing. "Not ideal? I'll tell you what's not ideal - your fucking incompetence."

Nobody protested, not even Miren; who, beside Minnie, was looking anywhere but the front of the room.

"Let's just hear out the police," said David in a tone that was clearly intended to lower the tension in the room, "and then we will answer your questions. We're happy to converse with every staff member today."

"Let's hear them out," said Stephen, resuming his seat. "Over to you, *Officers*."

"Our forensics team will arrive within the hour to collect DNA," said Officer Holgate. "Also, we are treating Kane Liu as a missing person."

This had a greater response than the homicide announcement.

"Oh my God," said Miren.

"What? How is he missing?" asked Kate. "He's in Tasmania."

Officer Holgate looked over her shoulder at Kate. "There is no evidence of this. We have exhausted all avenues of contacting him. He's now an official Missing Person."

"We need to close the school," said Judy, her voice quivering with barely withheld stress. "We can't be expected to exist in this shit show and teach."

"To clarify," said Officer Holgate, her voice rising in an attempt mute the various voices of support, "we hope that by collecting a complete set of DNA submissions from all staff that we can quickly eliminate potential suspects. Also -"

"No, no," said Miren, standing up. "I'm sorry," she added quickly, waving her hand in a single gesture to the police that made Minnie instantly respect her gumption. "I'm not a lawyer but I know that you *cannot* make requests for DNA without a *reasonable* suspicion of involvement in a crime. It has to be voluntary unless you charge us or get a court order. I'm not just going to sit here - and I think I speak for many when I say this - and just hand over DNA when I don't know any facts in the case. I don't know if you're investigating them as being linked or independent of one another. We've not been given time to even *call* a legal representative and you have forensic people coming here to just swipe cheeks like we're going to hear your request and think 'Oh, yes - reasonable!'"

Stephen clapped. "Yes!"

Miren resumed her seat after throwing a withering look toward Henry and David.

"We are requesting that your cooperation at this time is voluntary," said Officer Holgate in such a calm manner that she seemed to be practised in combative negotiations. "We suspect that Ms Keys and Mrs Rodgers were murdered on school grounds for reasons that are classified at this time. We have spoken to a number of persons who have brought to light various pieces of evidence that have led to two people being classified as 'Person's of Interest'."

"One being the victim's own husband," said Stephen, disgusted.

"Mr Carrs, while we are sensitive to the fact that you have all worked with the victims and are defensive of all potential persons involved, it does not remove from the facts of the case."

"Do you think there's a danger to other staff?" asked Wes, raising his hand like a student.

"There's no evidence indicating that," said Officer Clarke.

"Please take the time to contact your legal representatives," said Officer Holgate. "We will be leaving the school this evening after all voluntary samples have been given. We appreciate your openness and ability to provide clear and effective support in this investigation."

Minnie's head was pounding when the police left the room.

"Meet me before dinner, outside the stables," Miren said quickly, pretending to adjust her shoe before leaving swiftly.

Chapter 11

Sinners within the Gates

It was a quarter past four when Minnie set off for the stables. The day had been mild compared to the beginning of the week, absent of rain and dark clouds. As the evening set in, the sun began its descent below the horizon, casting a beautiful purple and orange illumination behind the mountains. Sunsets and sunrises were Minnie's least favourite time of day. She much preferred the height of the day and night, times that had purpose rather than the waiting rooms that were the hours of three to five, whether they be a.m or p.m.

The stables were closing; some students were completing the chores required to look after their horses. Two of the students, girls, greeted her as they brushed their horses. One of the supervisors, a physical education teacher who was a retired Olympic champion equestrian, raised a hand in greeting. He was leaning against the barn door.

"How are you, Ed?" she asked.

"Getting through it, ya know?" he said, shielding his eyes against the setting sun with his hand. "Should'a brought me hat."

"It's an early sunset," said Minnie, turning her back to it so she could see him clearly.

"What brings you out here?"

"Needed some air," she said. "I usually go toward the gardens. Thought I'd see more of this side of things."

"Mind you be careful - after what we got told today, seems we're all on the potential chopping block," he said.

"Did you... *volunteer*?" She attempted to be cryptic given the proximity of the students.

"Yeah, no harm in it - way I see it. You?"

"Same."

"What do ya make of it all? Phoebe, make sure your gear is all up on the wall," he added as a student made to leave. "Ya brush and blanket are still on the barn door. Sloppy won't do it, mate."

The student rolled her eyes and did as asked.

"Sorry," he said to Minnie, giving her a pointed expression that told her this was not the first time he had had to remind the student to complete her chores correctly.

"Ah, I honestly don't know what to make of it," said Minnie.

"You found Jenny, didn't you?"

"Yes."

"How are you coping?"

"Well, considering. Kate's been really affected by it. She cries a lot. I do what I can but it's difficult. I just hope the police sort this all out asap."

"Agreed, agreed. You expecting someone?" he asked, pointing behind her.

Miren was walking speedily toward them, waving. She had swapped a long, finely knitted dress for luxe sportswear, including a thick coat and hat. "Hi Ed," she said quickly. "Shall we go? I want to see if we can catch the sunset over the hill."

"Bye, Ed," said Minnie.

"See ya, ladies," he said, resuming his lazy recline against the stable doors.

Miren steered Minnie away from the stables and they walked up the stony, dirt path she had taken on a previous walk toward the woods. In anticipation of their meeting, Minnie was bubbling with questions that she hoped Miren would answer. The staff had been at their most combative and many cancelled classes in protest for dealing with police during office hours. The union was present in the form of a small, red-headed woman who caused Henry's already frayed nerves to completely disintegrate, and they could be heard swearing and shouting from his office, which was located behind Olivia's reception desk. "Passionate negotiations," was Olivia's response when Minnie queried the shouting. The school administrator did not look up from the computer screen, nor did the clacking sound of her acrylic nails falter in their dance across the keyboard. The school was a revolving door of suited visitors, including members of the Board of Directors and lawyers representing various staff. Many staff refused to provide DNA to the police, preferring to wait for a court order. The lawyers that came to assist their appointed clients found themselves suddenly providing their legal services to three or four. They were surprised by the situation, astounded that the media had not yet discovered more on the potential story. *Well,* thought Minnie, *it's only a matter of time.*

Once deeper in the woods, over the hill on which Minnie had once observed the school from its high vantagepoint, Miren stopped walking. With burning thighs and her lungs working overtime, Minnie leaned her head back and took deep, grateful lungfuls of air. Miren stood with her hands on her hips, catching her breath, before unzipping her coat in an effort to cool down.

"Why did you want to see me?" asked Minnie.

"I think you're looking into the deaths on your own," said Miren with a look that urged her to deny the accusation. "You and Wes."

Well, obviously. You did catch me coming out of Kane's apartment. What would be the benefit of denying it? Attempting to find out more about the deaths was not a crime, it was not forbidden. Outside of Miren being involved in some way, she saw no harm in telling the truth. That was, unless Miren planned to attack her if she deemed Minnie to know too much. At which point, it had been a careless decision indeed to be alone with her in the woods. "So?"

"I want to help." Miren handed Minnie her phone. "Jenny sent me this before she died."

Minnie gasped. It was another photo. A girl was standing in see-through lingerie, her back to the camera, facing a naked man. It looked to be the same room as the other photo, but not the same man. This was not Stephen Graham. This man was muscular, had olive skin and dark hair, as evidenced by the short strands visible. His face was hidden by the woman's torso.

"This isn't Stephen Graham," she said, zooming in to the figures. As with the previous image, this photo did not show the woman's head. "How did Jenny get this?"

"Apparently it was sent to her by Kane," said Miren. "She got it earlier in the year. Showed me at the start of this term."

So Stephen had already passed away.

Minnie remembered observing Jenny showing Miren something on her phone the first time she met the staff. "In the dining room," she said.

Miren nodded. "You saw. You're so observant."

"It's a habit."

"What else have you noticed?"

"There's something very off about the staff," said Minnie. "I think someone knows what's going on."

"Me too." Miren held back tears. "I think Sandra knew. I think Kane found out. And I think Jenny began to put some pieces together."

"You don't think maybe Sandra and Jenny were having an affair?"

Miren looked so astounded that a burst of laughter escaped her lips. "What? And Jeff killed them?"

"It's not unbelievable."

"It is to me. I don't know what's more unbelievable ... that those two might have been gay or that Jeff is capable of killing."

It's really not that unbelievable. "They're all gone - in one way or another."

"It's why I want to help sort this out. This school was *never* like this - secretive and *dark*. We used to be close. Yes, we're far away from town and from society in general, but we like it that way. Everyone is walking around accusing and gossiping - hoping to smear others so they aren't looked at."

An element of caution tugged at Minnie. She had no evidence to prove or disprove Miren's words. She wanted to believe it was real, to believe Miren was speaking out of genuine concern. She was not the girl in the photo; that much Minnie could tell. While Miren was tall and looked after herself, she was not as young as the girl in the picture. Miren was in her late forties, but the girl in the photo could not have been older than her early twenties. That was one element in her favour - she was not acting to cover her own involvement in the images; if that was indeed a potential theory.

"So where do we start?" asked Minnie, throwing caution to the wind. "What have you been able to find out? Do you have any clues as to who the girl is?"

"I don't think it's a student," said Miren.

"You *hope* it's not a student," said Minnie.

"We have so few senior girls and only one or two *might* fit this body type," said Miren. "The girls are a bit ... well, let's just say they aren't as concerned with their fitness as we might have been at school."

It was true but Minnie did not have the time to consider the physiques of the female students. She had to take Miren's testimony as gospel on this occasion.

Miren continued to assess the picture. "She clearly looks after herself - she's fit. She could be anywhere from late teens to late twenties. Good taste in lingerie. That's Fleur du Soleil. Could be from town. Well, she has to be."

Minnie was familiar with the brand and was unsurprised that Miren, with her excellent taste in fashion, would put the same amount of investment in her underwear. Unless... Miren caught the sudden flickering in her expression.

"I don't own this set, if that's what you're thinking," she said firmly. "Besides, I don't look as fit as this anymore. Satisfied?"

The prickliness emanating from her was testament enough for the moment.

"It's the same room as the other photo," said Minnie, moving to stand next to her. "It's the same bed, the same wall."

"I think..." Miren peered closer. "That's... that's the old butlers bedroom."

"How do you know?"

"No one's given you the 'historic tour'?"

"No."

"Let's go," she said, and set off at once.

Minnie was intrigued, in fact, exhilarated. She was finally getting somewhere. When they reached Main House, Miren turned left toward the kitchen gardens and then right, stopping at the back of the property. It was evident the schools money was dedicated to the upkeep of the front of the property and the gardens. Even the stables were in infinitely better condition than the back of Main House.

"This is the original servant's entrance," she said, motioning to a heavy wooden door. "It should be open." It gave way with a turn of the knob and a hearty push.

As they crossed the threshold into the servants quarters, a gust of cold air, chillier than outside, prickled her face. Miren flicked an old lightswitch and they had a decent view of a servants hall that led into a kitchen. She had seen many kitchens similar to this in period dramas on television, all of which doused the spaces in warmer light than was even possible in reality. Minnie imagined the dozens of men and women who would have been in service in this house across the centuries, bustling about in starched collars and heavy skirts. Whether convicts, free people or First Nations people, life in service was not pleasant or worth romanticising. The walls were bare and limewashed, the floor was made of slate and the furnishings were as plain as any she had seen on the same period dramas.

They walked slowly through the space, quiet, barely breathing. As Miren turned left to pursue a separate hallway, Minnie paused and looked into the kitchen. Many of the original objects were present, including a stove from the 1930s, a long and heavily used wooden table and a lineup of servants bells on the right wall. Under each bell, of which there were eight, a small label told of the room for which it rang. There was a brick fireplace across from the stove and a worn-out armchair. Over half-a-century's worth of dust coated the room; including shelves and old crockery. Minnie dipped a finger into inch-thick grey dust, dragging her finger along the edge of a display shelf. It seemed surreal that the once busiest room on the property was now as still as a cemetery. The floor, on the other hand, was a different story. Tracking the journey from the door through which they entered and down the hall, a dust-free pathway was visible. This place had not sat completely empty.

Finally, Minnie followed Miren down a hall of rooms.

"Male staff bunked down here, with the butler," Miren clarified from the threshold of the furthest room, indicating to the other doors. "The female staff were up in the attic."

Naturally, thought Minnie. *Make the women walk the furthest.*

"When did the school stop using servants?"

"Second World War, I think. This is the butler's bedroom," said Miren, leading her inside.

"Oh, you were right!"

Miren held her phone up, moving to stand in a position that mirrored the angle of the image. "It was taken around here," she said, standing in the far right corner of the room.

It made sense. The bed, side table and lamp were on the left hand side, closest to the door. What was curious was that the bed was made.

"There must have been a third person," said Miren. "How else do you explain it?"

Minnie laughed. "A camera. Timer, recording... controlling it from a mobile device. I don't think there was a third person. I think whoever comes down here to get their rocks off likes to film it."

"*Why?*"

"People do strange things," she said, walking around the bed. "There's a lot I can't wrap my head around."

Miren opened and closed the bedside table drawer. "Empty."

"This is definitely the room." Minnie left, leading the way back to the kitchen. "Where does that door lead?" She pointed to the door on the far side of the kitchen.

"You know the little mahogany door next to the escalator?" asked Miren, opening the door to reveal a short flight of worn out wooden steps.

"Yes."

"There."

"Shall we try?"

Miren closed the door. "No! What if someone sees us?"

"I'll say you were giving me the historical tour."

"What if it's the killer and we get murdered just in case they think we know something?"

"Are you serious?"

Miren made a face. "We can't be too careful."

"True."

Minnie followed her outside and pulled out her phone, making notes as Miren locked the door and led the way back to the front of the house. As they strolled through the kitchen garden, Minnie paused, suddenly aware of a decent point.

"Do you think Sandra saw something she shouldn't have?"

Miren paused. "Yes."

"Maybe it's plausible that Sandra saw something in the servants area and was killed for it."

"That seems possible. Sandra knew about the servants quarters."

"Maybe..." Minnie paused, gathering her thoughts before saying them aloud. "Here's a theory. For whatever reason, Sandra found out that someone was doing *the devil's tango* in the servants quarters and on the night she died, she went to check. I think she either startled someone or saw something she was not meant to see, and she was killed."

"Ok, let's poke some holes in your theory. Firstly, how did she know people were having sex there? Secondly, Sandra was scared of the dark. Why would she go alone?"

"Well, she either saw a photo or someone told her."

"Why would she need to *see* it though? Why didn't she report her suspicions or take evidence to Henry so that watching this area became formal amongst the staff?"

"I think she wanted to see it for herself before she raised the alarm. Rumours are only rumours until there's a witness."

"Why that night?"

"She might have seen them go in? She might have been told, in confidence? Could be any reason."

"Wasn't she found at like 2am? Sandra was a cup of tea at 7pm and bed by 9pm kind of woman," said Miren. "I never saw her up past 10pm and that was only for the Christmas party."

"At least it's a theory," said Minnie, feeling deflated and tired.

"Well, she was Stephen's wellbeing mentor."

"What if he told her?"

"She would be duty bound to report it to the family," said Miren. "Child Protection Law. He would have had to clarify consent and the age of the girl and from there she'd have had to report it to DHS."

"Was Sandra close with Jenny?"

"Suppose so - they did pottery together, in town."

"And Kane sent the photo to Jenny? Who then sent it to you."

"Yes."

"That means Kane knew as well. But why didn't he follow up?"

"And now he's missing."

"He is indeed. Or in hiding."

"Who would be in hiding because of this?"

"My husband used to say that people either do everything in their power to leave a stressful situation or they become comfortable in the stress," said Minnie. "Maybe Kane is the type of man who needs to be far from the kind of situations that can land you in prison."

"Prison?"

"It's the dissemination of child pornography," said Minnie. "Just by forwarding it, we're complicit in its spread."

"But it's evidence. We're just trying to do what the police can't seem to," said Miren, leading the way through the newly renovated entrance hall, past Olivia's desk to the dining room. Interestingly, they passed the mahogany door leading to the downstairs servants quarters.

~

"I swear to God this shit is going to end me," was Wes's greeting upon opening the door to his office.

"I'll explain," said Minnie upon Wes's immediate silence and glances between the two women. Minnie and Miren arrived after a hasty dinner, in response to a text message calling Minnie to his office.

"Please do," he said and motioned for them to enter. "I'm so strung out - my head's pounding and I feel like I need to call the FBI."

"We're *not* in America," said Miren.

"The version of the FBI that we have here," said Wes, pouring three glasses of whisky.

"I'm good," said Minnie, hoping he'd pause at the third glass.

"You'll need it," he grumbled. "Trust me. What I got out of Jeff today... I showered but I still feel dirty."

"What did he tell you?" asked Miren.

"First of all..." Wes downed the whiskey. "Explain."

"Oh, Miren wants to help solve the killings," said Minnie. "We found the location of where the photos were taken."

"The sex photo? Did you say photos like an error or you have more than one?"

"I have another one," said Miren, pulling out her phone. "Sent to Jenny from Kane."

"How do you have it?"

"Jenny forwarded it to me."

"When?"

"Start of Term 2."

"You've had this for like six weeks? You've said nothing?"

"No - I was scared!"

"Shit, you didn't even tell Henry?"

"No!"

"No pillow talk for you, I see," he said, sitting down heavily in his office chair. "Ok - so where is it? Where are people fucking and taping it?"

"The old butler's bedroom - down in the servants quarters," said Miren. "We just came from there."

"The *fuck*?"

"Weird but we saw it all."

"Oh my God... so this is happening right under us?" Wes grimaced. "I feel tainted all over again."

"Tell us what you discovered," said Minnie, eager to hear if they had any chance of uncovering the identity of the killer.

Wes lay his hands on the desk and straightened his shoulders, gathering himself. "Ok, went to see Jeff - as we all know he's resigned and he's leaving the school at the end of the Term. Went to offer my condolences for Jenny, offer to help with packing - all the rest of it. He gets emotional. Starts saying he 'should have listened' or 'should have believed her'. Turns out, Jenny had told him that she saw something in the woods."

"Which woods?"

"Stable side, not church side," said Wes. "Took some work but I got it clear from Jeff that Jenny told him she'd seen someone having sex in the woods in the first week of Term 1."

"Staff or students?"

"That's the thing. This is why I needed a shower. Jenny said it looked like a staff member and a student."

While the natural reaction should have been to protest, perhaps ask if he heard correctly or to cry out in rejection, the three sat in absolute silence. It was the kind of silence observed during a funeral; heavy and carried on because nobody wanted to be the first to break the seal and thus show that they were perhaps the least affected by the situation.

"Did..." Miren cleared her throat when her voice faltered. "Did she say *which* teacher or student?"

"Yes, but Jeff wouldn't say. He was adamant."

"Do you think he told the police?" asked Minnie.

"I think he did."

"Then why is he a person of interest?"

"Maybe it was him," said Miren.

"*What?*" asked Minnie, pushing the image from her mind.

"Oh my God..." Wes rubbed his eyes.

"Let's face it, we don't know if the student is male or female."

"Well, we know one of the students - Stephen - was a boy."

"But the girl could be a student too," said Miren.

"But if Jenny saw ..."

"Jenny might have seen a male teacher with a female student. What if it was Jeff she saw in the woods?"

"Her own husband?"

"Maybe he went to the police to admit it and that's why he's a person of interest," said Miren.

"He'd be in custody if it was a student," Wes corrected.

"This is getting confusing. So there are multiple people doing this now?" asked Minnie.

"Wouldn't surprise me," said Miren.

They looked at her.

"Well... we don't know what goes on behind people's closed doors! How do we know there isn't some sort of secret cult? It might not even be sex... what if it's an initiation? All Grammar schools have secret clubs. What if all this is some kind of culty-secret society initiation?" she babbled defensively.

Minnie and Wes shared a look; he pulled an expression that read, 'She could be right.' Minnie added the suggestions to her list of questions.

"Let's stick with the first theory," said Wes in a tone that suggested he was trying to regain some order. "If we theorise that the males in both photos are students, and the females *might* be not students," he said. "But then we're assuming there are two women giving these boys a hell of a good time."

Miren shot him a look. "It's child abuse."

"I know *technically*, but Stephen wasn't a baby - he was seventeen!"

"Sixteen," said Minnie.

"Whatever, split the hair."

"Wait!" Miren pulled out her phone. "Wes, bring up the original photo. The one with Stephen in it."

Wes did as she asked and they put their phones on the desk, side by side. Wes's phone displayed the photo with Stephen Graham, and Miren's phone displayed the photo with the unnamed couple.

"What're your thoughts, Mir?" he asked, blankly observing the phones.

"It's the same girl. Look - same body, same lingerie brand," she said, pointing at the matching features.

"Cheap?"

"Expensive."

"Which lends to it being a woman with a good job. Someone is town?" said Wes.

"No, it doesn't," said Minnie. "These are very wealthy students. I think they're both students."

"Ok," said Wes, agreeably. "But it's two different boys. We're saying now that there's a hussy girl getting off with multiple boys and recording it for fun?"

"Maybe," said Minnie. "This happens all the time."

"But why? And why Stephen? He wasn't exactly known for his looks."

"Can a student be 'known for their looks'?" Miren admonished.

"Listen, I'm as professional as anyone else but I call a spade a spade in the sanctity of my office," said Wes, flushed. "The kid was *challenged* in his *appearance*, shall we say? You're going to compare him to some of the other kids, especially the sports nutters and say he's the first choice for a frisky, fit girl? I'm saying something's off. It's a little off."

By Miren's expression, Minnie could tell that she agreed.

"What if it was some kind of initiation ceremony?" asked Minnie. "Let's go with the secret society theory. Would this be something they'd do?"

"Maybe. I don't pretend to know everything these privileged kids get up to."

"I think it's highly likely," said Miren. "Perhaps they had to have sex on camera as part of the initiation?"

"That would mean Stephen was brought in last year at some point?" said Minnie, considering the timeline. "And who knows when this other one was filmed. Could be recent…"

"This is from last year's spring collection," said Miren, pointing to the lingerie on the image in her phone. "So this is as recent as October last year to presently."

Wes gave a short theatrical clap, embodying the enthusiasm of a stage-mother. "She's done it!"

"Fucking queen," Miren murmured, taking a seat opposite the desk.

"Ok, theory one: illicit student/student relationships, including possibly some kind of club initiation. Theory two: student/teacher relationships. Theory three: what Jenny saw in the woods and these pictures are not related. Theory four: the girl in the photo is not a student or a teacher, but a local from town," said Minnie, typing quickly.

"It's quite the trek from town," said Wes.

"I think we just wrote more questions tonight than we answered," said Miren.

"Time to start crossing some off," said Wes, yawning.

"No matter the theory, I believe Jenny and Sandra died because they saw something they shouldn't have," said Minnie.

"And Kane is either in hiding or at the bottom of a well," added Wes.

"Jesus *Christ*," said Miren in protest to his lack of tact.

"What else did you tell her?" asked Wes, looking pointedly at Minnie.

She understood he was referring to Kane's computer and phone. "Nothing."

"You two know more?" asked Miren.

"Not really," said Minnie, feeling the need to keep something from her for protection. "Just theories that usually come to nothing."

She was grateful when Wes followed her lead and kept quiet.

CHAPTER 12

The Excursion

"WHAT ARE YOUR PLANS for the holidays?" asked Kate, serving two bowls of curry.

"In my dreams - two weeks in the Maldives," said Minnie, building the fire in the living room. "Reality - I'll stay here and maybe do a few days in Melbourne. See my family. You?"

"Same."

Thunder struck close to the grounds; the lightning that followed illuminated the room for a moment. Minnie and Kate shared a wide-eyed look as the room glowed a brilliant white then faded to the warm hues of lamp and candlelight. They were exhausted from completing a marathon of marking papers; full days of teaching were bookended by hours of marking and blind cross-marking in subject-year levels, ensuring quality results. Competition and stress was palpable amongst the staff, especially when comparing projected results with other schools. Henry was particularly keen to 'encourage' the staff to see 'positive' outcomes in the student work; it had been a meeting wherein Minnie understood they were being clearly instructed to mark up where reasonable. Minnie had sat there, silently seething at the audacity of the veiled comment. It had been clear, when the Year 12 English team met to blindly cross-mark (marking without knowing the name of the student) one another's papers, that she was the harshest marker of the group. She had no interest in arguing with her colleagues about the grade she gave some papers, merely commenting that it was what the grading criteria saw to provide and it was in their hands to either take her feedback or ignore it. She refused to 'fluff grades' for the sake of expectations and hurt feelings.

"Everyone here wants to be top dog," Kate had said in support when Minnie expressed her frustrations. "At least you're being honest. Don't worry - Edna always gets the best results for her classes because she rounds up. Everyone knows that."

As it was early June and the end of term was three and a half weeks away, Minnie and Kate had spent most of the afternoon clearing the lounge of stacks of papers and books, filling boxes and rubbish bags depending on what needed to be stored and what needed to be thrown out. It had been a cathartic experience, discarding and clearing. The apartment had never been so uncluttered. They had thrown open the windows, vacuumed and dusted the space in a symbolic ridding-of-stress ritual and settled in armchairs by the fire enjoying a curry. Due to the horror week of marking, Minnie had put aside her amateur investigation and focused solely on her job. Now, as things slowed down and they prepared to introduce the literary texts for the second semester, Minnie's mind was once again returning to the dark cloud that hung, both figuratively and literally, over the school.

"You should come on the ski excursion," said Kate, dipping naan bread inside the curry. "It's good fun."

"For who?" asked Minnie, who could not imagine a worse passtime than freezing on a ski slope.

"Us," said Kate. "We stay in the lodge most of the time. It's a paid three days in the mountains."

"Don't you supervise the students?"

"We do - most of the time the Phys-Ed team are doing all that. We just make sure they're in their cabins at night ... boring stuff."

It did not sound too bad at all.

"Who else is going?"

"From Phys-Ed: Andrew Cohen, Otto Friers and Ian Younger. They handle most of everything. Then, me, David, Rachel Simmons - for wellbeing purposes. Miren goes occasionally."

"How many students go?"

"Just the ones in competitive ski sports from Year 10 up. Should be about 12-15 kids."

It did not seem an outrageous amount.

"Oh come *on*," Kate pushed. "You need it. It's five stars."

Minnie doubted if anything related to looking after children could possibly be five stars. Yet, two days later, with her classes covered and carrying an overnight bag, Minnie and seven colleagues made to board the bus with twelve overly-enthusiastic students in sleek sports gear. The bus looked like a live advertisement for expensive ski clothes - from 'thermal technology' coats and the latest designs in leather snow boots, both students and teachers would make a fashionable entrance to the resort. Minnie had raced to town to purchase the necessary boots and outerwear for the trip, knowing the blistering cold that awaited in the mountains.

"Let me take that for you, Minnie," said Andrew, taking her bag by the handle before she could protest. She craned her neck, attempting to smile in thank you at the Welshman. "I'll put it here safely," he said, sliding it into the baggage hold.

Otto Friers, a teacher in his late forties whom she often saw running in the early hours of the morning, was standing at the head of the bus, beside the bus driver, and providing instructions for when they reached the ski resort. "... can be a tight turn in the front so we might need to stop at the gate and walk the rest of the way."

"Right-O," said the bus driver, a thin man who apparently thought this uniform of shorts and puffer jacket were appropriate for alpine mountains.

"Who's going to carry our gear then, Sir?" asked a girl with fine, pale hair that she had pulled into a tight ponytail and covered with a sweatband. She sat in the second row.

You, Minnie thought, not yet willing to indulge in the expectations of the students.

Otto seemed to ignore the girl. David, Kate, and Rachel Simmonds were already on the bus, seated at the front. Rachel had a knitted hat pulled firmly over her cropped brown hair, and was unzipping her jacket in a flustered manner when Minnie and Miren boarded the bus.

"Sit here," Miren muttered in her ear, nudging her into the second row. "Away from the students. They can get bloody rowdy on these trips."

"Nice of you to join us, Miss Fox," called a deep voice from the middle of the bus.

Kate raised her eyebrows but continued texting. David frowned, uncrossing his arms and glancing back. To Minnie's pure dislike, Ralph Astley's smirking expression appeared from behind a seat as he poked his head out into the isle. He sat beside Adroa Okello and behind Kai Watanabe, who, in that moment, turned to look at Ralph before slumping back in his seat while rolling his eyes. Minnie ignored Ralph and slid into the seat as directed by Miren.

"What was that about?" asked Miren.

I should've checked the list. "What's to say?" said Minnie, taking off her bag.

"Yes, he's a little shit," whispered Miren.

"That's kinder than what I'd call him," Minnie muttered, buckling her seatbelt.

Otto was busily consulting his tablet. Ian Younger, a stocky man in his late thirties who headed the school Sports and Health Education Department, boarded the bus carrying four full duffle bags. While wondering how his arms had not yet fallen off from the weight, Minnie watched as he threw the bags into the first seats on the bus.

"All good to go," he said to Otto as Andrew boarded the bus.

"Good." Otto raised his hand in the air and waited for the bus to fall silent. "Good work. Under three seconds - I like this. Keep it up, Team. Ok, I am going to mark the roll, then I'll introduce the teachers coming on the trip and their roles. Then we'll head off. It's about a 45 minute drive up the mountain. Schedule: arrival at 9.45 approximately. You'll be shown to your cabins. You'll have 10 minutes to sort your gear. You'll meet outside the cabins at 10.15am. Your instructors will be at the slopes waiting for us so it's imperative we respect their time. You will be training until 3.30pm. Then showers and free time until 7pm. It's dinner and lights out by 9.30pm. Seems early but you'll be competing tomorrow morning. It's essential to get a good night's rest. Ok, roll call: Ralph Astley."

"Here, Sir."

"Leslie Cartwright."

"Here, Sir," called the girl in the sweatband at the front of the bus.

And so continued the roll: the name of the student was called and they responded with an identical 'Here, Sir'. "Amelia Donahue, Rosie Fortescue, Samantha Gallager, Luca Gonzalez, Xavier Holmes, Hugo Isaacs, Solomon Jacobson, Jasper Jansen, Liam Maine, Noah Romano. Adroa Okello. Kai Watanabe."

"Here, Sir," said Kai, slipping on a pair of sound-blocking head-phones and slumping in his seat.

"What's the plan for tonight, ladies?" asked Kate, who sat across the aisle from Minnie and Miren.

"Should I see if the spa is open tonight?" asked Rachel, who sat next to Kate, pulling her phone out.

"Who is on duty tonight?" asked Miren.

"Surely the guys will do it if we want tonight, then we can swap tomorrow," said Rachel.

"I'm good with that," said Andrew, turning in his seat to look back at them.

Otto made a face of agreement. "Easy done."

Minnie was surprised by the ease with which they made agreements. She did not feel comfortable going to a spa and relaxing while on active duty. It seemed a breach of responsibility somehow but they were organising themselves in a practised manner. It wasn't her place to buck the system.

"So there's always someone available for the students?" Minnie asked Miren.

"They will do tonight, and we'll do tomorrow. They just need one person on hand near the cabins really. Our rooms face the cabins, so even if we're all in bed, they can access us," she explained. "The girls have their own cabin - and the boys have two others between them."

"So shouldn't one woman be on hand in the night just in case one of the girls needs something?"

"We'll check on them before we go," said Miren. "They have our numbers and the guys don't check on the girls. It's against policy."

"Is it against policy for us to check on the boys?"

"We can't go *into* their cabin."

Who'd want to?

Minnie spent most of her time admiring the natural views from the window seat. As Otto and Andrew exchanged stories from their travels around the United Kingdom - Andrew originally hailed from Wales, and Otto met his wife in Scotland while backpacking - Minnie fiddled with her wedding rings and watched as the scenery grew more wild and the roads narrower. She wished Jamie was there to hold her hand, to remind her to look away from the edge as he had done on their ski trip to Japan. She grew nervous as the bus made ever tighter turns up the mountain's edge, sliding past four-wheel-drives on their way down, and leading a growing train of cars slowly up the road. They passed the first carpark wherein intrepid skiers were leaving their cars and carrying their gear to buses that would take them the rest of the way. She understood the journey was coming to an end when snow appeared all around. It made the ground sludgy, and pockets of white dusted the forest floor. A few minutes later, they rolled past a set of iron gates that opened to a beautiful modern resort. A man and woman in coats with the resort name and emblem on the back were waiting for them at the top of the driveway. The woman waved enthusiastically, smiling. She was stocky, well-presented and kept her red hair in a bob. Her colleague, a tall, broad-shouldered man stood with his hands tucked in his jacket pocket.

Otto stood as the bus came to a stop. "Well done on keeping the noise reasonable on the drive. Disembark and wait to the left of the bus and collect your bags."

Minnie followed Andrew off the bus.

"Janine Liddle," said the woman, offering her hand. "This is Matt Tengku."

The resort played host to two other schools, both of whom seemed to have already arrived and settled into the cabins. Their direct competition, Geelong Grammar, appeared moments after their arrival and were preparing to leave for the slopes. The staff exchanged pleasantries and light banter about the competition before continuing on. Minnie supported Kate by settling the female students into their cabin, ensuring they had their gear and lunches packed before leading them back to the bus.

Despite the restful intention of the trip, Minnie felt tired. After putting their belongings in their room, she and Kate met Miren and Rachel for lunch in the resort restaurant and quickly dove into discussion about the murders.

"We should be careful," said Miren, when the waitress departed with their orders. "It's not public information."

"I wonder why," said Kate. "You'd think it'd be a headline."

"Henry's probably keeping it quiet," said Rachel, wiping her eyes of tears

"Can you blame him?" asked Miren. "Think of the school's reputation."

"I'm still working through it," said Rachel. "It's got to have been an intruder."

"From town?" asked Kate.

"Why not?" Rachel asked defensively. "If not, then it's someone from school. *One of us.*"

"Surely the police would have said so."

"They've told us nothing except that it is... you know," said Rachel, dropping her voice dramatically, "homicide."

"How long do you think it'll take them to find the killer? Now they have our DNA?" asked Minnie.

"Not all," said Miren. "Lots of staff refused."

"Fair enough," said Kate with a shrug. "They do need a reason."

"Or a court order," said Minnie.

"Do you think it's all connected to the photo?" asked Rachel.

"Might be," said Kate, buttering herself a slice of sourdough.

"You know what I heard?" Rachel looked around significantly and leaned in, forcing them to do the same. "I heard the man in the photo was Stephen Graham."

Minnie raised her eyebrows; she felt Miren was purposefully not looking in her direction.

"What makes you say that?" asked Kate with a mouth full of bread.

"I heard it from Olivia who overheard the police talking," said Rachel as though the matter could not be disputed.

"That doesn't make it a fact," said Kate as the waitress settled their wine orders in place.

Minnie, who rarely drank alcohol, had ordered sparkling water and wished she had ordered a gin and tonic. Miren gulped her wine when Rachel responded with, "Maybe it will when they search Stephen's computer."

"Stephen's computer?"

"Apparently the police investigating the photo - not the ones who've been at the school - have been looking into Stephen's computer," said Rachel.

"What makes them think it's Stephen, I wonder," said Minnie.

Rachel shrugged and dipped her bread into an olive oil and vinegar infusion. "All I know is that. Maybe they have it wrong, and it's not Stephen. But if it is - it answers a lot. At least from our wellbeing perspective."

"What do you mean?" asked Kate, concerned.

"Well, now this is all confidential - between us - we can't really discuss student profiles outside of meetings," said Rachel.

"Of course," said Kate.

"Naturally," said Miren.

"What's said on the ski trip, stays on the ski trip," said Minnie, hoping that Miren was paying as much attention as she was.

"Stephen was up and down emotionally," said Rachel, "we all know that. And Sandra, being his wellbeing mentor, copped it all. When she saw that photo she said immediately that she suspected it was Stephen. She suspected that Stephen might have become obsessed with one of the girls in his year, hence why he was so depressed. Inconsolable sometimes - Sandra always looked more worn out when she finished seeing him."

"Who's the student?" asked Kate.

"No idea. I thought it might have been Tabitha Myles? But I'm likely wrong," said Rachel.

"Might have been someone from town?" offered Miren.

"Maybe," said Kate.

"What did you think of him?" asked Miren. "He was always fine in my classes but Year 11 was a tricky one for him."

"Mostly fine," said Kate. "Work went downhill last year. He really struggled to get things in on time. I wasn't the most patient with him. I guess I feel bad about it. I'm trying to do better with Kai."

"Another one struggling with his emotions," said Rachel, sympathetically. "He's taken Stephen's death very badly."

"It's been tough for them all."

Late in the night, Minnie woke to the sound of movement outside the room. Her room was on the ground floor, outside of which was a small veranda. The student cabins were opposite. Groggily, annoyed that her peace had been disturbed, she lay still and listened. There were definite footsteps outside. Minnie sat up. A shadow loomed through the sheer curtain. This was not the night she wanted to catch teens engaging in a lust-and-thrust but better to stop them before anyone was subjected to noises that would make skin crawl.

"Kate, I'm just going to see what's going on," she whispered to the sleeping form in the bed beside hers. "I think someone's going for walks in the night."

Minnie pulled on a pair of boots and a coat, pushed the sliding door open and stepped outside. The night air nipped at her warm cheeks, blowing her dark hair across her face. She zipped her coat up to her chin and peered out to the student dorms. The lights were out. The grounds seemed to be quiet.

"Over here."

Minnie jumped. The voice came from her left. "Who's there?"

"Over here, Miss."

Minnie made to go inside, intending to get a torch. That blew her theory of frisky teens out the window.

"*Here*," the voice urged.

"For God's sake," she muttered, slinging her leg over the balcony and into the snowy ground. "Show yourself, *now*."

Nobody answered. Minnie hesitated. The area around the hotel was dark and thick with shrubbery and trees. This was her least favourite scene in horror movies. The idiot protagonist always walked into the dark.

"Please, Miss!" A flash of light appeared behind the trees a few feet in.

"This is a mistake," she said, stepping toward where the light had shone. *I'm the idiot in the movie.*

She was not a few feet into the darkness when a warm hand clasped firmly around her mouth, while the other blindly snatched her right wrist. The pressure was immense. Instinctively, Minnie grabbed the hand around her face.

"Now, now. No struggling, Foxy."

The man was bigger than her, taller and wider. The cheek against her ear was clean shaven. She made to dig her nails into the hand around her mouth, struggling to scream.

"You're living up to your name. Stop moving now, or I'll break your wrist."

Her attacker held her arm out at such an angle that she did not doubt the sincerity of the threat. She stopped moving immediately. Her heart pumped in a vicious rhythm, slamming a heavy beat in her ears. Her lungs tightened, eliminating any chance of catching her breath.

"You and I are going to go somewhere nice and quiet," said the man, moving backwards and tightening his hold on her face. "Be good, be good. I don't *want* to bruise."

Minnie looked desperately for a sign of movement, a hint that someone was out there whom she could call to. The hotel was mere metres away. If she was loud enough, surely Kate would hear and come running. If she allowed herself to be dragged away, there was no telling how far from safety she would end up. If she fought, he could easily damage her arm, even kill her. Minnie closed her eyes, bracing for the snap. She was dizzy with adrenaline.

"It's a matter of willpower, in the end, isn't it?" Jamie had said, sweating under the weight of the solid bookshelf.

Minnie struggled to keep hold of the other end and attempted to readjust her grip. The old tshirt clung to her sweaty back; she was grateful Jamie had made her wear shoes for this task - she could easily see herself dropping the bookshelf on both of their feet before it made it near the living room.

"Shall we pause?" he asked.

"We're in the doorway," she said, moving into a squat to ease the pressure on her back. "Whose decision was it to move house, again?"

Jamie laughed. "'*It's got an original fireplace*'," he imitated.

"It's all my fault!" she said dramatically, remembering the day she convinced him to buy the house.

"Look at me," he said, breathless.

Minnie did so, locking her green eyes to his darker ones. "We got this?"

"We got this," he said intently. "We are going to carry this in there -" He cocked his head to the newly painted living room complete with fireplace, "and we're going to put your million books on it. And then I'm having a beer."

"Ok," she had said, reinvigorated though suspect that callouses were developing on her hands.

"Just a little brute force, Minnie!"

As the memory slipped from her mind's eye, Minnie slid down to her knees, aware of the tightening grip on both her face and arm, until the hand loosened from her mouth. She turned and bit the man on his thigh with all the strength in her jaw, feeling the immediate release of her arm. She fell onto her back and kicked out, landing a decent attack on his knee.

"Help!" she screamed.

Her attacker was struck, stunned by her escape and made furiously to grab her. She kicked out again, landing a solid heel into his shoulder.

"Help!" she screamed again.

A light glowed from behind her. Her attacker, masterfully covered in a balaclava and heavy coat, seemed to take heed of the alert and scrambled into the forest.

"Oh my God," Minnie gasped, falling flat on the ground.

"Minnie?"

It was Andrew. From her perspective, he appeared from behind her clad in his pyjamas and holding a torch. Seconds later, Miren appeared, frantic.

"What the fuck happened?" she demanded.

"Let me help," said Andrew, moving to assist Minnie back to her feet.

"Someone attacked me," said Minnie, finally upright. She touched her face where the man's hand had gripped her.

"You look it," said Miren, putting her hand to Minnie's left cheek. "Someone dug their nails into your face."

Minnie took a moment to compose herself. After taking in a series of deep breaths and pushing aside the urge to cry, she said, "It was a man."

"Which direction did he take?" Andrew demanded, shining his torch through the trees.

"That way," said Minnie, pointing in the direction he was searching.

"Both of you go inside," Andrew said firmly. "I'll see if I can find anyone."

"He could be armed, Andrew," said Miren, dusting leaves and snow from Minnie's coat. "We should call the police."

"I'll be back in a few," said Andrew, disappearing into the darkness.

"Come on," said Miren, wrapping a comforting arm around her. "Let's get inside and see the damage. I can't believe this."

"You and me both," said Minnie, furious at her own stupidity. "I shouldn't have gone on my own."

"What made you go outside at this time of night?"

"Someone was moving out here and then they called me," said Minnie.

"Sounds like this was an opportunist."

Minnie shook her head. "They knew me."

"How do you know?"

"He called me Foxy."

"As in... like, sexy, foxy?" asked Miren.

"No, as in my *name*," said Minnie.

They entered her room through the balcony. The light was on. As soon as they opened the sliding door, Kate was standing there with her sleep mask pulled up to her forehead.

"Fuck's going on?" she asked, half asleep.

"Minnie was attacked," said Miren, pushing her side.

Kate's expression hardened. "*What*?"

"Some crazy person," said Minnie, wanting to minimise the commotion. Embarrassment was creeping in. "It's my own fault. I shouldn't have gone on my own."

After recounting the ordeal, Miren put a warm cloth to Minnie's cheek. Otto and Ian appeared at their room a short while later, sent by Andrew who apparently had gone to search the students dorms and alert the authorities. Both teachers were shaken, demanded as many details as possible from Minnie, and considered cutting the trip short. Despite their best intentions, and their genuine concern, Minnie could not help but wonder if either of them could possibly be responsible. They were strong enough ... and clean shaven. It was not without merit to be suspicious. They were away from the school and their families. Perhaps it was an opportunity too tempting to miss. As quickly as the suspicions rose, she rebuked herself for being suspicious. They had shown her nothing but kindness since she started at the school.

"This is an attempted sexual assault for sure," said Otto.

"We don't know that," said Kate. "Maybe he just wanted money."

"Nobody wants money in the middle of the night in a sky resort," said Ian. "Minnie, is there anything about the man that you could use to identify him?"

He's at least six feet tall, clean shaven and knows me, she thought.

"No," she answered.

"Height? Voice? Smell?" asked Ian.

"I might think more clearly in the morning," said Minnie, nervously rubbing the wrist that had been in the man's clutches. The heat of his hand lingered on her skin like a dirty smear.

"This has to be related to the homicides," said Otto.

"How?"

"What if this is how the killer got Sandra and Jenny?"

~

The ski field had been made perfect by the application of artificial snow, layered on the mountainside in an effort to provide the skiers with ideal conditions. Unwilling to make a spectacle of the attack, Minnie spoke to Officer Clarke discreetly in the morning and headed to the competition by mid-morning.

"We should be on a first name basis," said Officer Clarke, surveying the area of the attack in the bitter cold of the early morning.

"Nicknames, even," said Minnie, appreciating her attempt to inject humour into the situation.

"Is this space making you uncomfortable?" asked Officer Clarke.

"It's making me wonder why I was stupid enough to come into the dark on my own," said Minnie. "It was a dumb thing to do."

"You thought it was a student. You were just being a good person," said Officer Clarke. "But you need to be more careful."

"Rodger that."

"He ran into the woods, you say?" Officer Clarke was looking over the ground, walking carefully, surveying for evidence.

"Yes."

"What made you fight back? Why didn't you go with him? Did you suspect he didn't have a weapon?"

"It didn't occur to me," said Minnie. "If he had a gun to my head, I wouldn't have gone anyway."

"Why not?"

"If he had a knife and I was led away, I'd have been too far for anyone to hear me. If he shot me, people would have heard. Besides, I figured it would likely surprise him into releasing his grip if I just fought back," said Minnie.

"It's quick thinking."

"It worked."

"Yes, it did," she said pensively.

Officer Clarke left the mountain after joining the teaching staff for morning coffee. The students rolled into the breakfast room just after 8am, sleepy and unaware of what had occurred. While they loaded onto the bus, each student carrying skis and backpacks, behind sunglasses, Minnie observed their movements, their demeanour. If they stumbled it was because of their heavy gear, not any injury she had made to their legs. No one seemed out of sorts; their spirits were high and competitive.

"What do you say, Miss Fox? We should have a bonfire if MG wins on the slopes today," said Adroa, who was busily encouraging his classmates to seek support from the teachers.

"A bonfire?" she asked.

"Sure!" he said, straightening his sky goggles on his head. "You'll love it, Miss."

"What happened last time?" asked Miren pointedly.

"That was *other* seniors, Miss Sorensen," said Adroa with practised charm. "You know this class of seniors is *much* more responsible. I'll even smooth it with the gardeners."

"You'll have to convince Mr Waterstone," said Otto, whose presence indicated the beginning of their journey to the snowfields.

The bus was flooded with student requests for a bonfire and promises of good behaviour. Minnie sat down, regretting coming on the trip. When the bus arrived at the ski field car park a message from Wes appeared on her phone.

'Call me when you're alone. More details.'

Minnie was intrigued. The call would have to wait half an hour, at which point, she stood on the side of the slopes, watching the students complete warm-up runs down the field. She hid her bluetooth headphones beneath her hat and dialled Wes's number, hoping he was not in class. Kai Watanabe was descending the side of the mountain, moving gracefully across the snow. As the phone rang, she observed half a dozen teachers from competing schools, all wearing school-embossed coats and milling; swapping friendly banter about rankings and weather conditions.

"The phones moved," was Wes's answer to her call.

"Which phone? What?"

"Kane's phone. Lily looked up the IP again - it's moved."

"To where?"

"Have a guess."

"Tasmania?" It was the best she could think of. If the phone turned up in Tasmania, then Kane was where he said he would be and perhaps the technology was in error? Had they begun an amateur investigation on faulty information?

"It's on the mountain."

"Which mountain?" Minnie demanded.

"Mount Bulla. Where *you* are!"

"You're talking shit," she retorted, looking around with a vague notion that the person with the phone would be in the vicinity.

"No shit - we checked *twice*. The phone moved. It pinged off wifi on the mountain."

"That means-"

"That Kane or the person who has his phone has gone to the mountains at the same time as you."

"What about the computer?"

"Still here."

"Because it's too cumbersome to carry. Why though? Why bring it? Why come here?"

"I don't know but I'm starting to think you need to be really careful. We don't need another body," said Wes.

"Someone attacked me last night."

"*Excuse me*?"

Minnie told him a brief version of events, watching as Kai took instruction from the ski coach at the base of the run. The boy was not smiling, nor did he seem particularly interested in what was being said. He nodded somewhat mechanically, then proceeded to take off his skis and walk back to the chairlift. As he departed, Ralph finished his run and met the coach for feedback.

"What did the police say?" asked Wes when she finished the story.

"What's to say? It could have been anyone."

"You said he called you Foxy? So he *knows* you."

"That's the impression I got."

"Any chance it was staff?"

"I don't know. I can't tell."

"Student?"

"I don't think so," she said, turning back as Amelia Donahue finished her run. "I just wish I had answers. Why is nothing clear?"

Wes sighed heavily. "It's all bullshit."

"Yes, it is."

"Miss Fox!"

Minnie looked around. "Hold on…"

"Miss Fox!"

Kai was walking down the mountain, carrying his ski's on his shoulder. He waved. "Miss Fox!"

"I'll call you later. Kai needs something." She tapped her headphone and tucked the buds into her pocket. Kai lumbered toward her, his black hair sticking up around the thick band of his ski goggles. "What happened, Kai?"

"Wonder if you had a minute. Everyone's a bit preoccupied and I needed a word," he said.

"In a wellbeing capacity?"

"Sure."

"Alright." She waved to Ian who was amongst a group of teachers from Methodist Ladies College and indicated she and Kai would be departing the area for the cafe's about one hundred metres away. The scent of cinnamon donuts was most welcoming on this frosty morning. Kai left his ski's in the designated area amongst dozens of others and they walked toward a popular kiosk. It was being manned by a young man with a long, cultivated beard in a thick sheepskin aviator jacket and tattoos on his knuckles.

"What's on your mind?" she asked as they joined the line of customers waiting to order.

"Just some stuff's going on and I need someone to talk to. Rob said you were cool. When Miss Keys died … I tried to get on with stuff on my own but I haven't done a good job," he said.

Minnie regarded him for a moment. Despite his towering height, Kai seemed like a fragile young boy. Tall as she was, standing confidently at five-foot-nine, Kai was shoulders and heads above her. "I'll do the best I can, Kai. Has the school not designated a new mentor to you? Even after our last conversation?" She remembered distinctly when Kai had taken the time to see her after class. She assumed he had gone to leadership and asked for another wellbeing mentor.

"I kind of asked for you but the school said you weren't in wellbeing. They told me Mrs Simmonds would be my new mentor," he said flatly.

Rachel, thought Minnie. She would be a perfectly decent mentor to Kai but she knew that Kai did not want to hear that in the present moment. "Well, what can I help with today? Are you feeling nervous about competing this afternoon?"

"Nah, I'm not fussed about it. One of the others will take the Champion Trophy. It's more... I want to ask your advice. If you knew something, something *bad*... something that could get you in trouble, what would you do?"

Minnie tried not to show her surprise. Kai was the type of person who would respond by closing himself off if there was a hint of disapproval. Her training had taught her that students, especially those seeking assistance needed reassurance not judgement. They were three customers away from ordering. "Firstly, I would decide if there was a danger posed to me or someone else," she said conversationally.

"No danger."

"Then, I would ask myself where my morals stood. Do I let injustice win? Do I do the right thing?"

"What if you want to do the right thing but you have no one to trust?"

"There is always someone - even someone unobvious."

"Who do you trust, Miss?"

Jamie.

They were two customers away from ordering. "Well, I have a very good friend," said Minnie, "who helped me through a terrible time in my life. Other than her, my parents. Do you have someone, Kai?"

"Maybe," he said, frowning. "But I don't think they want to hear about my issues."

"Who is they? Your parents?"

Kai smiled uncomfortably. "Should I speak the truth?"

"I find the truth is better than lying," said Minnie. "All secrets come to light eventually."

"Yes, they do," he said as they stepped forward, one away from ordering.

"I don't think I have said anything you don't already know."

"Just needed the assurance," said Kai, shrugging.

"Go to the police," said Minnie, understanding what he was alluding to.

Kai unzipped his jacket, looking uncomfortable. "Why?"

"It's anonymous and you'll be helping the investigation if you know something that could help. Do you know something?"

"I'm not sure yet. Rob said you were with him. He said you made it easier."

"I don't think I made it easier," she admitted. "I am happy to support you. Donut?"

Kai smiled at her. "Sure, thanks, Miss. You're alright, you know that?"

"I try, Kai."

~

The following day, Minnie boarded the bus to the sound of cheers as the revelry of their win was yet to be satiated. Adroa Okello won the

Championship Trophy for Mansfield Grammar the previous evening and his elation could not be subdued. The staff and students had erupted when his name and points appeared at the top of the board following his third successful run of the slopes. Their competition clapped cordially, teachers consoling their students. David had filmed the moment for Adroa's parents, holding his phone to the scoreboard after they witnessed their son's final run.

"Miss Fox, hold the trophy!" said Adroa, holding up the silver cup.

After dropping her overnight bag in the front seat of the bus, she moved to pick up the trophy. It was heavier than expected. "Where will you put it?"

"It goes in the entrance hall at school," said Adroa. "So everyone can see it."

"But it's your trophy," said Minnie, confused. "Don't you want it on your shelf in your dorm?"

"It's the way things go, Miss," said Ralph. "There's an order to things at MG."

Minnie ignored him and returned the trophy to Adroa. "Congratulations again."

"Thanks, Miss. Maybe this will be enough for you to give me a week off English homework?"

"Dream on, kid," she responded to a busful of chuckling.

Andrew, Otto and Ian took their seats amongst the students, leaving the front for Minnie, Miren, Kate and Rachel. A message appeared on her phone screen. 'You never know.' It was from Wes. He had forwarded a phone number.

Minnie was confused until the intention behind the message clarified itself. With sweaty palms, she tapped the number - then hesitated. Kane's phone had pinged from a phone tower on the mountain. She looked down the length of the bus; it was the vision of innocent revelry. Even the teachers had given up on asking the students to calm down - the excitement had won them over. Minnie tapped the call button and picked up a bag of sweets. She tucked her phone in her pocket, allowing it to ring and began to offer sweets to everyone. Nothing was out of the ordinary; Kate took some, Miren and Rachel declined. Each student plunged their hand into the packet, some hardly looking. Her heart skipped a beat when, while holding the packet out to Ralph, he held her gaze and pulled out his ringing phone. Minnie looked at the glowing screen, her heart in her throat.

"Hi, mum."

Minnie let out a long, shaky breath through her nose and moved on. The noise of the bus was too loud to hear any phones ring or vibrate. No one else moved to answer a phone. It had been a good idea - well intentioned. She returned to her seat, deflated. Meanwhile, a few seats behind hers, her phone number flashed below a 'Missed Call' message on a phone buried deep in a duffle bag.

Chapter 13

The Next Victim

Hospitals were hell. If they ever had a baby, Minnie made Jamie promise they would have a homebirth. They were cold and the smell of disinfectant and death induced the need to escape. It was June 28th when Jamie drew his last breath, tied down to the ugly white bed with an unreasonable amount of machines surrounding him. The sound of high-pitched pulsing had made Minnie want to take a bat to them more than once. The sound was disturbing his peace, interrupting the last pure moments he had on earth. Nothing was pure about hospitals. He should be home, tucked in their bed, surrounded by family and his favourite music. Time had not allowed for such arrangements to be made. The horrific call had come at two o'clock in the afternoon and she was a widow by 10 o'clock that night.

'Drunk driver,' the police had said, though she hardly heard them.

Minnie had nothing in her except to lie beside him in the bed, much to the disapproval of the doctors and nurses, and cradle him in her arms. She spoke to him softly, kissing his cheek as she did each night as they lay together in bed, talking until they fell asleep. On this occasion, the scent of his body wash was replaced by blood and chemicals, and where he usually would pat her to sleep, he was motionless. "Can you hear me? I'm *right* here," she repeated, kissing him again.

Jamie's mother knelt by the bed, patting his feet; his father sat beside him, holding his hand. Numerous times, he had attempted to soothe Minnie, to touch her, but she tightened her hold on her husband. Perhaps they thought she had lost her mind, perhaps she had. Her parents certainly thought so, especially when she swore at the doctor who asked her to consider whether to allow Jamie to be an organ donor. Her mother-in-law sobbed heavily, but where she was vocal in her grief, Minnie was beside herself to such an extent that neither tears nor prayers did justice in expressing the agony - the physical and emotional *agony* - she felt the moment he was pronounced dead.

The pain was exacerbated when she came face to face with Jamie's killer in court. The woman was suitably supported by a lawyer and her family. She was an affluent middle-aged woman, or as her lawyer had stated, "A devoted mother to three school-aged children and a wife," who, "always found the time to support children's charities." When the time came to read her victims impact statement, Minnie made note of her devotion to children and charities and felt every bit in the right to retort that, "No amount of charity will clean you of the stain that your actions have made upon my family and your own. You chose to drink to excess and you knew you were drunk. You chose to drive. You ruined my life and stole my husband from me."

The memories were yet so raw that the face of her husband's killer was still fresh in her mind. Olivia, the school's meticulous administrator, watched as Minnie stared down at the stack of mail forwarded from her home address. The first envelope was addressed in a child's hand. Minnie lifted her thumb from the envelope, unwilling to touch it but unable to throw it away. She suspected it contained a letter - the three identical envelopes before this one had contained letters. Whatever compelled the little girl to write for forgiveness on her mothers behalf, Minnie was unwilling to give it her energy. Had the girl been older, she would have responded as such, but compassion, perhaps made tender by her years as a teacher, led her to simply ignore the letters. Some things in life, despite what the motivational speakers or the online positivity army said, were unforgivable. There would be no social media worthy moment of mutual grief when the woman was sentenced. Rather, Minnie left feeling the sentence was too lenient and the killer's family thinking it too harsh.

"It's back at the school." Wes appeared beside her. He spoke in a low voice. "Minnie?"

"Yes," she said, tucking the envelopes under her arm.

"It's back at school," he said purposefully.

"I imagine it would be," said Minnie, following him to the library where Lily was looking intently at the monitors on her desk.

"You look unwell," Wes said, concerned. "You ok?"

"It's been a big week," said Minnie, avoiding discussing the upcoming anniversary of her husband's death. "Still catching up on sleep."

"Is it the attack? Do you feel unsafe?" asked Lily. "I honestly don't know how you're coping."

"Oh, it's fine. It's been a few days. Nothing else has happened. What have you got here?"

"It's back in the area," said Lily, nodding to the screen. "The IP bounced off the school wifi."

"I've got a list," said Wes, taking a seat on the office chair beside Lily and motioning for Minnie to sit beside him. "Everyone who went on the ski trip with you. Teachers at the top - students below them. What do you think?"

"Think about what?" asked Minnie, consulting the names.

"Did anyone act strangely?" asked Lily.

"Not that I could tell," said Minnie.

"I think whoever attacked you is the same person who took Kane's phone," said Wes. "It's got to be."

"Why?"

"Maybe, whoever it was, saw us in Kane's apartment or thinks we're onto them. Maybe the plan was to attack you in the woods and make it look like a random person was responsible," said Wes.

"It would certainly take some heat off the school," said Lily.

"Let's start with staff," said Wes.

"Well, I hardly saw Otto," said Minnie, already disliking the task of trying to find oddities where none seemed to be. How could average human behaviour be quantified into something potentially sinister? "Just at breakfast and on the ski field. I've not spoken to him much either. Andrew and Ian were fine - they're quite personable. Kate, Rachel and Miren were fine - their usual selves."

"Did Kate say she heard something when you were being attacked?" asked Lily.

"She said she woke up when I was calling for help," said Minnie. "Miren heard me first though."

"Wonder why."

"Might have been up at the time? Her room was next to ours."

Wes was tracing the bridge of his nose, deep in thought. "What about the students? Did anything stand out?"

"Well, no," she said, not wanting to betray Kai's confidence entirely. "Kai was nervous, but I think that was more related to the competition."

"What about the little shit?" asked Wes.

"Which one?" asked Lily.

"Ralph Astley."

Lily pulled a face, grimacing as though a foul smell had come under her nose. "He's got some opinion of himself, that one."

"He's a little fucker," Wes said agreeably. "Maybe it was him."

"In the woods?" Minnie found that difficult to comprehend. She disliked the boy deeply but believing he could attack her was a step beyond what she could allow herself to consider. He was a pompous teenager - wealthy, likely lonely and a bully - but someone capable of assault? "The man who attacked me was tall."

"Beard?"

"No."

"They're all skiers, Minnie. They're all tough."

"I think I injured his knee," said Minnie. "I kicked him in the leg."

"Ralph's been in physio," said Wes pressingly.

"So has half the ski team," said Minnie. "It doesn't narrow anything down. I even tried calling the number when you sent it to me. The bus was too loud to hear anything."

"Are you sure this thing can't find the exact location of the phone or computer?" Wes asked Lily.

"If I could, I'd have done that. I don't work for ASIO," said Lily with barely restrained frustration.

Wes was visibly disappointed. Minnie wished she had useful knowledge of computers but beyond the basics, she simply did not. They were once again at a standstill.

"Is it a party?"

The three froze, glancing silently at one another as a set of footsteps drew closer. Minnie breathed a sigh of relief when Miren appeared; freshly showered and dressed in a tracksuit. Upon finding them, her expression seemed to be frozen in one that, while smiling, beheld cold suspicion.

"Just tell her," said Minnie. It would be a relief to share the secret, to be rid of one element of their covert operation so that someone else could assist in shouldering the burden.

"Tell me what?"

Wes broke; he seemed to have finally decided, like Minnie, that if Miren knew some details of the mystery she might as well know them all. He told Miren of their suspicion regarding Kane and that they discovered his phone and computer were still on school grounds. Miren asked the questions they expected, testing their theory a number of times, before she too agreed that Kane was both suspected of being involved in the murders or a victim himself.

"Is this why you were in his apartment?" Miren asked Minnie.

"Yes, I thought he might have left something behind."

"Does Henry believe Kane is in Tassie?" Wes asked firmly. "Has he been able to get in touch with him?"

"No. Henry is of the belief that Kane is in Tasmania, yes. But they have not been in contact as far as I can tell," said Miren. "We have to tell Henry. We *have* to."

"No!" said Wes. "We've been working on this for weeks."

"And got *nowhere*."

"What if he's involved?" asked Wes. "I'm not even 100% sure that *you're* not involved."

Miren fixed him with a hard look. "What would I be involved in?"

"Well, we can't know you don't know more about the photos."

"You're fucked," said Miren. "What in the fuck would I know about those fucking photos?"

"You were close with Jenny. Sure she didn't ever tell you anything? Slip a name in there?" Wes asked testily.

Miren's face twitched from offended to hesitant.

"Miren, share if you know something. We're only stronger with all our information on the table."

"Jenny... Jenny..." Miren struggled; she placed her hands on her hips and took a breath to compose herself. "Just thought a teacher was involved."

"I. Fucking. Knew. It."

Lily clutched her hands at her chest. "You mean ... with the photo of Stephen?"

"Jenny thought that someone was being inappropriate with some of the boys in senior years," said Miren, clarifying. "She long suspected that Stephen had a crush or fallen in love with someone. That person ended their relationship at the beginning of this year and then he... well, killed himself. Jenny thought she saw them once - in the woods."

"Just going for a stroll?" Wes asked lightly, as though inquiring after a common item in a shop.

"Don't be flippant, Wes. It's a serious issue," Miren snapped.

"Fucking kids *is* a serious issue," he responded, nodding. "Did you tell this little tid bit to your *boyfriend*?"

"Certainly."

"So, the Principal was aware of a suspicion of children being interfered with and nothing happened?" he asked with what seemed to Minnie as withheld fury masked in lightly placed questions.

"You know," said Miren, abandoning her poise, "despite what you think of Henry, he is decent and wants what's best for the students *and* the teachers. Of *course* I told him but there was *no evidence*. You can't just go looking into people's personal lives without reasonable suspicion and due process."

"That's bullshit and you know it. Everyone in this room knows that if there is the slightest suspicion of harm to a child then we are duty-bound to follow it up."

"Then I'll assume you've made reports of *everything* you've found in your little amateur investigation here, shall I? Made reports on your tracking IPs, Lily? Made reports on looking into Kane's office, Minnie? Made reports on your suspicions, Wes?" Miren pinned them each with a look of furious frustration. Minnie felt ashamed, brought to quiet contemplation. "Your 'evidence' is non existent," she said, underlining her point.

"What about the photo that Jenny sent you?" asked Minnie. "Isn't that evidence?"

"Of what? What does that photo prove that the photo sent to everyone else doesn't?"

"That it's more than one male student, but the same female."

"It's a variety of evidence," said Wes.

"Two photos?" Miren waved him off dismissively.

"What if Stephen wrote about her?" asked Minnie, struck by an idea.

"So?" asked Lily.

"What if there are clues in his writing?"

"How do we get a hold of his writing?" asked Wes.

"I have some," said Minnie. "A book, actually. They belonged to Kane. Someone passed them on to me. I found them in my room when I arrived at the school."

"Why would anyone give you Kane's copies of Stephen's work?" asked Miren.

Minnie shrugged.

"That's weird. Who was it? Kate?"

"Not sure ..."

"Can you show us?"

"Sure," said Minnie. "It's long."

"Shall we call it a night?" asked Miren. "We can look over Stephen's papers tomorrow?"

Minnie nodded. "I think we need to go to the police."

"We don't have any real information," said Lily.

"We have enough for them to take the suspicions seriously," said Minnie, convinced they'd come to the end of the line.

"We have to tell Henry before we do that," said Miren. "It's not fair otherwise."

"It is," said Minnie, annoyed by her sense of loyalty. "We don't have to go up some 'chain of command' to get permission."

"Not permission but time to prepare. All this has come from left field and it's not fair..."

"You know what's not fair?" said Wes, cutting Miren off. "Getting hung. Sandra and Jenny knew something. I'm willing to bet that's what killed them. I'm not giving Henry a second of lead time before I call the police when the time is right. I think he knows something."

"Again - where's your evidence of that?" Miren scoffed and walked off, leaving them in an uncomfortable silence.

"If she pre-warns him, then I'm suspecting her too," said Wes.

"The time is right," said Minnie.

"I agree," said Lily. "I can make copies of all the evidence and give it to the police."

"Call in the morning?" said Wes.

"Ok," said Minnie, leading the way out.

Exhausted but relieved they were ready to contact police, Minnie made up her mind to wake extra early to map their findings. There was something not quite fitting together. For all their evidence, or lack of, something was both obvious and obscured from their consideration. She needed to visualise it on paper. No wonder crime television displayed the board of suspects and theories in police stations. She needed to acquire her own extended red string to draw the connections of this impossible situation. With her key in hand and fantasising about diving into bed, the hairs on the back of her neck stood up a fraction of a second before a firm hand gripped hers.

"Just couldn't help yourself could you, Foxy?"

Minnie gasped, at once aware of the sharp pain in the back of her head and instantly rendered immobile. She collapsed, unconscious.

Chapter 14

Kane Liu

S ome nights they walked across the virgin forests of Switzerland, other nights they strolled through the dunes of the Sahara. Wherever they were, their hands were locked, entwined at the fingers and pressed at the palms, gliding ever peacefully through the world under a navy sky that displayed the brightest stars; their plane beholding neither life nor death. On this night, Jamie danced with her in the streets of Valencia. They were alone but for the gypsy musicians, dancing across the cobblestones in the light of the shop-front candles. While aware that none of Ginger Rodgers talent was present in her movements, she allowed herself to be led by Jamie, who without doubt had talent and enthusiasm to match Fred Astaire. As they moved smoothly to the music, dipping and swirling, Minnie became aware of a rhythmical tap on her face. She looked to Jamie; he was holding her close, one hand on her waist, the other her own hand. Once more - this time, firmer.

"Miss Fox."

Minnie lifted her head from his shoulder. "Jamie?"

"Miss Fox!"

Jamie smiled and kissed her nose. "Sounds like it's time to go, darl."

"Miss Fox! You *have* to wake up!"

"No," she said firmly, tightening her grip. "No, Jamie."

Jamie continued to smile. "We'll dance again."

"No!" The slap that woke her stung beyond her initial awakening; hot and prickling. She opened her eyes, fighting tears and the sense of egregious injustice at having lost the sense of floating euphoria. "Kai?"

The teenager's unshaven face hovered above hers. He looked frantic and pushed her to sit upright. He pulled at the ties around her ankles, having already untied her hands. Minnie held her head; her brain pulsated. The base of her head was tender and as she pressed her hand to the skin beneath her hair, she felt the texture of something recently dried and crumbly. The residue on her fingers told it was blood. Using the torch function on his phone, Kai checked her face and her hands. He carefully put the phone down, muting the light while not altogether turning it off.

"Where are we?" she asked as the cold air withdrew an involuntary shiver.

"We can't talk," he whispered as softly as possible. "We're not alone."

"What do you mean?"

"They will be here soon. We have to *hide*."

"*What?*"

"Just follow me," he whispered desperately.

Minnie followed his lead and crawled along uneven floorboards. They emerged from a small room with a narrow closet. They exited through a hall to a door that led outside. Minnie did not recognise the area until - crouching low - they emerged around the side of a white picket fence. It was the church. The long, tree-lined path leading back to the school was dimly illuminated in the moonlight. No one else seemed to be around. Kai raised a trembling hand, indicating to remain low. They waited a moment, hovering in a squat so low that her years of pilates practice were being put to the test. Growing impatient, Minnie was tempted to ask what he was waiting for, and then, as though sensing her disquiet, he pressed a finger to his lips. A cloud emitted from his mouth, bringing the bitter cold to Minnie's full attention. Adrenaline and shock had struck her so fiercely that the evening chill was yet to seep into her skin. Without a coat, it would take minutes before her body slowed and shook. She hoped Kai had every intention of leading her back to the school.

When Kai deemed it safe, he guided her forward. They did not return back to the school by way of the main road. Instead, he diverted her into the thick woods, slipping between trees, hovering behind others, and pausing intermittently to listen. After ten minutes, they paused at the treeline, hovering behind the barn.

"It seems oddly quiet," said Minnie.

"Not for long," said Kai. "It's dinner time. I think some of them might go to the church to look for you. They will wait for the dead of night to do anything."

"Who's *them*? Do what?"

Kai motioned to the front steps of the senior dorms where Ralph Astley and Harry Dormer were talking. "I saw Ralph carrying you to the church."

"Ralph knocked me unconscious?" Minnie was suddenly warmed by anger. "That little *fucker*."

"I think that's what he intended, essentially."

A sliver of bile rose in her throat.

"Ralph is dangerous, Miss Fox. He's been fascinated by you since you got here. It's not a school-boy crush, either. Don't mistake the situation."

"What situation?"

"You're one of the few people in the world with a true white light, Miss Fox," he said, smiling briefly. "Sometimes, when people like you come across predators... you end up the victim."

"You'll have to explain yourself better, Kai," said Minnie, not quite piecing together his cryptic message.

"Watch," he said, motioning to Ralph and Harry. "They're probably heading for the church."

"What will they do when they see that I've gone?"

"They'll go to her and admit what they've done. No one else could cover it up."

"Who is *her*?"

"I'll explain. Follow me."

"I don't have my phone," said Minnie, patting the back pocket of her trousers.

"Yeah, he took it."

"But we need to call the police," said Minnie.

"I'll do it when I've told you everything. Come."

"Kai, if we don't call the police we're going to end up like Sandra and Jenny. These boys knocked me unconscious ..."

Kai rounded on her. "I know. But we *have* to go to the cellar for evidence. It's all in the school."

Frustrated by the lack of control she had in the situation, Minnie followed as Kai led the way back to Main House, through the back of the kitchen garden, past the servants entrance of which she was familiar, and to a small wooden door. A small 'Cellar' sign swung forward on its squeaky hinge. Minnie stared down at the rickety wooden steps, wondering when she lost her sense of self preservation. She had no reason to trust Kai, excluding his saving her from the church and whatever evil machinations Ralph had in store for her. What was more, a seventeen-year-old was leading her around as though the student-teacher roles were reversed.

"What's in there?"

"I think ... you said honesty is best," he said.

"Yes."

"I think it's Mr Liu."

That should have rattled her. "Mr Liu?"

"Yeah," he said as though the answer was obvious.

"Why is he in a cellar?"

"I don't know for sure he is yet."

"Do you know how to give a straight answer?"

"How do you think I stay out of trouble?"

I need another career, she thought while rubbing her temples.

There was no evidence that Kai was in any way attempting to do the right thing, nor was there that he was leading her into a trap, though the location and the lack of information as to what exactly he was leading her toward did influence her to lean toward the latter. Trust. Calculating his behaviour over the term, his friendship with Rob, and his demeanour, she was led by an element of trust. Despite her better judgement, she followed him down the stairs, where he lit the path using the light of his phone.

The cellar, though dusty, was not abandoned. They had not stumbled on a centuries old cellar worth millions but it was not kept in the immaculate conditions expected of such a wealthy school. Isles of wine and liquors filled the space, some were incredibly old and others were new additions. There was little evidence that it was used regularly. The ground was dusty enough that a few footprints were visible, but, curiously, something seemed to have swept the ground from the cellar door along the first aisle of wines and around the corner. Perhaps they were storing heavy bags of rice down there.

"How do you know he's down here?" asked Minnie, following the path.

"I heard Harry talking about it."

"Surely he can hear us coming," said Minnie, and as she made to call out, Kai raised his hands in protest.

"Shh!"

"What?"

"Be *quiet*!"

"Why?"

"You want to alert people that we're here?" said Kai, cautiously stepping forward.

"But you said he was down here."

"I said he might be down here." Kai led the way, holding his phone high. "Ugh," he grimaced. "There's a smell."

Minnie's breath hitched in her throat in anticipation of the vulgar smell that would hit her in the nose. A large tarp was wrapped around a long but indecipherable shape. While Minnie held hope that the tarp merely wrapped some closed outdoor umbrellas or gardening equipment, Kai, with courage only given to teenagers when in a state of discovery, leaned forward, still holding the phone light high, and pulled it back.

Minnie gave an involuntary shriek; Kai jumped back, swearing. A body lay against the far wall wrapped in plastic from head to toe like a cling-wrap mummy. Curiously, there was evidence of food and a few bottles of water also wrapped in the tarp. Minnie inched closer, lifting her jumper over her nose as Kai made dry retching sounds.

"Hold the light closer, Kai," she instructed, squinting.

Despite the lack of clarity due to the plastic wrap, it was clear the body was bound at the hands and feet. There was no blood visible. It was a man.

"Does it look like Mr Liu?"

"It's him," said Kai. He looked anguished.

Disappointed, Minnie sighed. "He's just been discarded down here ... like he doesn't matter." *Three bodies*. "Oh my God," she whispered, stepping away. "There is an actual murderer at this school. What in the *fuck*?"

"A serial killer."

"Sandra, Jenny and Kane... that's all you need. Three. There's a serial killer at one of the most prestigious schools in the world. There's a body in the cellar." Minnie felt herself spiralling, becoming lightheaded and emotionally frantic. There was no telling if someone would return to check on the body. It was likely to be a nightly duty, afterall, who would leave the discovery to chance? "Kai, where are we with regards to upstairs? What are we under?"

"Well, the old servants quarters are on the other side of that wall," he said, pointing to the wall against which the body lay. "The stairs go up to the entrance hall."

Minnie remembered being there with Miren when they discovered the room in which the videos had been recorded. How did Kai know how to access the servants quarters?

"I don't know if there's a door that ..." Kai fell silent, looking past Minnie.

"It's alright."

Minnie turned. Henry was halfway down the stairs, holding his hands up in an attempt to show he meant no harm. He looked on edge, exhausted, if not apprehensive. While she felt momentarily relieved to see the Principal, hoping to close the whole ordeal once and for all, she was guided to immediate distrust when Kai pulled her back and pointed at the older man. "*Stay there*," he ordered.

Minnie was taken aback. Henry complied, keeping his hands up.

"It's alright," he said evenly. "I know you're afraid."

"Not afraid. I'm just cautious. You stay there."

"I won't come any closer. Miss Fox, you'll need to listen now and step away from the boy. I'm not sure what you have him doing down here but this is inappropriate."

"Excuse me?" Minnie understood what irked Wes about the Principal. He was an actor through and through.

"You don't have any authority to be down here with a student, Miss Fox. I'm going to have to ask you to come with me," he said.

"She's not going anywhere. There's a body down here," said Kai, holding his arm out so Minnie did not pass. "But I think you know that already, don't you?"

Minnie looked over her shoulder at the sound of an opening door. Part of the cellar was now lit, illuminated by the bright lights of the room behind. It was a secret door, naturally, that led to what looked like a furnished room.

"Kai," said a soft voice.

Kai's hand trembled. He turned, lowering his phone light. Kate appeared at the threshold. Minnie's mind was racing. Nothing made sense.

"Kai, you weren't supposed to know," she said kindly. "Come up here. Let's get you out of there."

"What the fuck is going on?" Minnie demanded. "Is this a cult?"

"It's ok, Minnie," said Kate. "It's just a misunderstanding."

Kai looked from one exit to the other, calculating their success at escape. Minnie knew that if he were alone, he would bolt for the door being blocked by Henry. He was big enough to take the man, but she had little chance, especially without a weapon. She wished with every fibre of her being that she had demanded they call the police when they had the chance.

"Kai, call the police," said Minnie, looking from Kate to Henry.

"There's no need for that," said Henry, stepping forward.

"I said *stay back*," Kai shouted. "I can take you on, Waterstone."

If Henry knew about the body, there was a chance he was involved in the murder, or was the killer. "Kai, call the police *now*."

As Kai made to dial the number, Kate said, "There's no reception."

"She's right," Kai said softly, defeated.

"Why don't you come in? You can join, Lily."

Join Lily? "Kate, what the hell are you doing?" Minnie demanded, unable to compute the absurdity of the situation.

"It'll all be sorted in no time," said Kate.

Minnie felt a visceral hatred for the icy calm in her voice. She glanced at Kane's body and wondered, morbidly, if she was going to join him, wrapped in the tarp and buried somewhere on the grounds.

"We'll talk," said Kai. "Outside. We're not going in there."

"It's cold outside," said Henry. "I *promise*, no harm will come to either of you. This is all a misunderstanding."

"A misunderstanding... *there's a dead man in here*!" said Minnie, outraged. "You let everyone believe he was in Tasmania!"

"They all know, Miss," said Kai, glaring at Henry.

"Minnie, she knows we've been tracking the IP address," called Lily, her voice thick with tears.

Because you couldn't keep your mouth shut, Minnie thought be-grudgingly, knowing full well it was undeserved. Lily was likely fright-ened out of her wits. Who knew what they might have done to her?

"They won't hurt us," he said, nodding to Kate. "I have *insurance*."

Confused and desperate for clarification, Minnie could not find the will to respond as he led the way toward the open door. It was Henry's office. A fact that made her stomach turn. How could he function day-to-day knowing an innocent man lay dead beneath his feet? Henry came up behind them, closing the door. Minnie stepped away from him. Lily was crying hysterically in one of the two chairs opposite Henry's desk. Minnie felt a pang of annoyance at the sight of her smeared makeup, the guilty expression and the fact that the young woman seemed to have no feelings for the situation outside of crippling fear. This was how people ended up dead in the movies. Showing this much fear made the enemy look at people like Lily as easily expendable. Attain information, then *bang*. Bullet.

"Why don't you take a seat, Miss Fox?" Henry gestured to the chair next to Lily.

"No. I'll stand."

"Suit yourself," he said coolly, sitting down behind his desk. "How did you find the body?"

"We're not answering a thing," said Kai.

"I think you have miscalculated your position in the room, Watanabe," said Henry. "You're a student at this school. You follow the orders, not give them."

"Listen, asshole. I'm following no orders. I'm making it clear now. I have protections around this situation. I have evidence timed to go to police, social media and my parents by 6am."

"On what?" Kate demanded. "Kai, how could you betray me?"

"Betray you?" Minnie asked, thoroughly confused.

"It's *her*!" shouted Lily, pointing at Kate. "She was fucking Stephen Graham. It's her in the photo! It's all her!"

Minnie felt suckerpunched. Raising her hands in protest, she rejected the idea, even when Kai's expression reflected that Lily was telling the truth. Kate did not flinch and Henry was rubbing his temples. Minnie held Kate's gaze in the hope that her roommate would leap to denial and reveal the truth behind the sordid situation in which they found themselves. As the seconds ticked forward, and

Kate remained infuriatingly mute, Minnie took her silence to be an admission of truth. Minnie looked to Henry, disgusted that he had attempted to insinuate that she had been in the cellar with Kai for a malevolent reason, all the while knowing that Kate had molested a child. A marrow-deep loathing rose in her and as her hands balled into fists, her chest tightened.

"It's in the manuscript, Miss," said Kai. "Did you read it?"

"How do you know about the manuscript?"

"I'm the one that left it in your room," he said, ignoring Kate's angry demeanour.

"You? You knew?"

"So did Mr Liu," said Kai. "He found out who Stephen was in love with. It's all in the manuscript. It's essentially his suicide note. You didn't read it?"

Minnie shook her head. "Not the whole thing."

A vein pulsed in Kai's forehead. "It's the last page that's most important. *'Goodbye sweet, Conqueror. Though you have lain waste with my love, I am, even in death, forever yours,'*" he recited.

"How does it direct to Kate?"

"Her last name," said Kai.

"How's your Latin?" asked Kate, adjusting her curly hair in its tie.

Minnie hesitated, unwilling to admit that 'Carpe Diem' was as far as her latin went.

"Vincini - Conqueror. To defeat, to vanquish... to conquer," said Kate, looking pleased with herself.

"Did Stephen ever tell you *outright* that she was the one he was in love with?"

Kai sighed. "There's so much to explain. This goes beyond the manuscript, beyond Stephen... I hoped that if you had the photos, you'd put the pieces together."

"How do you know about the photos?"

"I sent them!"

"You..."

"Kai!" Kate shouted, furious. "Why would you do that?"

"Because this is a sham!"

Henry, who had fallen silent, had laced his fingers around the back of his neck and was looking at the far corner of the room with a vacant expression. Minnie wondered if he was having an out of body experience, brought on by the clarity of the horrific situation. What was his role in all of this?

"Wait..." Minnie's mind was ticking furiously. "Wait a minute. There was another photo. Jenny had it. It was not of Stephen though. It was another person. A man..."

"Care to reveal?" asked Kate, looking pointedly at Kai.

"It's me," he said. "The other photo is of me."

The statement brought Henry to life. "You said it ended with Stephen!"

Kate responded with a sigh of irritation, and she glared at him as though to ask whether he truly believed her.

"You've been having sex with and filming children?" Minnie asked Kate.

Kate laughed. "Does he look like a child to you?"

Minnie was revolted, livid and in that moment did not care if it showed and who heard. "I don't care how tall they are, or how much they don't 'look' like kids. They're *minors*. They are your students. You've gone against everything teachers are bound by - both morally, ethically and professionally."

"*Spare* me," Kate said dismissively.

"No way. No," said Minnie. "You have just admitted to rape."

"It's not rape if they consented. We were in a relationship."

The cognitive dissonance was such that Minnie could not retort effectively. She felt the urge to throw herself across the room and punch the woman she was beginning to call a friend. Instead, she turned to Henry, a man whose petulant face she was most tempted to slap. "You're remarkably quiet. I take it you were aware of this?"

"Unfortunately. Ah, hell..." Henry pulled a bottle of whisky from his desk. "Kane came to me at the end of last year with - what I thought - was some bullshit story about our dear Miss Vincini giving extra favours to some of the boys." He pinned Kate with a look that squarely lay the blame on their predicament to her. "Kane and I spoke to Miss Vincini about it but not long into first term, I go down to the cellar and find Kane tied up."

"He was alive?" asked Kai.

"Young man, he is nowhere near decomposed enough to have been dead all the time he's been 'in Tasmania'," he said, signing the air quotes.

"Who killed him then? You?" Kai accused Kate.

"Gosh no," said Kate, looking offended. "You know the others enjoy doing that kind of activity."

Minnie began to feel lightheaded once more. "Can someone explain this? Who is *they*?"

"The Crew," said Kai. "Ralph Astley, Harry Dormer, Lincoln Friers, Leo Garcia, Stephen Graham... and me."

"What do you do in this 'crew'?"

"Like stupid boys, we fight for Kate's attention," said Kai, holding the gaze of the woman whose expression was melting into one of aggrieved betrayal. "With Stephen dead - because she abandoned him - there was an opening. Rob was next on the list - wasn't he?"

Minnie took a deep, slow breath in to stabilise herself.

When Kate didn't respond, Kai continued. "The point was - in The Crew, Kate would perform special favours for those she was most pleased with. For a bit, it was Stephen. He wrote stories. She liked them. He would do *anything* to keep her attention. But she got bored. Stephen spiralled."

"Why did you do it then?" asked Minnie.

"Because I'm no better than the others. I'm a fucking idiot. I thought sleeping with a teacher would be fun...harmless! After Mr Liu found out, I changed my mind. I haven't been able to keep up with school. Went down the same mental road as Stephen. When Mr Liu went missing I knew she was involved. That's when I got my little bit of insurance. I had to protect myself. I wanted it all out in the open. So I sent the photo. I hoped the police might get here and blow the whole thing open. Then she killed Ms Keys!"

"*Why* did you kill Sandra?" Minnie asked Kate.

"I didn't."

"But you were there."

"How can you tell?"

"You were out running. There's no reason for anyone to be running at 2am," said Minnie, remembering the way in which the short woman had gone against Kate's excuses. "Even if you can prove you didn't kill Sandra with your bare hands - which I don't believe - you were there."

"Sandra was killed by strangulation," said Kate. "I don't have the strength to do that."

"You do," said Minnie. "But I think you used one of the boys. I think it was likely Ralph. He seems to like coming up behind women and knocking them unconscious."

"It wasn't so much like that. I wanted her to *eat dirt*," said Kate with venom for the deceased woman. "So she did."

A disturbing flash crossed Minnie's mindseye; Sandra struggling to lift her face from the dirt, her head being forcibly pushed into a garden bed by Ralph as the Crew and Kate watched, smirking.

"But *why*?

"Stephen told her. She was his wellbeing mentor," said Kai.

"And she was dumb enough to confront me about it the night she died," said Kate.

"And you knew?" Minnie asked Henry.

Lily descended into tears once more, curling herself into a ball on the chair. Minnie pushed down the urge to tell her to snap out of it. This was a critical moment. They needed to demonstrate strength, not capitulation and fear.

"I suspected what happened," said Henry, side eyeing Kate. "Luckily I stumbled on the scene with David. You didn't have time to cover it up this time," he said to Kate.

"Don't be pathetic. This is in your best interests too," said Kate.

"If you weren't a whore then none of us would be in here."

"What were you and David doing up at that time?" asked Minnie.

"We got a security alert. Movement on the cameras."

"Had to turn them off after," said Kate.

"You covered this up for the school?" Minnie asked, disgusted.

"Don't be so high and mighty," Henry snapped. "The fucking cheek of people like you."

"People like me?"

"I have met plenty of women like you, Mrs Fox," said Henry, in a tone that suggested his tolerance for women - or at least, younger women - was fragile. "You're overeducated with no cash behind you and you begrudge career professionals who made the right decision to start in an *exemplary* educational institution. You look down your nose at people for rising to the top and *fighting* to stay there. Do you know the bullshit I deal with on a daily basis? Do you know how hard I have fought to develop this school? Making it co-ed was my idea! I have put blood, sweat and plenty of tears in this place. I wasn't going to let a small issue like this ruin my reputation and what I've built. Imagine the front page of the papers... 'Principal at Elite School at the Head of a Sex Scandal'. You think I was going to let that happen? If I had to bury some bodies... then so - be - it."

Minnie and Kai shared a look. The situation was all too clear. No one was going to leave the school alive if they could bear witness to the scandal. Lily gasped. Surprising them all, she bolted for the front door and threw herself out, running screaming through the atrium and out the front doors of Main House. Kate made to run after her. Minnie sprang forth and tackled her into the shelf, shielding her face by turning away as Kate tried to slap and scratch her way free.

"Ah, Foxy," said a low voice, grabbing her around the waist and heaving her off Kate. "Now, let's calm down. Shh shh. I really don't want you to go the same way as poor Jenny."

Chapter 15

Murky Waters

M INNIE MADE THE SPLIT second decision to flay and kick and elbow, striking everyone in her vicinity in an attempt to get free. She caught Kate in the shin, flung her elbow, painfully, into someone's face by the evidence of their profanity-laced outcry, and attempted to bite the hand trying to cover her mouth.

"GET OFF ME!" she screamed, feeling her throat rasp and tingle with the force. "HELP!"

"Shut her up!" Henry slammed the door.

Then, she was on the floor. She had been wrestled into compliance by a grip so tight on her wrists and arms that nothing she did with her legs was fruitful. "Now this is nice," said a voice in her ear.

Minnie leaned forward, shrinking away.

"You fucking *dog*," said Kai. "She's a fucking teacher, man!"

The Crew must have been waiting on the atrium side of Henry's office door. Kai was being held back by Lincoln Friers, who was also sporting a bruised eye. Harry Dormer, the shorter of the three, was hovering by Kate, and Leo Garcia, a boy Minnie never imagined capable of being involved in such behaviour, was watching with an apprehensive expression by Henry's desk. That meant Ralph was tackling her, and the humour he seemed to find in the situation was entirely lost on her.

"We seem to have this little dance, you and I," he said, his breath hot on her neck. "You're always *slipping* away. I don't think you will tonight though, Foxy."

Abandoning all pretence of professionalism, Minnie said, "You're a sick little shit."

"Astley!" Henry commanded. "You are not going to manhandle a teacher."

"We've had this little chat, Waterstone," said Ralph, his voice dripping with airy arrogance. "We compensate you *handsomely* to look the other way."

"No!" Henry approached them, and for a second Minnie hoped he might be able to release her from Ralph's painfully tight grip. "I will not allow you to assault a woman in my office."

"Then I won't do it in your office," said Ralph, agreeably. "I like a little privacy."

"Are you serious?" Kai screamed. "Back the fuck off me," he said, shoving Lincoln off him violently.

"Ralph, man ... what the fuck?" asked Leo, approaching skittishly.

"I helped with this whole drama, and now I'm getting my pay," said Ralph.

Minnie twisted herself in his grip and a sharp pain twinged in her wrist.

"No, no... sit quietly."

The idea of being ordered around by a student, a spoilt rat none-the-less, accompanied by the condescending tone, encouraged an atomic amount of rage within her. She was suddenly hot with the need to see her foot meet his obnoxious face in a swift kick.

"This is an outrage, Astley. Release her immediately!" Henry demanded, holding a pausing instructional hand to Kai.

"We can't keep her alive anyway," said Kate. "She knows too much."

Minnie wanted to believe Henry's morals would take precedence over his loyalty to the reputation of the school. His expression betrayed his dilemma. Where killing her would remove the problem of her bearing witness to their guilt, questions would be raised and the police would surely emerge at the school in full force. Three teachers were dead, only two known to police. If they killed her, their secret was blown. It seemed the room was contemplating the absurdity of Kate's statement; the ticking of tense seconds brought to reality the likelihood of her impending death.

Henry narrowed his eyes. "How much?"

It took a moment for Minnie to realise what he was asking her. "Much what?" *Time to run for my life? Seconds. Time to call the police? Even less.*

"Money? To keep you quiet."

Minnie smirked. The question did not deserve a serious answer. "It would be in the millions, mate."

"How many? he asked, humourlessly.

"Get him off me," said Minnie. "I'm not talking with this fucker touching me."

"I've dreamed it," Ralph said passionately, pressing his cheek to the back of her neck.

Craning herself away, fruitlessly, Minnie and Kai shared a look of pure incredulity.

"You're seriously going to pay her off?" Kate demanded of Henry.

"If I remember correctly, you already killed *three* other staff. Imagine what the police will do when another one is found dead? Or missing?" said Henry, raising his eyebrows to further punctuate the question. "Get Olivia," he directed Leo when Kate could not find a satisfactory response.

Henry turned to Ralph and motioned for him to release Minnie. His face became hard with barely restrained fury. As soon as his grip softened, Minnie shook Ralph off, rolling away from him and standing by the now open door. She wiped the back of her neck, disgusted at the idea that any residue of his would be on her. When Kai made to join her, Kate grabbed his arm.

Ralph smiled dreamily. "I'll think of your smell, Foxy."

"From prison? I hope so," she retorted. *There isn't a shower hot enough to get me clean now.*

"This isn't over yet," he promised.

Leo wheeled in the School Administrator, stumbling and shakily pushing the office chair through the threshold. Minnie and Olivia locked eyes, equally horrified. Olivia's hands were tied together and duck tape covered her mouth. How had no one noticed her in the hall in this condition? Where were the staff?

Henry's office phone rang. Eight pairs of eyes turned to the phone; Henry hesitated. Olivia and Minnie shared a glance, and then Kai gave Minnie a pointed look. Leo had left the door open. Minnie had the strength to tackle Leo if necessary; he was about her height and was half the bulk of Ralph. Minnie had a strange feeling that Leo purposely fumbled bringing Olivia completely into the room. Olivia gave a brief grimace and threw herself off the chair, struggling against her binds.

With a pang of guilt, Minnie took the opportunity and ran. She bolted as fast as her legs would take her, out of the atrium and into the gardens. After avoiding an almost fatal stumble on the stone steps, her adrenaline spiked to a point where she felt on the brink of simultaneous collapse and superhuman speed. She heard a commotion behind her; screams and great thuds alongside cussing worthy of truck drivers. She dared not look back as she sprinted into the kitchen garden. Her options were clear in her mind's eye. She needed her car keys. She used the dark to her benefit, having folded herself behind a rosemary hedge, listening. Tears pricked the backs of her eyes; stress and fear mixed into an adrenaline-filled cocktail that saw her involuntarily trembling.

Stop it. She took a deep, quiet breath. *Stop it. Cry later.* Second breath. She pressed her hands between her thighs and while it served the purpose of stopping her hands from shaking, her arms and shoulders now overtook the duty.

Fleeting moments passed - nothing. Perhaps they assumed she had run for the gates or the woods. Huddled in the dirt, pressed against the jutting rosemary leaves, she needed to take stock of the situation. The chances of being captured were high, as was the chance that other staff were involved. *Where the hell are they all?* It was the middle of the night; most likely they were headed to bed or already sleeping. Where was Wes? If he tried to contact her, there was no way she would know. Ralph had taken her phone. Where was Miren? Surely she would have been in contact with Henry around dinner time, they were dating after all. Was it she who had just called on his office phone? Olivia clearly knew nothing of the situation as she had been tied up and held hostage. What would they do with her now? Surely a payment to keep her quiet would not suffice. *Or*, Minnie thought, *it's an act and Olivia is well aware of the truth.* Was she also on the payroll?

The time to move had come. If she was brave enough, she would attempt to jump the fence and run for freedom. Town was far enough to reach before long, but the weather was against her; the cold was bitter. *Cold is a state of mind.* If people could bathe in arctic waters and breathe through it, she could walk to town. Without a coat. Or a phone. Or a clue.

With crumbling resolve, Minnie crawled out of the rosemary bushes, acutely aware of the silence. It was inconceivable that nobody was around. Neither an adult or skulking teenager. *That's a mystery for another day*, she told herself. While the teacher's apartments were the best place to look for a phone and seek help, she knew they were where she would likely be found if The Crew disbanded to find her. Rob was likely another primary port of call for them so she avoided heading toward the senior student dorms. Lily's desk in the library was her only hope of finding technology and calling for help. *Hopefully she made it out*. While crawling alongside the exterior of the library, taking care to stay in the shadows, she noticed a figure emerging from the second floor window. Nondescript in the darkness, it moved stealthily and with an agility that sparked a moment of envy, down an old drainpipe. *Has to be a student*. One of The Crew would not need to be acrobating down a drainpipe; they would just use the front door. This had to be someone else. When the figure landed with a soft thud, and Minnie reached out, the figure sucked in a high-pitched scream that was muted when they clapped a hand over their mouth.

"Rob!"

"Minnie!"

She was never more glad to see his flushed face. He looked astounded. Minnie pulled him behind the building, into the trees. "Why were you up there?"

"I got locked in there! Someone tripped a school-wide lockdown. Apparently there's an intruder," he whispered.

Smart little criminals.

"There isn't."

"There is! I saw someone grab Lily from her desk. I was hiding in an alcove so they didn't see me. I just managed to get through to police."

Minnie felt sick with relief. "You called the police?"

"Yeah! They are on their way."

"Why did it take so long to get through?"

"Phones were down."

"Rob, we have to hide until they get here."

"I need to tell Principal Waterstone that Lily's been kid-napped!"

"He's the one who kidnapped her," Minnie said quickly, her grip tightening on his blazer. "I just escaped the office!"

Rob's expression flickered from one extreme to the next. Minnie appreciated that he was likely trying to decide which question was most important to ask first. Then, they heard footsteps. Minnie was confident they would not be seen; she had hidden them in the thick of the trees. She motioned for him to remain quiet.

"I'm going to get that bitch," someone muttered.

"You shouldn't have attacked her!" said another, a woman.

Kate and Ralph.

"This is your fault anyway. If you'd just chosen me next..." Ralph muttered.

"Shut up. You're a whiny brat," Kate snapped. "If we don't find her, then everything is blown."

"Everything's blown anyway," said Ralph.

"What do you mean?"

"You can't pay her off. She runs on her ethics. Unlike everyone else around here. I say we bury her and Liu together behind the church and pretend like she went to Europe."

"How?"

"We fake it like we faked Liu."

"But I have Liu's phone. Faking it all was simpler."

Bingo, thought Minnie.

"And I have hers," said Ralph.

Minnie felt Rob tense beside her. He looked at her, silently questioning the truth in Ralph's admission. She nodded. It was then that a low whistle sounded from the library's front entrance. Kate and Ralph paused, listening. Another whistle sounded.

"Over here!" someone whispered frantically.

"Who's that?" called Kate.

"Here!" the whisperer implored.

Jesus, people really like whisper calling at this school. Minnie thought the voice sounded familiar but in her emotional turmoil she could not place it. They watched as Kate and Ralph backtracked, slowly approaching the library they assumed was locked down. It was likely the lockdown gave them a certain level of confidence to believe the person whispering was one of their own. Minnie hesitated, stepping cautiously out of their hiding spot, when Kate and Ralph entered the library. There was a grunt and the sound of a struggle ensued; Rob bolted to see to the commotion. Minnie followed and found Wes holding Ralph in a headlock, ramming him into the wall.

"Little shit!" screamed the heavy man, slamming Ralph's back once, twice and three times. A painting fell off the wall. "Stay down!" he ordered, keeping his tight hold on Ralph's neck. "Down! Take a knee! I might be a fat queen, bitch, but I'll break your privileged neck! Take a fucking knee!" After the fourth body slam, Ralph obeyed. He had turned a bright shade of bloody-purple and lowered himself to his knees, his eyes streaming with tears.

By the way Kate was beginning to sit up, having lain flat on her back for a few moments, Minnie assumed she had knocked her head. Ralph coughed and spluttered, massaging his throat. Wes wasted no time and tied Ralph's hands together with his belt. Halfway through, afforded by the length of the belt, Wes began to wrap it around Ralph's ankles, tying the boy so tightly he had no option but to lean against the wall, coughing intermittently.

"Are you ok?" asked Wes, flipping his thinning hair from the sweat on his forehead.

"We are now," said Minnie, thoroughly impressed.

"Did you get hold of the police?" Wes asked Rob.

"On their way. What happened here?"

Wes grabbed Kate by the scruff of the neck and dragged her to sit beside Ralph. "Beside your little sycophant, you dirty bitch," he said, throwing her between Ralph and the umbrella stand that usually acted as a door stopper.

"There are others, Wes," said Minnie. "They'll come this way."

"Who?" he demanded, pulling out his phone.

"Henry and their little possy," she said, pointing to Ralph. "Lily ran away. She's probably hiding somewhere. And Olivia. I don't know if she is in on it or not."

"Mir?" Someone answered Wes's phone call. "I've found Minnie. Police are on their way. Hold tight."

"What happened to everyone?" Minnie asked when he hung up.

"Someone triggered a school-wide lockdown. Didn't you hear the call?"

"I was unconscious. He knocked me out and tied me up in the church," said Minnie, glaring at Ralph.

"Why'd you do that, little creeper? Ha? Bit of sexual assault on the mind? Going to get daddy to pay the victim off again?" Wes sneered.

"Again?" asked Rob.

"Christie Bright," said Wes, as though it were obvious. "Didn't come back this year. This little fucker raped her in the church. Daddy paid the school and the Bright family to keep it quiet."

Ralph did not look at all ashamed but stared back as Wes with obnoxious petulance.

"You're about to get a lesson in consent soon, little shit," said Wes. "Prison will make mincemeat out of you."

"We'll see," Ralph responded, though there was clear concern on his flushed face.

"What does the lockdown do then?" asked Minnie.

"It was an intruder lockdown. All doors close and are controlled by a central mainframe. Two teachers would have to ring the security company with a code to have the school unlocked. I have one of the codes but I think Henry did it and used a different one to keep us all trapped. It was perfect timing. We were all off duty and in our apartments."

"I wonder why no one else has called the police?"

"They have," said Wes. "But it's psychology. Most people are dodos. They sit and wait like lame ducks because the alarm says, 'The authorities have been notified'. Me and Mir called the police a while ago."

"Why aren't they here then?"

"Likely confirming with the security company. We didn't know anyone had been kidnapped so we assumed the threat was real. But I saw some movement on the grounds from outside my window so I picked the lock on my door ... well, I drilled through it and broke the connection. I made it to the library. I was looking for help."

"Gosh that's impressive." Minnie closed the door to the library, hoping to avoid being seen by others who might be roaming. She was worried for Kai and hoped he had kept quiet, using the threat of his insurance - whatever it was - to stay unharmed. Kate was a sorry sight. Her bouncy, straight-talking persona was replaced with silence and an expression that spoke to her crumbling reality.

"You're awfully quiet for a child rapist," said Minnie, standing a foot from Kate's outstretched legs.

Kate glared at her. "I told you... it was consensual."

"You both seem to have a problem understanding the definition of consent."

"Are you the woman in the photos?" asked Wes, wide eyed. "Fuck me it all makes sense."

"Let's put them in the archive room," said Rob, hovering nervously around the front door.

The little room to the right likely served as some kind of game room in the original house. Presently, there were shelves of documents and a number of high-backed chairs. Grabbing Ralph by the belt, Wes used his considerable strength to drag him inside and thrust him against the leg of a solid wood desk. Kate sat in one of the chairs. Wes stood guard by the door; Rob remained in the hall, anxiously on the lookout.

"Call the police again," Wes instructed, throwing Rob his phone. "Get an ETA. This is taking too long."

Kate's eyes were vacant. She refused to look Minnie in the eye; focusing on the floor, sometimes the chair leg. Minnie felt her blood pulsating through her hands, her chest. It had come to this. Months of deceit culminated in the unmasking of the perpetrator. How had she done this under her nose? Why had she started the farce of this exclusive boys club? How long had it existed?

"Kate," said Minnie, observing her former friend through what she wanted to be a sympathetic lens, only to feel disgusted in herself. "Why did you end things with Stephen?"

"I got sick of him," said Kate, her blank eyes focused on the floor. She arched a fine, black eyebrow. "Stephen was a nice boy but I like variety."

"Why did you start this group? The Crew?"

"I didn't. They started themselves. I think they wanted my attention and I played along. Why not? It can get boring - doing the same thing, day after day. So it started as a little game."

Minnie glanced at Ralph. "Was Stephen always part of The Crew?"

"He was mates with Kai - so we let him join," Ralph said as though bored.

"Wouldn't have felt good - to have Kate choose him before any of you. How embarrassing."

"Seems a lot of people don't *choose* you, eh Astley?" said Wes. "I bet your parents put you in a boarding school cause they couldn't stand you either."

"You'll be fired before the day's done, Tubs," Ralph spat back.

Wes shrugged. "It'll be worth it."

"Stephen wasn't stable. It's not my fault he killed himself," said Kate, picking at the cuticle on her thumb.

"Yes, it is. Don't start removing responsibility from yourself just because you don't like the feeling. You led him on," said Wes.

"We were in a relationship."

The delusion was either a preconceived ploy or further evidence of Kate's disassociation from reality. "Adults don't have relationships with children. Teachers don't have relationships with their students. You led on a vulnerable boy," said Minnie.

"What about the others?" Kate snapped. "Does *he* look vulnerable to you? He was about to rape you."

"Oh shut the fuck up," Wes snapped. "You played this *fungus* masquerading as a student because you knew his shitty personality type. You knew he'd get more and more worked up because he only thinks with his dick and balls. He's a predator - like for like. But still a kid."

Two sociopaths, thought Minnie. "You likely didn't see Ralph as much of a quest. He was too easy to get onside because he's similar to you. Stephen was hard work and Kai would have been harder."

"They were *more than willing*," Kate protested.

"How did you respond when Kai changed his mind? When he called it off? Were you hurt?"

Kate chewed on the inside of her lip, silent.

Minnie let the question sit for a moment. "But you graduated from abuser to killer. I want to know why. You wanted to walk with me to the church that morning. You knew Jenny was there, hanging. Why did you make me see that?"

Kate's eyes shone with amusement then but she did not answer.

"They're on their way," said Rob, poking his head in. "Seems they called the school after I did and Henry told them the situation was under control. I told them what's happened since. They're sending a few patrol cars."

"The gate will be locked," said Wes. "I'll call Baldwin and tell him to unlock the gate. Hopefully he's not locked in somewhere."

Minnie and Kate held one another's gaze. "I deserve to know why. We were friends. I told you about my husband, my life before this school. How could you walk me toward a dead body - a murdered woman - knowing what I had been through already?"

"I suppose it was to see your grit," said Kate. "You always struck me as a fragile powerhouse, Minnie. You have a quiet strength to you that I wanted to crack. What's your tipping point? Besides, I hadn't seen the body myself and I guess I wanted to share the moment."

"What do you mean you didn't see it?" asked Wes.

"I'm talking to Minnie, you fat asshole," Kate snapped. "As I said before, I never actually killed anyone."

"So who killed Jenny?"

Kate glanced at Ralph.

"Who killed Sandra?"

"That was a group effort," said Kate. "Leo is stronger than he looks and did the grunt work, hoping I'd choose him to be my next lover. Ralph was good enough to keep her from thrashing around."

"Who killed Kane?"

"Actually, I think that was me," said Kate, looking lightly apologetic. "I hit him with one of the candleholders in our apartment. I thought he was dead when I was dragging him to the cellar but he was alive. So I kept him there."

"For how long?"

"A few weeks," she said casually.

"When did Henry find out?"

"Start of term. He was *not* happy."

"How did he find out?"

"Wine. Probably went to get wine for his escapades with Miren and stumbled on Kane. Lucky I checked every day or Henry might have let him go. I got there just in time..."

"*Absolute in-sanity...*" Wes whispered, pacing.

"How did you convince Henry to keep quiet?" asked Minnie.

"Convince Henry? Please... as he told you before, he's not having anyone ruin the reputation of his precious school. He just picked up a bottle of red and walked away like he never saw a damn thing."

"We've all been living on top of Kane's body?" Wes asked weakly.

Kate shrugged.

"Did David know?" Minnie asked. She heard a high pitched sound in the distance and wondered if someone was screaming.

"David?" Kate laughed. "David's straighter than six o'clock."

At least one person in leadership is, thought Minnie, relieved at the news.

"So which one of your lackeys killed Kane?"

"Me, but … It was avoidable. If he just kept his mouth shut…"

"How did he find out?" Minnie interrupted.

"Stephen's little novel." Kate sighed. "Then he got his hands on video footage of us. Yeah, I shouldn't have slept with them on camera… but I found it all really, well… hot."

Astounded as Minnie was by the casual nature of her confession, she was desperate for answers. She took a breath, calming her fluttering heart. The high pitched sound drew closer. *A police siren*, she realised. How did Kane get the footage? Had Stephen sent it? Had Kai also taken the footage of his escapades with Kate?

"You have Kane's phone," said Minnie.

"Yes."

"Did you take it with you on the ski trip?"

Kate frowned. "How do you know that?"

Minnie and Wes shared a look.

"*How do you know that*?" she repeated.

"I think Lily might have told you already," said Minnie, not allowing herself to be led. Lily had called to her in the cellar, confessing - essentially - to revealing their tracking of the IP addresses.

"Where's Lily now?" Wes demanded, though his voice was drowned by the siren. A flash of blue and white light peeked in rhythmic motion in the gap between the heavy curtains. Rob ran out, calling for help.

Minnie held Kate's stare as the police entered. It was the end. She got up, hiding tears, and was thoroughly relieved to see Officer Holgate appearing behind the two uniformed officers. Kate was a murderer who took innocent lives to cover up her affairs, her *abuse*, of impressionable teenagers. Her body was heavy with sudden exhaustion. It was over.

"These two," said Wes, pointing to Kate and Ralph.

"I want to press charges!" Ralph called.

"Shut up," Wes snapped.

"Are you alright?" asked Officer Holgate, landing a warm hand on Minnie's arm.

"Kane Liu is in the cellar," said Minnie as tears fell to her cheeks.

"He must be in a state," said Officer Holgate, reaching for the radio on her belt.

"He's dead."

Officer Holgate sighed, disappointed. "And these two?"

"Responsible for the deaths of Kane, Sandra and Jenny." Minnie wiped her cheeks with her dirty sleeve.

"Lies!" called Ralph as the police untied him. "This is bullshit. I'll be calling my lawyer *immediately*."

"You'll be coming down to the station for questioning, Sir," said Officer Holgate. "Both of you - on suspicion of involvement in homicide."

"Are we under arrest?" asked Kate.

"Correct. Parker, caution Ms Vincini and Mr..."

"Astley," Minnie answered.

"Astley," Officer Holgate continued. "You do not have to say anything, but anything you say can be used in evidence."

It was with great satisfaction that Minnie observed Ralph's belt restraint replaced with handcuffs. They were marched out and put into the back of separate police cars.

"Who tied him up?" asked Officer Holgate.

"Me," said Wes.

"He'll want charges laid."

Wes shrugged. "Self defence."

"Persons we should focus on?"

"Henry knew everything," said Minnie. "And there are three other boys - Lincoln Friers, Harry Dormer and Leo Garcia, who were part of it. Kai Watanabe was a victim of Kate's. Olivia is tied up. They kidnapped Lily... she ran and I don't know where she is."

"So... Kate Vincini...?"

Minnie took a deep breath, unashamed of the fresh tears. "Kate Vincini has been sexually assaulting students and filming it. She directed the deaths. But I'm sure she'll tell the rest. She has nowhere to go with her bullshit anymore."

"Including Stephen Graham?"

"Yes."

"Seems to be clearer now..." Officer Holgate sighed and led them outside where students and teachers were emerging from all corners of the school. Everyone seemed to be aghast; there was a great amount of commotion; questions, rumours, crying, phones on video calls. Where not twenty minutes ago the school had been unnaturally quiet, it exploded with energy now the lockdown ended. Half a dozen police cars were parked on the manicured front lawn. Minnie sat on the front steps of Main House and rested her head in her hands.

Rob sat next to her. "You might need a holiday, Minnie."

"I need to move to another country," she responded. *And a career change.*

To her great relief, Kai appeared from a distance. He waved, sporting a bloody nose. Rob went out and embraced his friend. Minnie was reminded of the fragility of youth and the idealism that drove their behaviours. The Crew had involved themselves in a passion-led behaviour that destroyed their moral centre. They behaved for want of immediate gratification, inconsiderate of the consequences. It was a game that fuelled the ego of a woman and the desires of the boys that chased her.

"Minnie!"

Miren, having clearly rushed from her apartment, paused on the steps, horrified. Henry was being put into the back of a police car. She was ashen, surveying the scene as though computing an advanced algebraic equation.

"Was he involved? Why is he being arrested?"

Henry, resisting the urging of the police officers to get into the car, looked expectantly at Miren; she hesitated.

"He was involved," Minnie answered, feeling a nasty twinge of satisfaction at seeing him being publicly arrested.

Miren ran for the police car, her velvet robe billowing behind her. "Henry! No, stop! I want to speak to him!"

A burly, bald policeman held up a hand, stopping her. "This man is under arrest, Miss. I'm afraid you'll need to step away."

Bristling, Henry stepped into the car without looking back. Minnie only wished she could be there to watch him being processed. She would never forget his audacity; firstly accusing *her* of being inappropriate with a student, then attempting to buy her silence. How many people would have been tempted by millions to keep quiet?

Miren plonked herself next to Minnie. "This is horrific," she said tearfully, watching the police car drive away.

"You might want to get another boyfriend," said Minnie as Rob and Kai approached.

"Did he kill anyone?" Miren demanded.

"He knew about it all."

"Thanks, Miss Fox," said Kai, smiling through the blood smeared on his face.

"Nonsense. Rob called the police, not me."

"But you fought. I thought I'd be alone in this forever."

What 'this' was remained unclear for quite a while. Deciding that this was neither the time nor the place to interrogate him, Minnie stowed the question in her mental repository for another time. "It was a group effort," she remarked simply, motioning to Miren and Wes, the latter of whom was busy giving a statement to the police. "Thank them."

Minnie felt Miren's burning unspoken questions but made no motion indicating she wanted to answer them. They sat quietly, observing the chaos without guilt; their colleagues seemed to have the students well in hand.

"Daddy says he's suing," said one middle-school student, walking with her friend as they clutched their phones. "Mum is on her way."

"Grans coming now. She's livid," said the other, shivering as they joined their homegroups.

Several teachers were exasperated by the lack of response from the students as they tried to bundle them into their homegroups and year levels. The situation was one they would not likely forget soon and they would not be torn away from their phones. Neither Minnie nor Miren had the energy to remind the students about the school's social media policy. So long as her face was not being filmed, Minnie could not care less. David, with shoulders slumped, was conferring with Officer Holgate. The school was now his responsibility. He paid no mind to his phone, which rang incessantly, glowing with the names of Board members, parents and one politician. Minnie admired the way he compartmentalised his priorities and gave his focus to the police and then, marching into gear, held an assembly for the students. Minnie did not attend.

Chapter 16

Clarity

"Mr Liu's laptop."

Feeling entirely stupid, Minnie dropped her spoon in her porridge. "Of course it was," she said, as though missing the obvious clue in a television murder mystery.

Kai did not hold it against her. "It was the Ace up my sleeve. In case anything happened to me."

They breakfasted in the student dining hall awaiting his parents. They were due at 10am, allowing Minnie and Kai a bit of time to debrief before he would be taken by his parents to give a formal statement to the police. The students were out of uniform and eager to leave for a time until the school was ready to have them return. The staff and some students, David explained to parents in a firm email, had undergone a grave trauma. The term would end early, exams would be undertaken as soon as possible, school fees would be adjusted, and counselling offered to anyone who needed it. The financial hit would be enormous, but prestigious schools always seemed able to straighten themselves out of difficult situations. David had a vast amount of work ahead of him in order to appease both the Board and parents, and indeed police, but Minnie believed he was suited to the job.

"How did you get it?"

"I snuck into his apartment," said Kai. "The day we were told Mr Liu was on leave, I snuck in and took it. I knew *she* had something to do with it and I needed proof. Stephen told me he sent some videos to Mr Liu. He trusted him."

"Mr Liu sounds like he was a good man."

"Stand up dude," Kai said agreeably. "I found the video footage on the computer and I decided to send a screenshot to the staff."

"But the email was from an anonymous address."

"I made it. Simple enough. But I sent it from Mr Liu's computer."

"Why?"

"Suppose... I wanted to start an investigation. I wanted the police here but I didn't know how to do it myself. I thought I'd get arrested."

"That's... that's also when you sent me email with the login details?"

"Yeah."

"What did you want me to look for?"

"I hoped you might be suspicious enough of Mr Liu's disappearance to actually log in and find something. If you found the videos then maybe you would call the police?"

"But I didn't..."

"Nah. I realised that early."

"How did Jenny get a screenshot of you?"

"I sent it to Ms Keys. She must have shown it to Mrs Rodgers. But... I think Mrs Rodgers saw us... early on."

"In the woods?" Minnie tried not to picture the rendezvous in her mind's eye.

"Yeah."

"Did Ms Keys or Mrs Rodgers ever ask you?"

"About the photo?"

"About Kate," she said, shaking her head. "It was my impression that Sandra didn't like Kate. Now it's obvious why."

"Ms Keys never knew the photo was of me. But I think she guessed."

"How?"

"Tutoring."

Another realisation. Minnie felt like an impeccable fool. "It was the tutoring," she muttered. "Right under our noses."

"Perfect cover."

Minnie had a few bites of breakfast and took the time to collect her thoughts. Father Baldwin was seeing to the emotional needs of the students at the far end of the table. She was reminded of their conversation about sin and wondered if he had an inkling of what had been occurring under the guise of tutoring.

"It was consensual," said Kai, interrupting her musings. He took a rough bite of toast.

Minnie did not respond because it would not be fruitful. Whether Kai had begun a sexual relationship with his teacher under some misguided belief that she had feelings for him, or with the full understanding of the game being played, it had no relevance to the fact that he was a minor. The law would not agree with his definition of consent, and it would throw the book at Kate, as it should. Despite the ethics of the situation, she was intrigued by Kai's perspective and countenance this morning. He did not proclaim himself the victim nor did he believe himself misled by Kate. He was confident in his proclamation of consent but equally clear that he had ended their relationship and knew she had been involved in the killings. It was an unusual angle and one she was sure his parents would reject in favour of proclaiming him the victim to save themselves the public shame.

"Why did you leave me the manuscript?"

Kai shrugged, buttering a third piece of toast and covering it with baked beans. "You look trustworthy. I thought it would be safe with you."

"How does someone *look* trustworthy?"

He shrugged.

"How did you get into the apartment?"

Kai gave her a firm look.

"Understood," she said softly, removing the image of him with Kate in her apartment without her knowledge from her mindseye.

At 10am sharp, Mr and Mrs Watanabe ushered Kai into their Mercedes. They uttered brief greetings but looked in urgent need to leave the school. They were mortified. Minnie felt nothing but sympathy for their position.

Two days later, Minnie and Charlie sat wrapped in a blanket facing an outdoor fireplace. Rob helped his father, Michael, with the BBQ; he had been careful not to discuss the details of the experience around his parents after giving his statement to the police. They continued to reel over how close their son had come to being involved with Kate. Charlie had taken a particularly rageful approach to the ordeal.

"In the end, it was all about Stephen," said Minnie. "He killed himself because Kate turned her attention to Kai."

"But this ... *Crew* ... they were all just there to play for her attention?"

"It's genius, if you think about it."

"It's *sick*."

"It's human nature," said Michael, approaching with appetisers.

"Being a pedo?" Charlie snapped, clearly in no mood to be generous to the situation.

"If you make an 'exclusive' group, Charlie, and pit the members of that group against one another, they will fight to be number one," said

Michael, topping up their wine glasses. "It's not right, darl, but it's nature."

"Nothing happened, mum," Rob pressed, setting a plate of corn down.

"I'm still unimpressed by your behaviour," said Charlie, tearfully sipping her wine. "You were playing right into her claws."

Rob shot Minnie a pleading look and went back to the BBQ. Michael kissed Charlie's forehead. "Be easy on him," he said.

Charlie scoffed, dabbing her eyes.

"Rob was heroic," said Minnie.

"I'm sure he was," she responded, blowing her nose. "Doesn't take away from the fact that he was in that fucking group. That dirty bitch ... my son ... *my* son played right into her hands. And what about that little shit? Astley? His parents will have lawyered up well. They're fuckers too."

"Sure they are."

"The *embarrassment*."

"I think the school is a bit cursed," said Minnie.

"Why?"

Minnie shared the details of an early conversation she had with Olivia about Jasper Millard, one of the owners of the school's original estate. The painting had portrayed him with a pocket watch with the hands at 2 o'clock. "What really ties it all together is that he was known to have killed himself at 2am. Sandra was murdered at 2am, and Stephen is believed to have killed himself around that time. And I'll bet that's when Jenny was killed as well."

"So Kate must have known about that," said Charlie, twirling her wine glass.

"She did," said Rob, blushing when his mother cast a sharp look at him.

"Was it all to push some kind of ghost narrative?" asked Minnie. *It didn't even get off the ground. Fail.*

"Yeah, that place is definitely haunted. *Honest,*" he pressed when they gave him identical sceptical looks.

"And what about that Astley kid? Are you pressing charges?" Michael asked, bringing with him the scent of fresh barbeque. He set the meat on the table.

"The police will," said Minnie, recovering from having to relive the ordeal. "It'll be a few charges, especially with Kai affirming what Ralph's intentions were when he knocked me out."

"Thank God that boy survived," said Michael. "He seemed to know a lot."

"I think he's going to need a lot of therapy," said Charlie, serving their plates. "Something Rob is going to do weekly, *aren't you?*"

"Yes," he mumbled.

"I'm grateful I got my phone back," said Minnie, tracing the case. "All my memories..."

"Jamie would have been proud of you," said Michael, raising a glass in salute.

They followed suit.

"To Jenny, Sandra and Kane," said Minnie. "And my Jamie... gone too soon."

Chapter 17

Conquered

Lara Holgate observed her prime suspect through the one-way glass. Her coffee had long gone cold but she held it out of habit, or comfort. The suspect was pretty, in her thirties, fit... *Why kids?*

"Hardly," Officer Clark had said, noting down the ages of the boys believed to be in The Crew. "Months off being legal."

It was a fine line, she had responded, all the while curious as to why the woman had decided to pursue boys rather than men. Their fledgeling beards - whiskers, more like - were certainly no sign of maturity, nor was their height. They had each crumbled under the fluorescent lights of the interrogation rooms, claiming innocence or fear. It had amused her, and her colleagues behind the glass, to watch the sons of the powerful and the privileged brought to size when facing murder and kidnapping charges. Barristers and lawyers who usually holidayed in Mansfield's chalet's had arrived just after dawn, some with staff. It had been a sight for the regional police department.

"God, just imagine the bill on all this," a sergeant had observed of the lawyer-lined reception office.

One of the lawyers, a friendly-faced man with a Sri Lankan name too long for her to pronounce accurately the first time, was whispering with Kate in the interrogation room. Lara did not need to turn the volume higher to know he was directing her not to answer any questions without his direction and to avoid details. It was their way.

"Heard anything?"

Lara did not bother to acknowledge the arrival of the detective whom she suspected had been sent by Victoria Police to take over the investigation. Mansfield had been warned the investigation required more resources than they had, a euphemism from the higher-ups that was over utilised to take over high-profile cases they saw as being 'above the purview of regional stations'. It was interesting to all regional police that missing persons or matters pertaining to the majority population hardly deserved the blessed resources of metro-police, but when a once-in-a-career case involving some of the nations most powerful families dropped in their lap, metro-police were on hand and ready to assist - or in this case, take over. Lara knew the unfortunately-named Zelda Springfield was only doing her duty but that did not stop her from holding an unfiltered grudge against her.

Go back to Melbourne, she thought while leading the way into the interrogation room.

Detective Springfield followed suit in her podiatrist-approved shoes and carrying an A4 notepad. Once the room was set up and the tape-recorder launched, Detective Springfield set her notepad on her knee.

"Interrogation commencing," said Lara, "with Detective Lara Holgate present, alongside Detective Zelda Springfield, Mr ..."

"Adam Jayawardena," said the lawyer.

"... and Miss Kate Vincini present. Kate Mable Vincini - can you confirm this is your full name?"

"Yes."

"Born 20th April 1987?"

"Yes."

"Can you confirm your current employment?"

"I'm a teacher at Mansfield Grammar School," said Kate, having glanced at her lawyer.

"How long have you worked there?"

"Eight years."

"In what capacity?"

"A teacher."

"What *kind*?" Lara emphasised. "Sport department, English..."

"Maths. I'm a maths teacher."

"What year levels?"

"All of them. It varies, year on year. Last two years I've had 10-12."

"Ms Vincini, I'm hoping to get a clear idea on a number of things. Beginning with your relationship with Stephen Graham."

"I'm not answering on the advice of my lawyer."

Lara looked at Mr Jayawardena. He nodded.

Switching tactics, she asked, "How long were you his teacher?"

Mr Jayawardena nodded to Kate.

"His whole secondary school life," said Kate, with a sigh.

"So from age 12 - 17?"

"I suppose."

"When did the nature of your relationship change?"

"No," said Mr Jayawardena.

Kate gave Lara a fake look of apology. "Lawyer's advice."

"Ms Vincini... you understand we have multiple points of evidence substantiating charges of rape, murder and kidnapping? You under-stand that cooperation is your best chance?"

"Best chance of what?"

"Demonstrating to a jury that you are remorseful," said Lara, taken aback.

"To what end?"

"Are you settled on life in prison?"

"I'm not going near prison," said Kate, shrugging. "I didn't do anything wrong."

"I have statements from various accomplices and witnesses claiming otherwise," said Lara.

"You have nothing."

Lara paused, collecting herself. "Ms Vincini, we have evidence that you engaged in a sexual relationship with Stephen Graham from the age of sixteen up to his suicide earlier this year. How do you respond?"

"Do you have any hard evidence?"

Lara did not want to reveal the existence of Mr Liu's laptop quite yet.

"We have further evidence that you engaged in a sexual relationship with Mr Kai Watanabe, aged 17. How do you respond?"

Kate merely shrugged. "This is a bit boring, don't you think?"

Lara pulled out the two photos that had circulated amongst the staff at Mansfield Grammar. Mr Jayawardena and Detective Springfield leaned forward to look at the images and began making notes.

"Ms Vincini do you recognise any of the people in these photos? Note for the tape that two photos have been presented to the witness. Photos are Articles 3 and 20 of the evidence files."

"I'm not answering on the advice of my lawyer."

"Ms Vincini ... we conducted a search of your apartment and identical underwear as seen in this photo was found in your bedroom," said Lara.

"You'll find they are in many people's bedrooms."

"The person in this image," she pointed to the second photo, which she knew was of Kai Watanabe, "has confirmed their identity and yours."

"But no faces are seen," she said lightly.

Lara hesitated, tempted to reveal that she had the footage from which the screenshot was taken. This woman was as smug as the parents of the privileged snots in her sycophantic group. She had wiped the smiles off their faces soon enough, but she believed in allowing people to reveal the truth of their own accord.

"Do you recognise the room in the photo?"

"I'm not answering on the advice of my lawyer."

"Can you remember when you started sexually abusing Stephen Graham?"

"I'm not answering on the advice of my lawyer."

"Can you remember when you started sexually abusing Kai Watanabe?"

"I'm not answering on the advice of my lawyer."

"Can you shed light on the workings of a group known as The Crew?"

"I'm not answering on the advice of my lawyer."

And so it continued. Twenty questions in, with frustrations at their peak, Lara paused her questions.

"I'm going to tell you a theory," she said, taking a deep breath. "You'll be free to confirm or deny but I want you to be aware that this theory is supported by evidence."

"I don't have anywhere to be," said Kate, yawning.

Pushing down the urge to inflict physical harm on her, Lara cleared her throat. "You began a sexual relationship - excuse me - sexually abusing Stephen Graham about a year ago and ended it early this year because you turned your attention to Kai Watanabe. Both boys alongside Harry Dormer, Lincoln Friers, Leo Garcia and Ralph Astley were part of a group called The Crew. This group of boys made it a game to get your attention, to play for your time and favour until you chose one of them to be your new victim. Under the guise of 'tutoring' you engaged in sexual activity with your 'favourite' at the time - beginning with Stephen and until recently, Kai. Stephen was a bit of a tortured soul, an artistic romantic and left evidence behind but I'll clarify that in due course. He told his wellbeing mentor, Sandra Keys, and she did not believe it entirely until she was given black and white evidence. Under great stress, she told Jenny Rodgers. You found out somehow across the course of the past ten weeks and proceeded to kill them..."

"I didn't!" Kate protested.

"... in order to keep your secret. You used your control over the boys in The Crew - except Kai - to kill both Sandra and Jenny. Stephen was a gifted writer - we have some of his writing as evidence..."

Kate sat straight, glancing at the photos, but remained quiet.

"... and it was remarkable that he was so detailed. He gave a lot of his writing to Kane Liu. He also gave other evidence but we'll focus on the writing for now. After Stephen's suicide, Kane opened each and every email that Stephen ever sent him and *wow*, did he leave a trail of tears. Kane put two and two together - didn't he? Did he come to your apartment to confront you?"

Kate's expression was stony. "So you were busy up at the school. And here we all thought you were enjoying the scenery."

Lara was unperturbed. "Is that when you killed him?"

"I'm not answering on the advice of my lawyer."

"After you attacked Kane and hid his body in the cellar, you went to his apartment and found his phone. Using this phone, you made it seem that he just upped and left due to stress. His apartment was packed up, his things sent to a storage locker, and you communicated with school leadership as though you were him. It's genius."

"I'm not answering on the advice of my lawyer."

"No fret," said Lara, undeterred. "What you forgot was the computer."

"Computer?"

"Computer," Lara confirmed. "Someone was on to you."

"This is a fantasy."

"Is it?" asked Lara, noting the fine sheen of sweat on her top lip.

"Can we get an idea of the evidence on hand?" asked Mr Jayawardena.

"All in good time," said Lara. "You notice that Jenny and Sandra are particularly cold toward you this year, I'm guessing. Then one night, Sandra confronts you. She has the photo *and* Stephen's testimony. But who sent her the photo?"

Asking was clearly on the tip of Kate's tongue. With great satisfaction, Lara watched her deflate, knowing that any questions would hint to her guilt.

"Can you reveal this?" asked Mr Jayawardena.

"Absolutely. But I just want to finish ... so, you and some members of your group, murder Sandra. Then, Jenny gives you a cryptic message. And you kill her."

"I *didn't* kill her," Kate said.

"Your hands or the hands of the boys, no matter. It was on your direction."

"Then, Kai breaks off with you. He removes himself from The Crew. You notice that he's talking to Mrs Fox. Was she next on the list?"

"This is bullshit," Kate said to her lawyer. "How can they keep me here with no evidence?"

Frustrated, Mr Jayawardena agreed.

Lara turned on her tablet and flipped it to show the video footage of the photo with Stephen Graham. "Sorry about the sound," she said before pressing 'play'.

Kate blanched. Mr Jayawardena looked at his client as her ecstatic face came into full view of the camera. He paused the video. "I'm going to need some time to confer with my client," he said.

"Confer away." Lara took back the tablet.

"What about security cameras?" he asked. "Is there footage demonstrating my client had any hand in the killings?"

"While we believe the footage was wiped by another party, we have not ruled out its existence," said Lara. "It is an ongoing element of the investigation."

"You won't find any," said Kate.

"Focus on your defence," said Lara, getting up. "Interview ended at 4.30pm. We will take a short break... allow you to convince your client to cooperate... and resume in an hour."

"I've done nothing wrong."

"Ms Vincini... I strongly suggest you get out of your delusion."

END

Other Titles